THE BRAZEN RULE

THE BRAZEN RULE

STEVEN BURGAUER

Northwest Publishing, Inc.
Salt Lake City, Utah

NPI

The Brazen Rule

For information address: Northwest Publishing, Inc.
6906 South 300 West, Salt Lake City, Utah 84047
ESH 01 26 95
Edited by: Debra Burgauer

PRINTING HISTORY
First Printing 1995

ISBN: 0-7610-0088-7

NPI books are published by Northwest Publishing, Incorporated,
6906 South 300 West, Salt Lake City, Utah 84047.
The name "NPI" and the "NPI" logo are trademarks belonging to
Northwest Publishing, Incorporated.

PRINTED IN THE UNITED STATES OF AMERICA.
10 9 8 7 6 5 4 3 2 1

To Debra, my editor and lover.

1

GEDULD

Considering the intensity of his many weeks of survival training, the elite soldier should not have been surprised how fleeting the desert's hold had been on the day's burning heat. But, he was. The sand, which just hours ago had been scorching the exposed skin of his dirty face, now felt uncomfortably cold, and the hair on his sinewy arms stiffened as the raw night air clung to his sweat-soaked body.

Hanging from his canvas belt, just inches from the fingers of his twitching hand, was a manual firebomb. It was circular at the top like a conventional grenade, but its hull was covered with a sheet of heavy plastic. At the base was a handle five inches long, a handle which enabled the thrower to hurl the explosive farther and with greater accuracy than an ordinary grenade. The trick was in the accuracy and the timing; for once the plastic shield was removed and the casing of steel-like adhesive was exposed to the air, the bomb itself would adhere instantly to any surface it contacted. The thrower had only fifteen seconds from the removal of the plastic covering until the explosion of the firebomb.

Doing his best to shake off the nagging sensation of numbness which had begun to envelope him, Specialist Wenger bent his left leg ever so slightly. Like the others in his unit, he had lain nearly motionless, hugging the hard sand for hours, while the day had passed from a blazing afternoon into a chilled dusk. In the valley beneath him he saw burnoose-cloaked figures sharing a cup of hot tortan as they huddled around the cooking fires. Jealously licking his own lips, he wished he too had something warm to drink.

Pressing his ears into the headphone, Specialist Felix Wenger listened intently for the whispered order he knew could not be long in coming. In a short while, Commander Patterson would order his squad to launch an assault on their quarry in the camp below, and if Intelligence had it right *this* time, Rontana would be among the figures lurking about in those smoky shadows. If not, Patterson's raiding party was about to needlessly slaughter a company of inconsequential underlings or, worse yet, a clan of innocent nomads.

Under normal circumstances the President would never have consented to assemble a hit team like this one, but these were not normal circumstances. Rontana was a murderous fiend, and everyone agreed that he had to be stopped at any cost.

Although precise details as to Rontana's origins were clouded in obscurity, sometime around the turn of the century he had swept out of the mountains of Persia leading an army of Moslem bandits. All the crazies of the world have had a manifesto, and Ali Salaam Rontana was no exception. His maniacal cry directing his followers to "kill their ideas by killing their genes" was merely the latest version of the age-old master race excuse for slaughtering one's neighbor. Rontana's particular sickness was infanticide, and in a flaw-lessly logical, yet seemingly rational way, he laid it all out in his manifesto, *Deicide, Infanticide, & Ecocide*, or D.I.E. for short. His treatise was pure, unadultered lunacy, but it was required reading to earn a spot on Patterson's strike force. The Commander believed that only by studying and understand-ing the diseased ideas of this deranged psychopath would a team member cultivate the necessary loathing to see this grisly business through to the end.

As Felix lay there on the cold sand waiting anxiously for the "go" signal, he thought again of the madman's handbook and how it had recited in nauseating detail Rontana's five reasons for committing infanticide in order to spare the environment.

First, there was the exploitation of infants as a food source, in other words, cannibalism. Felix remembered how he had endured the dry heaves when first learning of this.

Next, there was the competition for resources. By starving or murdering another man's infant—but not actually *eating* the unfortunate child—the killer would increase the nutriments available for himself and for his family.

Third, there was the competition between males for access to fertile females. By murdering another man's offspring, the killer gained the opportunity to utilize that female to produce more of *his* progeny. Rontana relished this "murder and rape" method as his personal favorite.

The fourth he labeled "compassionate infanticide." In the poverty-stricken areas where it was practiced, compassionate infanticide took place just after birth. It was typically rendered by the infant's mother with deep regret as she sadly realized that her thriving four-year old would die because she lacked the resources to raise both of her children at once.

Reason number five was pure social pathology: slaughtering for sport. There was no tangible gain of any kind for the butcher, except the sheer joy of killing.

As if studying D.I.E wasn't enough training for this mission, Commander Patterson had brought in a military psychologist who had done her best to explain to them what sort of man they were up against. She told them that fanatics like Rontana required a personality cult to be successful. In order to usurp existing lines of authority, such a man had to debunk any and all conventionally held "truths." No institution was exempt from the degradation— not God, not science, not even the rules of law. Only by debasing a culture's traditional heroes could a powerful lunatic hope to substitute his own warped personality for the idols he sought to dethrone. To Rontana's followers, religion and mysticism were more convincing than science or fact. To Rontana himself, life meant nothing and several hundred million people had already died at his hand by the time the President decided to act.

At the outset of this phase of their training Felix had found it difficult to understand how otherwise normal people could have lined up behind such a tyrant. Yet they had. And in spite of the terrible suffering Rontana had imposed on the peoples he subjugated, he had not been overthrown. This was an absurdity Felix could just not fathom.

The psychologist from the anti-terrorist unit had struggled long and hard to account for this apparent contradiction. She had said that a ruthless and cunning leader could remain in power even when he brings untold anguish to his people due to something she called the "paradox of collective action."

She summarized the paradox this way: The gains from removing an evil leader accrue to the population as a whole, including those who have done nothing to get rid of him. Yet, the extraordinary risks of *opposing* such a dictator—which might extend to the loss of life itself—are borne entirely by those who take action against him. Although everyone would surely gain if the totalitarian leader were overthrown, the gain to any *one* person, or even to a small group acting in concert, was too little to make the risk worthwhile.

Not only did the paradox she had so carefully spelled out for them account for the unwillingness of anyone in Rontana's inner circle to do the "job," it also explained Felix's presence in the Saudi desert this moonlit night in 2282—the President wanted this menace to society eliminated, and it was up to Patterson's team to carry out his orders.

Hidden now in the cold Arabian sand there were seventy-five brave soldiers like himself: men like Skinny, Tex, Oiler, Geek, and Matthews. Though surprise and stealth were their allies, Wenger knew that if they met stiff resistance there would be no second chances. There were no squadrons of airchops waiting to swoop in and save their skins, no backup troops standing ready to rescue their hides. They were on their own. The last team had failed miserably and now it was up to them. Get in, get out, and get back to the jeeps alive.

Finally, after what seemed like an interminable wait, the "go" order sounded in his earphone. Crawling on his belly, Felix "Flix" Wenger began moving cautiously forward over the ridge of the wind-sculpted dune. Unlike the men in Lead Corps or in Alpha Unit, he wouldn't actually approach the point of engagement; Flix's importance to the mission demanded that he remain safely out of harms' way.

Without twenty-year old Felix Wenger, their offense would be muted: he was one of just two pyrotech specialists assigned to this unit. That designation meant he was a first-class munitions expert proficient with nitro-projectiles, dynamite megaflares, plastique, and manual firebombs. His nickname mimicked the sound one's thumb made when spinning the flint cylinder of a lighter to ignite the wick of a fuse—Flix.

Even as the team of commandos slid silently down into the depression, their 9 millimeter submachine guns at the ready, Flix spied a glint of moonlight reflecting off a pair of night-vision goggles. He swore under his breath at this incredible stroke of bad luck. Like a warning beacon, if this flash of light was spotted by an attentive sentry in the camp below, the element of surprise would surely be lost, and the enemy would be alerted to the raid that was just getting underway.

Justifying his own worst fears, the sound of an automatic weapon being discharged rang out from the hostile lair. Splitting the night's silence, the tracers brought an immediate end to the careless owner of the infrared field glasses. As the man's pained gasps filled Flix's headset, Patterson's squad answered the death of their teammate in kind. Acting as if on cue, they pounded the encampment with machine-gun fire. Sparks filled the air as stray bullets blew burning logs from the cooking fires. Even as concussion grenades rocked the enemy positions, Patterson's Lead Corps moved in with their flame-throwers, scorching everything in their path as they advanced.

Executing the steps he had rehearsed so many times before, Flix anchored his megaflare launcher firmly in the sand. Across the valley he knew Lieutenant Matthews would be doing likewise. Supported atop a tripod no more than 18 inches in height, the size of this nasty little device did scant justice to its destructive capabilities. The launcher was designed to hurl baseball-sized globes filled with lyddite-gel high into the air over the field of battle. Upon reaching its apogee, a megaflare globe would shatter into a thousand fluorescent fragments, illuminating not only the battleground, but also burning and maiming the enemy as its glowing shards fell from the sky. Because no man struck by one of these fiery cinders could ignore the pain long enough to aim and fire a return volley, once this scorching rain began, retaliation became impossible.

For the fourth time in two minutes, Flix checked the direction and the speed of the wind; no one knew better than he that a hot cinder would burn a friendly just as severely as it would an enemy. Once he was satisfied that he would not be inadvertently unleashing a cascade of agony to rain down upon his buddies from the heavens, he catapulted his first megaflare skyward. As it reached the top of its flight path, the night sky was briefly as bright as the dawn.

Moments later, as the glare from the exhausted megaflare dimmed, the seared screams of the enemy soldiers reached his ears. Carried upon the light wind, the stench of their scorched flesh brushed past his nose. But before he could even put his hand over his mouth to keep from gagging, the sky went white again as Flix's counterpart on the opposite ridge launched one of his own megaflares into the night.

"Switch to nitro!" Commander Patterson ordered abruptly, his worried voice booming through the headphone.

Recognizing that Lead Corps had probably moved in too close for him to safely use another megaflare, Specialist Wenger reached gingerly into his rucksack. His adrenaline flowing, he carefully removed an aluminum canister marked, "Extremely Volatile."

A nitro-projectile was a most unpleasant incendiary device. In the first stage, a pressurized mist composed of pure oxygen and a highly flammable fuel was released over the target area, a circle of death with a circumference of perhaps

500 meters. Inasmuch as the explosive fumes would spread rapidly through the air, when the fog was ignited shortly afterwards, there would be a huge blast and a ferocious firestorm. In the circle of death, temperatures could reach more than 700 degrees Fahrenheit. The shock wave from the inferno could level buildings, explode minefields, blow out eardrums, implode eyeballs, and even suffocate unsuspecting troops as the firestorm literally sucked the air from their lungs. Anyone who managed to survive such a blast would be so badly burned they might have wished they had not been so fortunate.

"Thirty seconds to nitro from my mark," Flix announced over the comm as he set the timer.

"Do not enter central strike zone!" Commander Patterson warned his commandos. "Repeat, clear central!"

The light-burst from Matthews' second megaflare had already crested when Flix's nitro-projectile went incendiary. Because it burned so furiously and because it consumed so much oxygen so quickly, the detonation produced a curious effect. Instead of blowing things outward like a grenade or a bomb might, the inferno generated a violent inrushing of air, a torrent which had the blissful side benefit of drowning-out the screams of its hapless victims.

To Flix's amazement, when the nitro storm receded, a handful of Rontana's men were still standing. Though they had been fortunate enough to have been bivouacked just outside of the ring of death, the soldiers were obviously stunned by the blast and could not retaliate. They were shown no mercy by Alpha Unit. Illuminated by the blaze behind them, Rontana's men were quickly felled by bursts of machine-gun fire from Patterson's snipers.

Then all was quiet. From where he sat on the bluff, Flix could see no movement in the enemy camp. Minutes passed as the burning nitro slowly cooled.

At long last, the comm crackled, "Perimeter secure. Lead Corps, move in. Exercise extreme vigilance."

Flix observed the guarded movements of several of his

teammates as they cautiously advanced toward the decimated camp. They wore desert fatigues to conceal their bodies, and black balaclavas with eyeholes to cover their heads, necks, and shoulders.

"Alpha Unit, fan out and execute sweep," Patterson droned authoritatively over the comm.

Mobilized by his instructions, eight men broke cover and began a systematic search of the area.

"Delta Unit, swing left to cover flank; Epsilon, swing right," Patterson ordered, following the procedures they had practiced time and time again back at base camp. "Lead Corps, hold your…"

Lead Corps never heard Commander Patterson's order to hold their position because all of a sudden they were swamped by an unexpected horde of Rontana's men. Surging from a hidden, underground bunker, Rontana's soldiers counterattacked. In a vicious backlash, the enemy troops cut down most of Lead Corps and all of Delta Unit as they exploded from their subterranean hiding place. Seeing the tragedy unfold before him, Flix figured the bunker must have been sealed off before the nitro blew or else its occupants would have been incinerated by the firestorm along with everything else.

Although Flix and Matthews were in little personal danger themselves, there wasn't much they could do to stop the carnage. Not only had they been ordered to remain in the rear, away from the fighting, they could not dip into their pyrotechnic bag of tricks without unleashing the fury of their dreadful weapons upon their own men. With the battle already at close quarters, it would have been too late to call in for air support even if there had been any.

The savage duel raged for nearly an hour. Once the machine-guns were drained of their ammo, the contestants turned to pistols, and once the flame-throwers ran out of fuel, they turned to knives. Eventually the fighting degenerated into a brutal hand-to-hand contest. Possessing far superior cover, Rontana's people steadily gained the upper hand as the fighting wore on. It wasn't long before it had clearly become a desperate, one-sided affair. Flix's heart sank as he saw one after another of his buddies drop to the ground.

After what seemed like an eternity, his somber thoughts were interrupted by Commander Patterson's stern voice thundering over the comm, "Flix, you and Matthews are to finish it. Now! I want a nitro-projectile from each of you."

"But Commander," Flix protested strenuously, "you will be killed for sure!"

"We are dead already," Patterson replied stoically.

"But, sir, I can't..."

"Damnit!" Patterson shouted into the comm. "I *order* you to finish it! There is no other way."

Drawing a deep breath to flush the adrenaline from his system, Flix reluctantly catapulted the canister of nitro into the air as instructed. From the opposite ridge, Matthews did the same. Switching off his comm to shut out the anguished cries of his friends, Flix cringed at the thought of what he had just done.

As the circle of death engulfed and vaporized the enemy along with what was left of his own garrison, Flix sobbed quietly, his tears falling to the cold sand.

2

DESERT

Despite the fact that the moon had already marched its way across the heavens, when Flix awoke he had no idea whether he had been out for several minutes or for several hours. Though scattered lumps of glowing embers still lingered to remind him of what had happened, the fires of destruction had evaporated into nothingness along with the pained screams of his comrades. By this time, even the distasteful stench of burnt flesh had been irrevocably extinguished by the frigid night air. Indeed, it was not until the sun vaulted above the horizon that he was jolted back to reality. Feeling its profound heat upon his face, Flix instinctively sat up and switched his comm back on.Immediately it was alive with sound!

"Lordy, Flix! If yer still alive over there, give me a holler," Matthews urgently whispered into the walky-talky, his speech colored by his slow Missouri drawl. "Damnit, man, say somethin'!"

"I copy you, Tiger," Flix responded hoarsely, as he got up on one knee. "Sorry, but I must have fallen asleep for a while."

"Three hours is not 'a while' you rascal."

"Listen, I'm tired and I'm sore," Flix admonished irritably. "Let's just finish what we have to do and get out of here. This place gives me the creeps."

"Okey-dokey," Matthews nodded from the opposite ridge, "but let's take this real slow and easy like."

Shouldering his machine-gun first, then his rucksack, Flix struggled to his feet. But after so many hours prone on his belly, he found his legs were wobbly. Even as he glanced across the gap to where Matthews was standing, the sun silhouetted him with its brightening intensity. Signaling to one another with their weapons, the two of them began inching cautiously down the sandy incline from opposite ends of the valley.

The battle zone was a confused jumble of weapons and bodies. Machine-guns, their barrels grotesquely deformed by the heat of the firestorm, were strewn everywhere even as the charred remains of dozens of fallen soldiers carelessly littered the beleaguered camp. With little more than bones to go on, identification of the corpses was all but impossible, their former allegiance to one cause or the other having been extinguished by the flames.

Standing shoulder to shoulder as they surveyed the disaster, the two men were a study in contrasts. Nathanial "Tiger" Matthews had blue eyes and was obviously of northern European stock; his buddy Flix had dark eyes framed by swarthy, Mediterranean features. Tiger had bushy, blond hair; Flix's was black and closely-cropped. Tiger was tall; Flix was short. Though the two men could not have been more different—or closer friends—what lay before them was a revolting sight. They looked at each other in shocked horror. It had never occurred to them that they would be the sole survivors of this encounter.

"Do ya think we got 'im?" Tiger asked, his voice cracking.

"Got who?" Flix questioned without thinking. "Oh, you mean Rontana? It's impossible to tell. Every soul here is burnt beyond recognition."

"I just hate to return home without some sorta proof that we got 'im," Tiger insisted, kicking his boots through the grimy sand.

"I know how you feel," Flix remarked unhappily. "We'd all sleep a whole lot better tonight knowing that the reign of terror was finally over."

Shaking his head in agreement as he walked further afield to examine the casualties, Tiger recalled their platoon leader's final briefing. "Listen, Flix," he pointed out, "we had better git outta here and back to the jeeps. If ar' buddy Rontana *was* here, he will soon be missed. Remember what Patterson told us about the revenge squads?"

Nodding, Flix popped the protective cover off his wrist-watch. Of the many survival tricks Patterson had taught him, one of the simplest was how to convert a standard wrist-watch into a compass. With the watch held parallel to the ground, all one had to do was point the hour hand in the direction of the sun. Precisely halfway between the hour hand and the 12 o'clock position, an imaginary line would point due south. Taking a quick but expert reading, the two of them set off across the desert at a fast clip. Their jeep lay concealed with the rest of the platoon's equipment under a canvas tarpaulin about three miles due east of here.

As the sun climbed ever higher above the horizon, the temperature rose rapidly. They had to move quickly enough to avoid dehydration but not so swiftly as to become winded. They knew there was ample water stored in a reservoir tank mounted on the rear of their jeep, but until they reached their destination they had to rely on a small canteen Tiger had hanging from his belt. Checking the heading on their improvised compass every four minutes, they dashed over one dune and on to the next. After the third reading, Flix realized they were in trouble.

Gazing through his field glasses, Matthews groaned as he confirmed their misfortune with his own eyes. Just ahead of them, about a dozen horse-mounted troops were milling about the camouflaged equipment their unit had left parked in the desert. The bandits were heavily-armed and were shielded from the debilitating effects of the sun by their kaffiyeh, the traditional Arab headdress.

"We'll have to move in loads closer if we're gonna use nitro on 'em," Tiger whispered to his friend as they lay on the ground hugging the sand. "We're not even in range."

"No!" Flix countered firmly, shaking his head. "If we use nitro, we'll not only vaporize our Arab guests down there, we will also vaporize our transportation home. Not to mention our water and our provisions. Don't forget, it's nearly a hundred miles across the desert to the coast. We could never make it on foot."

"Yer right, a course," Tiger replied sheepishly, "but if not nitro, what then? A megaflare? A manual firebomb?"

"Maybe," Flix answered thoughtfully, wiping the sweat from his brow as he judged the distance that lay between them and their adversaries.

"Ah kin tell from the look on yer face that you have something *else* in mind."

Grinning slyly, Flix offered, "How 'bout a near miss?"

"Say again," Tiger demanded with a quizzical stare.

"What if we try to disperse them with a blast which is near enough to scare them off, yet far enough from the mark to avoid melting down all our equipment?" Flix offered matter-of-factly. "With *our* lousy aim, I imagine we'll kill a few of the bad guys in the process one way or the other."

"Flix, yer brilliant!" Matthews declared excitedly, his dirty face beaming. "Ah swear, you'll be a general one day!"

"Not me, Tiger," Flix objected. "The military's no life for a running-dog capitalist like me."

"We'll see," Tiger retorted. "We'll see."

"Will you forget about the future already!" Flix snapped irritably. "Right now we have a more pressing problem, wouldn't you agree?"

"We sure do," Tiger admitted, nodding his assent. "To pull this one off, we'll have to work ourselves in real close. If it works and they *do* disperse, we'll have a minute or two at *most* to make it to a jeep, and git the hell outta here," he emphasized, his twang belying his Missouri upbringing.

"Makes sense," Flix agreed. "And since they are on horseback, we should be able to easily outrun them in a jeep."

"Flix, you drive—ah'll ride shotgun."

"Good enough," Flix replied. Then, with a false tone of

sternness, he commanded, "On your belly, soldier! We have got to scoot in much, much closer."

"Aye, aye, mon general," Tiger returned playfully. Saluting his friend, he got down on all fours.

Nearly a quarter of an hour passed before they were able to work themselves into position a hundred yards downwind of the scruffy-looking army of bandits. Although a handful of the turbaned outlaws had remained in their saddles scanning the horizon for intruders, most of the thieves had dismounted from their steeds and were searching hungrily through the vehicles for food and for weapons.

While Tiger took wind readings, Flix set up his megaflare launcher and began adjusting its sights. With the day's heat rising in full force, a stream of perspiration poured off his face and onto his hands, making it impossible for him to manipulate the small dials on the field-sights. Wiping his sweaty fingers against his desert fatigues time and time again, he struggled to get the setting just right. It was absolutely critical to their plan that the explosion be oriented close enough to the bandits to scare them away, and yet far enough from their equipment to leave at least one of the jeeps intact. Without a four-wheel drive vehicle at their disposal, they had no hope whatsoever of escape.

Working in tandem, Flix and Tiger launched their assault. First, they catapulted a nitro-projectile into the air. Then, in rapid succession, they launched a megaflare, followed by another nitro canister. As soon as the first of the nitro canisters began spewing its deadly incendiary fumes across the target area, the two young men broke cover and dashed across the uneven sand for the nearest vehicle. The going was painfully slow.

Though they had taken the precaution of covering their mouths with a swatch of cloth, being in so close, they were caught off-guard by the enormity of the explosion. It was as if they had given birth to their very own hell-on-earth. As the furiously burning nitro gulped down all the available oxygen, their breath was sucked away, and as the inrushing torrent gained in intensity, the loose sand beat them mercilessly. Unable to see through the swirling dust, neither of them could prepare themselves for what was to happen next.

The torturous vortex generated by the nitro's firestorm shifted the path of the descending shrapnel in a most unfortunate way. Instead of falling only upon the swarthy outlaws as Flix and Tiger had intended, the megaflare's rain of pain fell directly upon them as well. It was a terrible miscalculation.

Instinctively, Flix dropped to the ground and began burying himself in the sand. Knowing that a layer of sand was the only body armor capable of withstanding this onslaught, he frantically screamed at Matthews to do the same, but it was too late. Even as he watched, Tiger was repeatedly struck by shards of fiery-hot shrapnel.

Dazed by what was happening to his body, Tiger stood outside himself and observed the spectacle with feigned disinterest. Screaming and writhing against the most profound pain he could ever have imagined, fortunately only seconds passed before he lost consciousness.

Moments later, time was bent by the pounding detonation of the second nitro-projectile. Even as horses melted into gooey blobs, grains of sand were instantly transformed into slivers of glass. Jeep tires vaporized, and engine hoses became blue puffs of smoke. Food rations incinerated, and jugs of water evaporated on the spot. Gasoline tanks exploded, and to a man, the enemy perished. It was a gruesome sight to behold.

Once the fires had burned themselves out, the sand cocoon which Flix had hurriedly dug for himself slowly cooled. Cautiously testing the temperature of the outside air, he worked his fingers free. Satisfied that the worst of the fury had run its course, he unburied himself, only to be confronted by a rather unpleasant picture.

Lying in the fetal position next to him on the sand— his body peppered with terrible burns—was his friend and companion, Tiger Matthews. Considering how little blood there was, Flix guessed that Tiger's wounds must have been instantly cauterized by the searing shrapnel. But judging by his pale countenance, weak pulse, and shallow breathing, Flix knew that his friend was in trouble. These were the classic symptoms of trauma, and time was of the essence.

"Stay with me, buddy," Wenger whispered to the haggard-looking Matthews. "I'll get us to safety," he promised in a trembling voice. "Just don't die on me you hear?"

Running frantically from one wrecked jeep to another, and from one demolished truck to the next, Flix tried to find a four-track which hadn't been destroyed by the terrible havoc they themselves had caused. But none were operable!

"Damn!" he swore, feeling his collar tighten.

Again he tore from vehicle to vehicle, this time in a fruitless search for water, for food, for medical supplies. Nothing! All incinerated!

Straining to control his panic, he took a deep breath to calm himself, but it didn't help. "Damn!" he swore again as he attempted to mentally grapple with the enormity of his dilemma. Here he was, deep inside enemy territory: he had just assassinated this country's most beloved leader; his best friend was little more than half-alive; a hundred miles of impossible desert lay between him and the coast; and he had no water nor any transportation!

As he digested the hopelessness of their situation, anxious fear began to grasp at his bowels, and for one long moment, he thought he would be ill. He stood there frozen for an eternity until something deep within him said he had to try.

Kneeling down, Flix slung Tiger's motionless body over one shoulder, took a one-handed compass reading with his watch, then set off due east at an unsteady pace. Mindful of their slim chances, he reckoned he would walk mostly at night when it was cooler, but for starters he would have to put a few miles between himself and the jumbled mess of disabled trucks and broken bodies.

As he began his unlikely trek across the blazing desert, the intimidating words of his survival-training instructor rang prophetically in his ears: "Water is the largest component of our bodies, yet we have little to spare. In the hottest desert we can sweat water out at the rate of two gallons a day while resting in the shade, or at up to four gallons a day while walking. Since the human body loses water at a constant rate even when it is already dehydrated, the only way to stretch your life is to reduce your water needs: stay put, stay shaded, and by all means, keep your clothes on!"

Smiling glumly, Flix debated what he might have done differently to avoid his present predicament, and what inner force was driving him to blatantly ignore the survivalist's advice to stay put.

"Thirst is first felt when the body has lost just one half of one percent of its weight to dehydration which, for an average-sized man, amounts to a mere pint. With a two percent loss—say, two quarts—the stomach is no longer large enough to hold as much water as the body needs, and even if they are given ample fluids, people at this stage stop drinking well before they have replenished their loss."

Swallowing hard, Flix struggled to flush the cobwebs from his parched throat as he drudged onward. Not only was his head pounding, his back was starting to feel the strain of Tiger's weight upon his shoulder. Though he tried his best to suppress them, feelings of resentment for the burden he had to bear were beginning to bubble to the surface.

"At a five percent loss, the symptoms include fatigue, loss of appetite, flushed skin, irritability, increased pulse rate, and mild fever. Beyond that lie dizziness, headache, labored breathing, absence of salivation, blue skin, and slurred speech."

Shifting Tiger's weight higher on his shoulder, Flix sought to spirit the emptiness in his stomach away. But, he could not. As each step he took seemed shorter than the one before, his kneecaps felt like they were about to explode.

"At ten percent a person can no longer walk. The point of no return is around twelve percent when the tongue swells, the mouth loses all sensation, and swallowing becomes impossible. A person this dehydrated has lost about three gallons of fluid and cannot recover without medical assistance. Be aware—it may take as little as half a day to get to this stage!"

By this time, Flix was completely drenched in sweat and he was totally winded by his effort. Licking his cracked lips, he sadly reckoned that he hadn't gone more than half a mile since he began.

"Now the skin shrinks against the bones and begins to crack, the eyes sink, even as vision and hearing become dim. Urination is painful. Delirium sets in. The blood thickens. The end comes with an explosive rise in body temperature, followed by convulsions and blissful death."

Exhausted, Flix stumbled and fell to the ground, dropping Tiger unceremoniously in the process. There was no way he could go on. Without a vehicle, he would never be able to cross the ninety plus miles to the coast on his own, much less with Tiger slung over his shoulder.

Specialist Wenger was not a man given easily to defeat, but unless he found some water and some shade soon, he knew death could not lie more than a few hours in his future. Even as the sun beat against his upturned face, he laid back on the hot sand, closed his eyes, and cursed his stupidity and bad luck.

For a time, he debated whether he should temporarily abandon Matthews, trek back to the jeeps in search of tarps and poles, then build a lean-to to protect them from the sun's murderous rays. The shade might just keep the two of them alive a while longer. Maybe he could even find a flare gun for signaling, or a puddle of radiator coolant to drink from. Surely there had to be some way to avoid such a miserable end!

Even as panic gripped him, he felt the cooling presence of a shadow as it fell across his face. But rather than relishing in the pleasant change, he steeled himself for action.

Only "things" generated shadows, and in his state, the only "thing" Flix could think of was an enemy soldier.

Convinced that one of Rontana's men was standing over him, Flix reached for his sheathed blade. Rolling swiftly to one side with his last burst of energy, he sprung expertly to his feet. Grasping the blade in his powerful right hand, he prepared to plunge it into his assailant.

Startled by what stood before him, Flix thought for a second that he might be hallucinating. If it wasn't a mirage, it was proof positive that a merciful God was indeed looking after him.

Squinting his eyes to be sure of himself, he smiled as he realized that the figment of his imagination was genuine. Pawing the ground not five feet from where he stood was a horse: a fine Arabian stallion, its dark coat wet with sweat, its sinewy body speaking of its strength in battle. Hung at the steed's flanks was a tooled-leather saddlebag, its seams obviously swollen by the full water-bladder within.

It was a miracle!

As Flix edged noiselessly toward the stallion to avoid spooking it, he reckoned that for the mount to have been spared, it must have been tethered at a respectable distance from the explosion. The horse undoubtedly abandoned its rider when it bolted, then wandered off in precisely the right direction.

Now the three of them at least had a fighting chance!

3

SEASONED

Campaign Headquarters, Farmington, Missouri
Many Years Later

The confetti had settled to the floor, the tones of the statesmanlike music blaring from the municipal band had died down, the overzealous electioneers had gone home, and the lobbyists were lining up to collect their due. In other words, Nathanial Matthews, Jr. had won the election. It had been a close, hard-fought campaign with plenty of old-fashioned mudslinging, ritualistic name-calling, and time-honored back stabbing. Yet, Nate—as he preferred to be called—had come out on top. At this junction, however, the pressures of the campaign, coupled with the death of his wife shortly before election day, had left him exhausted and troubled. In the heat of the battle, he had never had the opportunity to properly mourn her loss, and as he sat here now, reveling in his victory, his thoughts turned to her.

Darna had flown to China in October as part of a goodwill trip sponsored by the University of Missouri. While she was there, she had toured a panoply of scientific research laboratories plus a slew of cultural establishments. Unfortunately, she had taken ill somewhere along the way, and by the time she disembarked from the suborb in St. Louis, she was already running a high fever. Within a matter of days she was on her deathbed, her doctors unable to even identify what it was that was killing her. At the end, she had a drawn, dehydrated face and great big bulging eyes. It was a ghastly sight for a husband to face in a woman so young. Undeterred by her death, he had not withdrawn from the race, but now that it was over, he felt as if his world was about to close in on him. If it hadn't been for his sometimes girlfriend and tireless campaign worker, Musette Lafayette, he might never have made it through the ordeal.

Though Nate had always been hesitant to admit it, he had married Darna more for her family's money than for her unrequited love. Even so, they had managed to live together peaceably all these many years and sire one pathetic specimen of a boy. For Nate, however, his marriage of convenience wasn't enough and—as was not uncommon for a man of his standing—a mistress came with the territory. Despite the fact that Musette was not terribly bright—or perhaps *because* of it—she made for an adequate diversion from his otherwise staid existence.

Now that the election had ended in success, Nate felt a tinge of remorse for the people he would have to leave behind, if only temporarily. First there was Musette, of course, and his son Franklin, but there was also his father and his good friend, Police Chief Munson. Without a mother to watch over Frankie, and without an engagement or contract of marriage with Ms. Lafayette, Nate had decided to leave the boy with his aunt and uncle at least until the end of the school term. Believing himself to be fully capable of handling the boy, Nathanial, Sr. had not been happy with this decision, nor had Frankie, but until Nate could get settled into a home in D.C., he felt he had no other choice.

The first item on his post-election agenda was to select a man to be his new chief of staff. Having just been deposited here by his secretary, the man he wanted to see sat before him now.

"General," the younger man began, obviously intimidated by his guest's rank, "I understand you saved my father's life once."

"Yes, Senator," the older man replied, content to hold his interviewer in awe. "Tiger and I go way back," he reminisced, drumming his fingers against the crown of his cane.

"Tiger?" the Senator cross-examined curiously, as he surveyed the rows of medals pinned to the man's uniform.

"That was your father's nickname in our unit," the General explained, "but you wouldn't know that, would you? Hell, you weren't even *born* yet. Indeed, I hardly think you're old enough to be a Senator *now*," he added, waving his arm through the air in vague reference to the room full of campaign posters and colorful streamers.

Ignoring the taunt, the younger man smiled and moved closer to the window, the morning sun revealing his round, gray eyes, and his light, almost blond, hair. He was muscular, but not rock hard like an athlete. There was the faintest hint of a cleft in his chin. "You're right, of course, I never knew he went by the name of Tiger," the Senator admitted. "And what did my father call *you*?"

The General grinned broadly and answered, "In my younger days, I was a pyrotech specialist. They called me Flix."

"Flix," the Senator repeated thoughtfully as he continued to gaze out the window. There was a light cover of snow on the ground. Though it was only November, winter had come early to this portion of Missouri. "Well, Flix, they tell me that you are a hero in some circles."

"How's that, boy?" the General snapped, his dark eyes and swarthy features not revealing his great age.

"You are quite modest," Senator Matthews suggested, again avoiding a confrontation on the issue of age. "You and my father were the only survivors of a commando-team which assassinated that fiend Rontana more than half a century ago."

"Ancient history," Flix countered nonchalantly. "Just doing my duty, son. I never planned on being a hero. Monsieur Rontana was a troublesome parasite. He had to be eliminated, and I just happened to be there."

"So I've heard," the Senator agreed. "But General, these too are troubled times," he pointed out with a dramatic sweep of his hands.

"Young Matthews, do get to the point!" Flix boomed insistently. "You certainly didn't ask me all the way out here to discuss ancient history—or the weather!"

"Quite right," Senator Matthews acknowledged, turning from the window. "My father—Tiger, as you call him—trusts you implicitly. Before the election he told me that if I won, I should ask you to be my chief of staff."

"Sir, I have already held every job in this man's army, only now I have retired from public life," Flix explained patiently. "Besides, I could never work for someone who does everything his daddy tells him to."

With that, the older man rose to leave, his medals clanging against one another as he reached for his cane.

"Damn it man, I need you!" the Senator exhorted. "I am young, I have no experience, and I am in desperate need of a seasoned adviser. My father suggested you because..."

"Seasoned, eh?" Flix confirmed, hearing a word that caught his fancy.

"Older, then," Matthews offered, thinking he had offended him.

"No, I prefer seasoned," General Felix "Flix" Wenger declared, collecting his thoughts. "And just what does a *seasoned* adviser to a newly-elected U.S. Senator actually do?"

"General," Senator Matthews began, "it is apparent that ..."

"Please, Senator," the General interrupted in a respectful tone, "call me Flix."

"Flix it is," the Senator returned amicably. "Officially, I am Nathanial Junior, but my friends call me Nate." As the air warmed between them, Flix and Nate exchanged a cordial handshake.

"Flix, so much of the world has been destabilized that our strategic military alliances are worthless pieces of paper. And under Chester Nolan, the Presidency has been weakened so severely that the Senate is practically running the nation. And by committee, no less! The Senate has become the unofficial Executive branch for God's-sake! Fortunately, out here in Missouri, we have been insulated from the worst of the turmoil, but the nation itself is on the verge of being balkanized. The man's even talking about turning over control of the Pentagon to the Council of Nations, if you can believe that! We have become so hobbled, so beleaguered, I fear we will not survive another large-scale war intact."

"So far, Senator Nate, you have told me nothing new," Flix reported coolly, though he too was quite contemptuous of their President. Over the many years of Nolan's long tenure, he had fed the people more and more bread and circuses to appease them, and he had paid for it all by bargaining away more and more of America's military might. It was for this reason that Flix had aligned himself with the likes of Silas Whetstone, Nolan's vice president. Though Whetstone was as repugnant as a man could be, at least he understood the importance of a strong defensive capability.

"Please, Flix, give me a chance to finish. The crux of the matter is this: the Senate has become a battleground for a multitude of wrong-headed notions. My problem is that a coalition of midwestern Senators is maneuvering to fashion a whole host of policies regarding military spending and foreign policy. I have been asked to serve on the Military Oversight Committee because I am a freshman Senator, and they assume I will rubber stamp their every idea. I very much want this appointment—indeed, I have already accepted it—however, instead of just mechanically voting 'yes' whenever they say so, I would very much like to make a more considered contribution. Frankly, I would like to surprise the conceited sons-of-bitches, and that's where you come in. You know the territory. Goodness, as Chairman of the Joint Chiefs, you've *been* there. I want you to tell me what the hell I'm voting on. Not *how* to vote, mind you, but I want you to tutor me enough so I can understand the what and the wherefore of the topics I'll be asked to vote upon."

For the first time since their meeting began, retired General "Flix" Wenger smiled broadly. The fullness of his smile betrayed his Mediterranean features—the straight white teeth, the always-tanned look, the black hair.

"I've decided I like you, Nate. You are Tiger's son after all. Now I see it. I had to save him so there would be a you. I see in you his same sharp intellect; the same 'how to think, not what to think' outlook on life."

Nodding his head lightly, Flix signaled his approval. "Okay, son," he agreed, "you have just hired yourself one seasoned adviser."

4

WHETSTONE

Vice President's Mansion, Arlington, Virginia
BeHolden Day Eve

"I guess all I *really* want to know," the Vice President grilled, a concerned look furrowed into his brow, "is can he be trusted?" Both he and the General were sitting in the Vice President's study overlooking the duck pond behind the mansion. Armed guards could be seen patrolling the grounds. In the distance, the tip of the refurbished Washington Monument poked through the morning fog. The other two shorter obelisks were still buried in the haze which drifted lazily off the Potomac.

"Who, Matthews?" his visitor asked, his dark eyes a bit cross. "It's hard to say. He's not a stupid man you know. Like his father, the Governor, Nate's honest, if a bit naive."

"Nate, is it?" the Vice President cross-examined in a curious tone. "It sounds as if the two of you have become good buddies."

"Let's just say, I don't think he will be a problem," Flix explained in a tired voice as he tapped his fingers against the hilt of his cane. He wished he was up at his house in Maine, preparing a delicious turkey dinner for himself instead of here in D.C. arguing with Whetstone. For Flix, BeHolden Day had always been a joyous occasion, one which he hated to miss. Unlike Christmas or Easter, this late November holiday had no religious overtones, and so far as Flix could tell, its only ostensible purpose was to legitimize—if only for a moment—all of one's indulgences.

"If we are to regain control of the country, nothing must be allowed to interfere with our plans vis à vis Nolan," the Vice President made clear, his long, thin fingers gripping the arm of his chair.

"Don't you think I know that, Sy?" Flix retorted, miffed by the implication. "If anyone is in over his head, it is most assuredly me."

It was at times like these that Flix questioned his motives for getting into bed with this man. If it hadn't been for Nolan's total disregard for the nation's crumbling military strength, Flix probably would have avoided Whetstone like the plague.

"But can he be *trusted*?" Whetstone repeated in obvious reference to Senator Matthews. "Or do you think perhaps he can be bought?"

"I seriously doubt that," Flix replied, disquieted by the suggestion. It was bad enough that he was putting *his* career on the line; Flix certainly didn't want Nate compromised as well.

"You know McDonald is retiring, don't you?" Whetstone queried as he got to his feet and paced nervously about the room. When the Vice President walked, it was a comical sight. Like Ichabod Crane, Silas Whetstone was tall and hollow-cheeked; like Abraham Lincoln, he had spindly legs and a gaunt face. When he stood next to the much shorter, much more athletic Flix, Whetstone could only be described as a curiosity.

"Well, it's only about time McDonald quit. He's been Chairman of the M.O. Committee for as long as I have been a General," Flix declared, rapping his cane impatiently against the floor. As he did so, it reverberated with a faint metallic ping, a sound which wasn't all that unusual when one considered that the staff had been hollowed-out inside to make room for a rifled gun barrel which ran down its entire length. The weapon's single-action trigger was hidden in the well of the walking stick's curved handle, and when it was squeezed, a single large calibre shell was expelled from its mouth.

"What's your point, Silas?" Flix probed apprehensively as he fingered the business end of his cane.

"People owe me favors."

"Meaning what?"

"Meaning that perhaps we could arrange for Senator Matthews to succeed McDonald as Chairman of the M.O. Committee," the Vice President elaborated, his face drawing thinner as his eyes sank ever deeper into his skull.

"He's a freshman Senator," Flix objected as he rose unsteadily from his chair to join the Vice President at the window. "They'd never go for it. Besides, Senator Duncan is the heir apparent."

"Forget about Duncan, will you? He's a sap. Look here, anything can be sold if it's packaged properly," the gaunt man explained in a condescending tone. "And with you visibly on the scene as Matthews' trusted advisor, I am confident the others can be persuaded that he is the right man for the job. By the way, wasn't his wife Darna—God rest her soul—the heiress to the ASARCO fortune?"

"Yes," Flix answered, almost choking on the words, "but what's *that* got to do with anything?"

"Don't you get it? I know the truth about the silver cannonball incident," Whetstone announced, obviously pleased with himself. "I know what *really* happened, and I wouldn't hesitate to use that information to my benefit if I needed to."

"You really are a bastard aren't you?" Flix snapped, looking as if he might rap Whetstone in the head with the butt of his cane. "Anyhow, that's ancient history—no one cares about that episode anymore."

"Even so, it would create enough of a scandal to keep the man in line if the need arose," Whetstone assured him wickedly. "Just like your little black book helps keep *me* in line."

"Don't worry yourself so; I have it safely tucked away in a place where even *you* can't find it."

"Oh, do you now?" Whetstone taunted as if he wasn't

afraid of what Flix knew about him.

"Yes, I do. But that's enough about me already, let's get back to Nolan," Flix redirected, his dark eyes revealing his concern for the nasty business he had set in motion. "I should be told who's gonna do him and when."

"My boss Chester has an eye for the ladies, and so I have set him up with a doozie—blond hair, blue eyes, big boobs…"

"Okay, already, I get the picture," Flix interrupted irritably, "but I want to see a dossier on her before we commit ourselves."

"Fine, I'll have one prepared," Whetstone answered almost too quickly.

"When will she do it?"

"Whenever I tell her to," Silas replied coldly. "Whenever I say the word."

"It's my considered opinion that to achieve the desired effect, it must be a public assassination—a *very* public assassination," Flix spelled out. "At a banquet perhaps, or at a political rally."

"Let me worry about the details, won't you?" the Vice President retorted.

"No, I won't!" Flix shot back, approaching to within inches of Whetstone's face. "If this thing blows up, it blows up in my face too!"

"But, Flix," the Vice President replied in a soothing tone, as he took a step backwards, "if we succeed, America will have been saved, and you will be a hero. You will be able to go to your maker in the confidence that you have saved the world, not once, but twice."

5

GUNNHILDR

Senate Office Building, District of Columbia
January

"Nate, your training officially begins this morning," Flix explained without elaboration. Unlike the first time the two of them had met, Flix was dressed leisurely, even casually. He held a bulky gym bag in his hand, and judging by the way he was struggling with it, the gunny sack was plenty heavy.

"What training?" Nate asked, irritated by the unexpected intrusion. Shooing Flix into his private office, Matthews shut the door behind them. In the outer reception area, his uniformed security man—known only to him so far as Dirk—grunted in a perfunctory manner as he jotted down the visitor's name and his time of arrival. Judging by Dirk's gruff demeanor, the newly-arrived Senator had obviously not paid him the deference an underling of his lofty position deserved.

"Geez, Flix," Nate objected, as he set down the box he had been lugging, "this is my first day on the job; I only just arrived in town."

That was no exaggeration. It had been just over seven weeks since the election, and between attending gala affairs to celebrate his success at the polls and making appearances at fancy receptions to herald the New Year, Nate had had little time to prepare himself for the duties of office. He had accepted the offer of a seat on the Military Oversight

Committee, and he had even met once with Vice President Whetstone to familiarize himself with the M.O.C.'s key battles in the upcoming session, but other than that, he had languished until today in that nether world between election and inauguration. With McDonald's announcement of his intention to retire, Whetstone had hinted that the committee's chairmanship could be his if only he would be willing to "play ball." Doing his best to conceal his excitement over the prospect, Nate had agreed to take it under advisement and render a final decision once he had formally taken the oath of office.

Early this morning, after bidding Musette a cordial adieu, and after delivering his son Frankie to his brother and his sister-in-law in Farmington, Nate had taken a suborb out of St. Louis and into Washington. When he finally got to his office, he was surprised to find Flix waiting for him at the door. Judging by the peeved glare on his face, he and Dirk had been arguing. Flix had refused to be searched, and the security man had refused to let him pass. Jumping in to mediate the crisis before Dirk could strike Flix with his metal detector, Nate separated the two men, and invited Flix to come into his office and take it easy.

"There's no time like the present to get started," Flix maintained as he barged into the room, still angry over his confrontation with Dirk. "You wanted a seasoned adviser, didn't you?"

"Well, yes," the Senator admitted as he offered the General a seat, "but the way I had it figured was that you would help me as I requested it, not the other way around," Nate pointed out as Flix set the gym bag on the floor and made himself comfortable.

"Well, then, you figured it wrong. It's a mighty dangerous world out there," Flix reported with a bit of a flare, "and you need to learn how to defend yourself."

"Here? In my *office*?" Nate debated incredulously. "I already *have* a bodyguard," Nate offered, gesturing toward the reception area where Dirk was just about to squeeze his eyes shut in preparation for his morning nap.

"That insolent dolt?! He's a damn civil servant, for God's-sake," Flix objected vehemently. "You can't expect a man who is paid by the hour to take a bullet for you."

"A bullet?!" Matthews exclaimed. "Are you crazy?"

"Are you really so arrogant that you don't think Senators ever get *shot*?" Flix boomed, rapping his cane against the hardwood floor for emphasis. When he was angry, his closely-cropped black hair and his dark eyes gave him a fierce look.

"Well…I guess," Nate interjected defensively.

"Nine assassination attempts in a dozen years," Flix tabulated, "*two* of which were successful."

"Yes…I suppose."

"Get serious, boy," Flix demanded emphatically. "You need to learn how to handle a gun, and your training officially begins today."

"I've never shot anything in my life," the tall, good-looking Senator revealed. "Dad was always against my learning."

"My, but you've led a sheltered existence," the General remarked caustically. "That doesn't sound like the Tiger *I* used to know—he was a *maniac* with munitions."

"You talk of assassinations, of killings, of guns, as if you were discussing the Dow Jones or the score of a baseball game!" Nate roared, getting to his feet. "What kind of a man are you, Flix?"

"Some men have to do what others won't—or can't—or shouldn't. There is no mystery here, no diabolical universities where such men are trained, no driving ambitions to destroy," Flix asserted passionately. "Men such as myself, such as your father once was, drifted into these shadowy occupations because there were voids to fill. And the candidates to fill them were remarkably few. With repetition you find that either you have the stomach for it or else you don't. *Somebody* has to walk the wall for God's-sake!"

"Flix, you're like a Catholic priest in a whorehouse," Nate declared disrespectfully. "You excuse yourself by saying that you are gathering material for a sermon, and then when you go home to write it, you end up playing with yourself."

"Let's just skip the holier than thou crap, shall we, and return to the real world? I have with me several unmarked pieces for you to try out for size," Flix explained as he reached into his gym bag for the guns he had brought along. "You are to keep one of these with you at all times just in case."

"Just in case of what?"

"Just in case sleeping beauty out there fails to stop an assassin in the outer lobby, and the bad guy makes it in here."

Even as he spoke, Flix silently propped open the door to Nate's office just enough for the Senator to see Dirk fast asleep at his desk.

"Goodness gracious, if I were attacked, I wouldn't know what to do," Nate admitted, listening more attentively now to what Flix had to say.

Switching to a professorial tone as if he had taught this subject before, the highly decorated General spelled out the steps Nate should take, "If you are ever threatened by an intruder, or if you are ever confronted by an assassin, the first rule of self defense is never hesitate. Get down. Stay low," he described even as he crouched defensively behind Nate's mammoth desk. "Survey the situation," he added as he peered around the desk acting out his own commands. "If you *must* move, move quickly. And by all means, get your hands on a weapon," he instructed, grabbing for one of the guns he had brought with him. "Always strike first, and *always* shoot to kill."

"Geez, Flix," Nate exhorted, overwhelmed by the older man's performance, "are you sure you know what you're talking about? That seems pretty severe."

"Never point a weapon at someone unless you are justified in killing him; then, if warranted, do so."

"Just like that?"

"Just like that. No warning shots. No wing shots to wound the fellow. If you were justified in pulling the gun to begin with, if you are faced with deadly force, shoot to kill. If you

leave the guy alive out of misguided softheartedness, he will
repay your generosity either by killing you or by suing you."

"Suing me?"

"He will sue you for causing his subsequent paraplegia,
and he will seek to force you to support him for the rest of his
rotten life. In court he will plead that when he attacked you he
was depressed because society had failed him. He will claim
that he was looking for Mother Teresa for comfort and to offer
his services to the poor. In that lawsuit, you will lose. On the
other hand, if you kill him, the most you can expect is that a
relative will bring a wrongful death action. In that case you
will have two advantages: first, there will only be your story;
you can forget about Mother Teresa. Second, even if you lose,
how much could the bum's life be worth anyway? A lot less
than fifty years worth of paralysis. Don't play games. Finish
the job."

"I don't know if I can do that."

"When the time comes, you'll know. Now pay attention.
Handguns fall into two categories: revolvers and semiauto-
matic pistols. Revolvers are made in both single and double
actions. That is, those that require manual cocking before the
trigger is squeezed, and those that automatically cock as the
trigger is operated. All come in a variety of sizes and fire a
bewildering number of different cartridges from the puny to
the powerful, but which to choose? Here, try this Colt .45 out
for size," Flix suggested, tossing him a hefty weapon.

"Do I really have to do this?" the younger man asked,
judging the Colt's weight in his palm.

"Only if you want to live. Or how about this Remington?"
Flix proffered, handing him another gun. "Or even this Smith
& Wesson .357 Magnum, the standard firearm of law enforce-
ment agents."

"Do they all have names?" Senator Matthews quizzed,
liking the feel of the second piece.

"For the most part, yes. Like most gadgets, they were first
named for their inventors. Men like Samuel Colt, Eliphalet
Remington, Oliver F. Winchester."

"So, smart guy, who was Mr. Gun?"

"Strange that you should ask that, because I happen to know the answer to your question. You see, I used to teach Strategy and Tactics at the Academy," Flix reported without boasting. "Our word gun derives from the name of a SKANDIA woman, Gunnhildr. A fourteenth century munitions account from Cornwall records a ballista which defended Windsor Castle as being called *Domina Gunilda*, literally 'Lady Gunilda'. Gunnhildr was an apt name for a war machine of that era because both 'gunnr', from the Indo-European to strike or to wound, and 'hildr', from the Old Norse to battle, meant 'war'. Bestowing women's names on engines of war is an old practice," he elaborated as he took a Luger in his skilled hands and began breaking it down on Nate's desk. "The most famous examples of this custom would probably be the huge World War One artillery piece, Big Bertha, named for the daughter of the twentieth century arms manufacturer Fritz Krupp, and Burping Betty of Australian Civil War fame, named for the gulping sound it made as it spat out its potbellied shells."

Even as he spoke, Flix snapped the Luger's trigger housing out of its recess and checked the weapon's bore under the light of the floor lamp; it was as it should be—spotless. Dismantling the gun as he might disrobe a high-priced woman, he tenderly oiled each mechanism until every inch of her dark metal glistened. A narrow smile erupted on his face as he affectionately reassembled the weapon, wiping every surface clean as he went. Depressing the long shells into the magazine with phallic implications, he cracked the clip up through the black slit in the handle with a lascivious thrust.

"This is the gun I want you to have," Flix said as he pressed it into the Senator's hand. "Next week, if it warms up, we will go down to the range, and I will teach you how to shoot her."

President's Ready Room, The New White House
That Same Morning

"Come in, come in," President Nolan eagerly motioned to his overdue guest as he pumped the man's hand. The Chief Executive was a handsome, middle-aged gentleman of boyish good-looks and undeniable charm.

"I was surprised by your invitation," Senator Duncan declared, reluctant to cross the threshold into the President's sitting room. Peering in, he could see that there was a regally-sized desk along one wall, and three couches forming a giant U along the other. Portraits of prominent commanders-in-chief hung all around.

"Duncan, it's been too long," Chester apologized before turning to his butler. "That will be all," he dismissed, shooing the tuxedo-clad domestic away. "Make yourself at home, Senator," he beckoned, showing the bald-headed Duncan to a seat. "I've been here in the White House so long—what it is now, six terms?—that I find myself ignoring those who have always been so supportive of my programs."

"Well, I'm flattered, to be sure," Duncan graciously replied.

"For crying out loud, man!" Nolan reprimanded. "You know what an inspiration you have always been to me."

"Do tell," Duncan snapped unenthusiastically. "You didn't ask me up here for a hymnal or a church service, did you? Let's drop the act, Chester, and get down to cases."

"Okay, already," the President relented. "I know we haven't always seen eye to eye but I need your help."

"Why me?"

"Because people respect you."

"Do you? Respect me, I mean," Duncan quizzed.

"How could you think otherwise?" he challenged with a Kennedyesque twist of the head.

"Do come to the point," Duncan insisted, feigning a bored yawn.

"I need your help," the President implored in as sincere a tone as Duncan had ever heard him use. "I don't trust Silas Whetstone anymore."

"So why did you take him in as your veep?" the Senator probed in an uncaring tone. Though he too was no great fan of

Whetstone's, Duncan had grown increasingly disillusioned with Nolan's continued refusal to adequately fund the Pentagon. To Duncan's way of thinking, both of them should be thrown out of office, and he had a mind to run himself.

"I had no choice at the convention," Chester correctly pointed out, "and now the man's just too damn popular for me to drop him from the ticket. Unless some scandal forces him to resign, I'm stuck with him for the duration."

"Chrissake! You want me to trump up some scandalous *charges* on this guy?" the Senator exploded, shrinking from the suggestion.

"For crying out loud, of course not! What kind of a man do you think I am?" Nolan petitioned sharply. "Considering what he has *actually* done, we won't have to manufacture a thing. All we have to do is ensure that the truth comes out," Chester clarified as he handed the recalcitrant Senator a sheaf of papers plus several photographs. "Here, take a look at these. But you had better make yourself comfortable, because I won't permit this file to leave my office."

After a few minutes' study, Duncan gasped with disbelief. "This can't be!" he exclaimed. "Silas beat up his wife? And his daughter too?"

"So far as I know, it's all true," President Nolan confirmed with a nod of his head.

"So what do you need *me* for?" the Senator probed suspiciously, handing the incriminating file back to Nolan as he spoke. "Just deliver it anonymously to the newspapers and let the scandal run its course."

"Not good enough. There's more."

"What?"

"I believe that, along with a couple of his chums at the Pentagon, my Vice President is running a clandestine, underground militia."

"How is that possible?" Duncan wondered. "I sit on the Military Oversight Committee for Chrissake. If that were true, I would have heard about it by now."

"Not necessarily," Chester countered. "Whetstone plays things pretty close to the vest. What do you know about this new Senator from the 'show me' state?"

"Who, Matthews? I've only just met him, but he's harmless."

"So how come I have a recommendation on my desk from Silas that Matthews be appointed Chairman of that committee instead of you?"

Bristling with anger over this unexpected revelation, Duncan shouted, "Why don't you go *fuck* yourself, Nolan! How should *I* know the basis for Whetstone's recommendation?"

Ignoring the bald-headed man's outburst, Chester justified, "The reason he's to be made Chairman instead of you is because of General Wenger. The good general is Silas' right-hand man, and I'd wager he's in it up to his crotch. And if I'm right—so is Matthews."

"At the risk of sounding like a broken record, I still don't see what you need me for," Senator Duncan questioned, getting to his feet as if he were preparing to leave.

"I want you to dig out the dirt on Silas; I want you to sniff around Wenger and see if you can't shed any light on this secret military budget of his; and I want you to go to Bethesda and try to talk to Clara, Silas' wife. As you may know, the Second Lady is institutionalized there."

"You want a lot. Give me one reason why I should do *anything* for you," Duncan jeered, digging in his heels.

"Because I won't be President forever, and when Silas is forced to resign, I'll be forced to appoint a successor to fill out his term, a successor who will take my place when I retire. I know you're ambitious, Duncan; there's no reason why that successor can't be you."

"Yes, I think I see your point now," Duncan nodded as he gathered his things to leave. "And you're right about one thing: I *am* ambitious."

6

NIKKI

Chevy Chase, Maryland
February

Kneeling astride his naked body, her well-oiled muscles rippling, she rode him like a professional broncobuster might have ridden an unbroken stallion. No matter how much he bucked, no matter how hard he thrust, her hips didn't loosen their vise-like grip around him. And when finally the two of them had both gone the limit, she dismounted her steed like a lady, without even breaking a sweat. Only, given the sum total of her effort, he didn't seem all that appreciative. In fact, no sooner had she rolled over and curled herself up in the silk sheets, than he sprang from the bed and made a bee-line for the bathroom, his feet making a deep impression in the plush carpet.

"I have to go," Chester mumbled indifferently, reaching for his toothbrush. As he stood there in the bathroom staring narcistically at himself in the mirror, Nikki concluded that this assignment was proving to be long on play-acting and short on genuine passion. Ever since she had accepted this job more than two months ago, she had been eager for the day when it would be over. President Nolan was so self-possessed, so full of himself, it made her skin crawl.

"Chester, honey, do you have to leave so soon?" she objected, her face painted with a big pout. "You only just got here."

"Listen, you," he retorted in an ugly tone from the lavatory, "if I had wanted to be nagged at, I could have stayed at home. I do have a wife, you know." Even as he spoke, he combed his wavy hair in the fashion that was his trademark on camera.

"Of course, I know you have a wife," she cooed, exposing her left thigh from under the sheets in such a way that he couldn't help but notice, "and I know how much you must love her; it's only we never seem to have the time to talk like we used to. Lately, it seems you only have time to do me, and then once you're done, you run off to some meeting, or some appointment."

"For crying out loud, woman, I'm the *President*!" he bellowed even as he admired his features in the mirror. "Don't you think my job is a bit more involved than just porking whatever bimbooker my chief of staff happens to drudge up for me?"

"Now that's mean," she whined as the tears started to flow. "All I wanted was a little affection."

"Now, now, my pretty," he soothed in his politician's voice as he buttoned his dress shirt closed, "Little Chester can come out and play with you again tomorrow, but that's all the time he has for you today."

"Can't he stay just a *teeny* bit longer?" Nikki begged between sobs. "Does he have to leave me now?"

"I can't help it, Nikki," he justified as he came to sit on the bed next to her, "but Ambassador Ling from China will be here in D.C. for just one night, and I *must* meet with him."

"What's so goshdarned important about a smelly old Chinaman that would make you want to leave these?" she taunted, wantonly fondling her breasts right before his eyes. Her body was scented like a cat in heat, her loins gladly parted for his inspection.

"Wouldn't *you* like to know?" he responded icily. Caught off-guard by her sudden interest in his affairs, but unwilling to let her see his surprise, Chester got up off the bed and scrambled to the closet in search of the right tie. She followed closely along behind him, squeezing his buns as they went.

"Yes, I *would* like to know," she admitted, taking the necktie from him and handing him another, more attractive one.

"Well, I'm sorry, but I can't discuss it with you," he explained, as he put on the neck piece she had chosen. "Anyway, if all goes well tonight, it'll be on the news before long. In fact, if this evening's negotiations are successful, the treaty could be signed as early as the upcoming Council of Nations dinner in April."

"Oh, that sounds so exciting!" Nikki sparkled, playing the dumb-blond role to the hilt. "Now, doesn't that tie go much better with your dinner jacket?" she verified as the two of them stood shoulder-to-shoulder admiring themselves in the full-length mirror, she stark naked, he in his tailored suit.

"Yes, darling, it does, and I must apologize for calling you a bimbooker earlier," he asserted in a conciliatory tone as he allowed his hands to indecently stroke her private parts. Even as he rubbed her into a frenzy, his eyes feasted on the reflection of his lewd movements in the mirror. "I feel as if I am being pressured by everyone around me to do things I don't want to do," he elaborated as he studied her reactions to his probing fingers. "I guess I must have been taking it out on you," he conceded as he massaged her to a crescendo.

"That's okay," she purred hungrily as she crested. "I understand. Just so long as Little Chester returns to take care of me tomorrow, I'll be happy."

"Did you plant the bug?" the gaunt-faced man asked, speaking almost reverently into the comm.

"Yes, sir, it is threaded into the weave of his tie," the assassin replied, proud of her handiwork. "Remember, it is an audio tap only; that's the best I could do on such short notice."

"Is he on to you?" Whetstone asked with half-hearted concern. It wasn't that he cared so much for her welfare, as he was worried about his own. This plot had been taking shape over several months, and he needed an excuse to bring it to a head. When he got wind of Nolan's meeting with the Chinese tonight, he felt he had to act.

"No, I don't think he has a clue," Nikki answered, reflecting on their just concluded liaison. "Our Chester's not the brightest boy in town. I suppose that's one of the reasons you want him out of the way, eh?"

"Watch yourself, my sweet," the Vice President warned. "He is more cunning than you may think. Anyway, this will be over before too long."

"It's only about time," the killer revealed, studying her own sculpted nakedness in the mirror. "This guy is in love with himself."

"Well, if you're not too busy, I may have another job for you shortly," Whetstone offered, his long, thin fingers wrapped around the hilt of the comm.

"Goody, goody," she exclaimed, her ample breasts bouncing as she hopped about the room. "Who will it be *this* time?"

"Are you acquainted with General Felix Wenger?" Silas asked as he prepared to cover his flank against one of his own.

"That old geezer?" she retorted in a carping tone.

"Be respectful, won't you?" Whetstone snapped. "The man's a war hero."

"What difference should *that* make?" she asserted coldly.

"Wenger has a code book hidden somewhere, a book which—if it fell into the wrong hands—could cause a global crisis. I need you to find that book and steal it for me."

"If you want me to sleep with him, that'll cost you extra."

"Don't worry, honey, there's plenty of money in the till," he declared confidently, "but for now, let's concentrate our efforts on Nolan. If you'll check the recycling bin out behind your flat, you'll find a brown corrugated box with a dingy yellow label on top. Inside the box is an unmarked piece plus two clips of durbinium-tipped shells. They're hollow points like you like. If the gun can be traced at all, it will be traced back to our General Wenger. When the time comes, that's the piece you'll want to use to kill Nolan."

"The man's a conceited lech, you know."

"And I suppose you're the virgin Mary?"

"I do believe in immaculate deception," she retorted naughtily. "Isn't that close enough?"

"I do hope you're as good as they say," Silas continued, "because this killing has got to be a very public event. Probably at the Council dinner Chester mentioned to you this evening."

"Isn't that being held at the Goldstein Center? How do you expect me to do it *there*?" she returned, suddenly suspicious of his intentions.

"Remember our good friend whose gun you will be using?"

"Wenger?"

"Yea, Wenger. He's one of my most trusted deputies. Taught at the Academy; was once head of covert operations at the Pentagon," Whetstone pointed out. "I'll arrange for you two to meet on a nonprofessional basis shortly. He needs a girl Friday to help him with a research project over in the law library. Then I'll see to it that he's in the audience the night of the hit. He will provide you with some sort of a distraction so the two of you can get away. When the job is done, he'll whisk you out of there and take you someplace safe—probably his cabin in Maine. Afterwards, if all goes well, you'll show him your appreciation for having saved your life by finishing the poor bastard off. But first, you must win his confidence. That way you'll already have your hooks in him, and he won't suspect a thing."

"Hooks?" she questioned. "That sounds so...so crass."

"My apologies," he answered insincerely.

"Indeed. Will there be anything else?" she asked, debating whether she was about to be double-crossed. "If not, I need to find that box out back, and I need to take a shower."

"No, that will be all," the Vice President replied, hoping that he wasn't leaving out some important detail. "After Nolan's meeting with the ambassador tonight, I'll contact you again. Sleep tight, honey," he closed in a fatherly tone.

7

TREATY

Embassy Row, District of Columbia
Later That Same Evening

The vestibule was superbly decorated, its wall-paper marbled and flecked as if it were a layer of thick frosting plastered generously on a cake, its carpet so plush each step left behind a deep indentation, and its divan so elegantly padded it would literally swallow up an unattentive guest. What looked like tiny grasshoppers were sewn into the weave of the seat cushions. Even the lighting in the antechamber was a bit garish, a fact which didn't go unnoticed as President Nolan impatiently paced back and forth across the room, his two bodyguards waiting impassively by the heavy oak door.

Accustomed as he was to making others wait on him, the President was more than a little miffed at having the tables turned. Under any other circumstances, he might have stomped indignantly from the room, but he needed this meeting, and he needed the treaty he hoped to negotiate. Even a weak leader knows when he's failing, and Chester was no exception to that rule. He could tell from the hushed whispers of his staff, from the suppressed snickers of his own Vice President, from the strutting, peacock-like ways of the Senate's powerful men like Benson and Duncan, and even from Nikki's probing questions, that his long-tenured administration had become a laughingstock. To save his Presidency, Chester needed to commit a bold stroke, and he prayed that this tête-à-tête with the Chinese would be just the cure for his ailing image. Perhaps sensing Nolan's desperation, Ambassador Ling could afford to make him cool his heels out here in the waiting room for as long as he pleased.

Even as Nolan stewed in a porridge of his own making, miles away—in the comfort of his Arlington home—Silas propped his over-sized feet upon his giant wooden desk. As Chester hummed an impatient little tune and made occasional small talk with his bodyguards, Whetstone eagerly listened to the short, staccato breathing of his boss. Lacing his fingers around a glass of tortan as he did his best to visualize the scene in the vestibule of Ambassador Ling's Embassy Row suite, the Vice President made a mental note to have Nikki plant a microcamera the next time around. When at long last, the door to Ling's inner sanctum swung noiselessly open, Silas couldn't picture the beefy guard who stood before Nolan, his bulk filling the portal. But he could hear what was being said.

"Ambassador Ling Tsui will see you now," the big man noted, bowing ever so slightly and beckoning to Nolan as he spoke. The man was huge and his muscles bulged with every motion.

Though Chester was still seething inside over the interminable wait, he couldn't afford to blow this opportunity. Swallowing his pride, the President addressed the mountainous man with all the politeness he could muster. "Are you certain I won't be disturbing the Ambassador?" he asked.

"If you will please remove your street shoes and put on these slippers instead, I will show you in," the sumo wrestler-sized attendant grunted.

Seeing the humungous man, Nolan's secret service agents sprung into action, their hands reaching into their vests for their revolvers. Moving with surprising speed for a man his size, the ambassador's man stepped between Nolan and his bodyguards. "Not them," he barked, a stern look on his face. "Only you."

"It'll be okay," Chester assured his two protectors, his

voice cracking with uncertainty. "Wait here until I'm through."

"But, sir, we could lose our jobs!" one of the men whined, less concerned with the President's safety than whether he got his next meal. "Our orders are to never leave your side."

"I'll be okay," Nolan insisted, slipping off his shoes as instructed. "This is an *embassy* for crying out loud."

As the President crossed the threshold into the next chamber, he entered another world. The room was dimly lit, its air clogged with the sweet perfume of burning incense. In the background, the sounds of a soft, twangy oriental tune filtered through the bamboo curtains separating the dining table from the lounging area where he stood. Two geisha girls, their jet-black hair in buns atop their heads, were tending to the ambassador even as two others beckoned to Nolan to join them on the low-slung sofa.

Lingering a moment at the doorway while his eyes adjusted to the darkness, Nolan swallowed hard as he digested just how much out of his element he really was. For an instant he regretted having agreed to leave his bodyguards behind in the next room, but gathering his courage as he tried to remember the correct protocol, he bowed servilely and introduced himself.

"Ambassador Ling, I am Chester Nolan, the President of the United States of America. After the many times we have spoken on the comm, it is indeed a pleasure to finally make your acquaintance."

Seemingly more interested in the girls fawning over him than in what the President had to say, the Ambassador remarked, "May I introduce you to Moira and Sona. They will be your pleasure-girls for the night. They will get—or do— whatever you tell them to. Please do not be shy."

Now that his eyes were fully acclimated to the murky atmosphere, he was able to bring Ambassador Ling into clearer focus. The man reminded him of the statues he had seen of the Asian god Buddha—a bald head, two fat hands, and a bulging stomach. Hanging from his thick neck was an amulet formed in the shape of a locust embedded in amber.

Next to him was a bong which he had obviously been putting to good use. Unaccustomed as he was to such practices, Nolan couldn't tell whether Ling had been smoking opium or hashish, or whether he had just been burning incense—all he knew was the Chinaman seemed stoned.

As Moira took his left arm and Sona his right, Nolan pointed out as sincerely as he could, "I really don't want to appear inhospitable, but I came here to talk, not to party."

"Business is pleasure; pleasure is business," Ling countered as if he were a great sage ready to spew forth some quotable passage every time his slit of a mouth opened.

"Where I come from, it's business *before* pleasure," Nolan retorted, digging in his heels even as he shooed the two girls away. "Come back in an hour ladies, and perhaps I will be in a mood to celebrate then."

Seeing that the President was serious, Ambassador Ling snapped his pudgy fingers and dismissed the geishas. When they had faded into the shadows, Chester demanded, "Him too," gesturing to the goliath-sized bodyguard who had first admitted him.

"Chang is harmless," Ambassador Ling objected.

"Harmless or not, these are *private* talks," Chester emphasized. "And if my secret service men must wait outside, so must yours."

"Agreed," Ling nodded dejectedly, "but I hope you are not so intransigent in *all* your demands."

"Once the table is set, I think you will find that I am not a very picky eater," Nolan replied, speaking in metaphor.

"An apt analogy," Ling complimented as Chang melted away. "May I interest you in a cup of ginseng tea?" the obese Chinaman asked as he struggled to his feet.

"Yes, I don't mind if I do."

When the ambassador had poured them each a demitasse of steaming tea, he asked, "So, Mr. President, tell me what is so urgent that we had to meet on such short notice? And what, pray tell, could trouble you to such a degree that we are forced to dispense with the many pleasures of women and wine? I would think that with all the problems facing America today, you would be concentrating your efforts on *domestic* issues, not worrying yourself over our intentions in the Pacific."

"A President can never afford to be sidetracked by pedestrian matters where national security is involved," Nolan explained in his politician's voice. "Ever since you conquered the island of Japan, we know you have had your eyes on Hawaii. It has occurred to me that perhaps we could do each other a favor."

"Go on," Ling calmly replied, his heart racing.

"Rather than the islands being a tempting target for you to invade, perhaps we could work out a *business* arrangement," Chester explained, gratified that he had the fat man's attention.

"I'm listening," Ambassador Ling advised, his eyes slanting even more narrowly.

"Our national debt has ballooned to such a level, I must find a way to cut it down to size or else we may be forced to default on at least one series of our outstanding Treasury bonds. China, for instance, holds all of our outstanding series K bonds," the President elaborated in a threatening tone. "As any good businessman will tell you, selling off assets to pay down debts is the swiftest way to correct a cash-flow deficit. Well, in an operation as big as the government of the United States of America, only selling thousands of acres of prime real estate can raise enough cash to make much of a dent in our IOU's. It occurred to me that since you already own most of the upscale hotels in downtown Honolulu and in Lihue, perhaps you would want to buy the whole place."

"What a novel idea!" Ling exclaimed, his bulging belly dancing. "But on who's authority are you negotiating? Hawaii is a state after all, don't *they* have a say in this?"

"Our constitution permits the President—and the President alone—the authority to sign treaties or to enter into contracts on behalf of the United States. If I am able to package this right, the rest of the country will agree that this sale is in the best interests of the other 56 states. I anticipate few problems obtaining Senate approval. They only need to be convinced that unless we sell, you will invade, and that defending against such a war would cost more than just giving it up outright."

"A declaration of peace without a declaration of war? I underestimated you," Ling acknowledged, wondering whether he had heard him right.

"All I have to do is convince them that Hawaii is no longer of strategic value to us."

"And how will you do that?"

"We bought Alaska from the Russians, didn't we?" Chester answered as if he were preparing a speech. "We can certainly sell a bunch of bug-infested, wind-swept islands to you. Now, where did those pretty girls go that you brought in for me earlier?"

By this time Whetstone had heard enough to click off the receiver. If he had ever harbored any lingering doubts regarding Chester, they were now dispelled. The man had to go!

8

SPRING FEVER

Each March, when the ice on the Potomac first starts to crack, it is a sure sign that winter has lost its bitter grip on the nation's capital. Though Flix had been here to witness the metamorphosis many times before, he never ceased to be amazed by the eternal changing of the seasons. Except perhaps for his lodge up in Bar Harbor, there was probably no spot on the eastern seaboard more beautiful, more tranquil, than Washington at the onset of spring. Even a man of Flix's age couldn't help but be moved by the balmy temperatures which had rolled into town ahead of schedule this year.

Bounding up the steps of the Jefferson Law Library—his gait quickened by the thrust of his own rising sap—Flix proceeded directly to the public information desk in the center of the library's main hall. After identifying himself to the clerk, he was sent on to the reference room in the basement.

Descending down several flights of stairs into the musty bowels of the block-long building, he came to a dimly-lit station in the midst of the stacks. Silas had told him to ask for a Miss Nikki, but Flix had no idea where in this gargantuan edifice she was sequestered, or how attractive she would turn out to be. He had expected someone as tattered and decrepit as the documents he sought, someone as yellowed and weathered as he himself was. What he found sitting there behind a broken-down giant of a desk was something else altogether—

Miss Nikki was a gorgeous specimen of a woman.

Though he should have been suspicious of her dazzling good looks from the start, once he laid eyes on her smooth-as-silk face and her tight little buttocks, his sixth sense began to fail him. Perhaps he was blinded by fears of his own approaching mortality, or perhaps he was confused by the debilitating effects of the season; either way, something caused him to drop his usual guard. Like Samson without his hair, or Popeye without his spinach, Flix was vulnerable to her advances. She swept him off his feet; he didn't have a chance.

"Are you Miss Nikki?" he stammered, blushing like a teenager.

"Why, yes," she answered, extending her hand in a lady-like fashion. Instead of sporting the long blond hair and soft blue eyes which had helped her seduce Chester Nolan so easily, she now wore a compact, auburn wig and a pair of contact lenses which made her blue eyes appear brown. Unless he looked closely, even Chester himself wouldn't have recognized her. Indeed, the only thing similar about this Nikki and that Nikki was her sculpted body; it was firm in all the right places, and deliciously soft everywhere else. And even though there were some vague similarities between Miss Nikki and the unnamed woman assassin profiled in the dossier Whetstone had given him, there were not enough to make him suspicious.

"My name is Nikki—Nikki Patterson," she pointed out as she escorted him past a row of stacks to a bank of info-terminals.

"I knew a Patterson once," Flix explained. "He was a commander in the special forces."

"See? We practically know each other already," she cooed, melting down his reserve. "We're almost family. Now, how can I help you sir?"

"The Vice President informs me that you have worked for him on several special projects in the past," Flix reported, blissfully unaware of Whetstone's prior relationships with this girl. "I need your assistance researching an archaic topic for my boss."

"And who is your boss?" she inquired sweetly, strutting her stuff back and forth in the aisle before him.

"Senator Nate Matthews," he replied, doing his best to suppress his obvious longings for this nymph.

"And what is the subject you need information on?"

"Before the Easter recess, there is to be a floor debate on the question of term limitations as it applies to the office of the President. It will undoubtedly be a partisan affair, but with Nolan having been reelected on five separate occasions, and with his popularity currently declining, momentum is building to amend the constitution and prevent him from running again. My boss, who was appointed by Nolan to be the Chairman of the Military Oversight Committee, has been asked to lead the opposition. I need to gain some historical perspective on this question, and I'm told you're the best researcher money can buy."

Beaming at Flix's compliment, she declared, "That may be a bit of an overstatement, but I'll admit I've done some work for Mr. Whetstone in the past and he seemed satisfied with the results. Please understand," she explained in a professional tone, her brown eyes seducing him, "I am only as good as our database retrieval system allows me to be. There are more than three-quarters of a million documents stored in these archives, over six million pages worth. It's all on fiche, and it's all cross-indexed by key words. For instance," she added, her fingers on the keyboard, "if I type in the word 'president', the machine tells me that there are 386,515 separate documents containing that word. We can bring them up alphabetically according to the title of the document, chronologically by publication date, numerically by document length, or by what we call frequency. That is, according to the number of times a key word is used in the story."

"Lord," Flix gasped, impressed by the girl's knowledge but not sure where to start. "How many delimiters can we use to get the list down to a manageable size?"

"Up to twenty."

"Okay then, let's begin," Flix urged.

"To access these records, I'll need your security code."

"My *security* code?" Flix exploded, taking a step back. "What the hell for?"

"These documents include some of the most sensitive materials ever gathered by the U.S. government. From the Federalist Papers, to the Nuremberg trials, to the Sommers Commission on the Assassination of Rontana, to the…"

"Okay, already," Flix relented, "I get the picture. But you must understand something as well: someone of my standing does not freely reveal his security code to a librarian."

"You may enter it remotely on that terminal over there," she declared, pointing across the aisle to a smaller unit with a black frame, "and then my screen will display only your name and nothing more."

Nodding his head, Flix moved to the terminal she had indicated and typed in his nine digit access code.

When she saw his name pop up on her screen, she oohed and aahed, "Oh, my. General Wenger! What a pleasure! I've read your public file—you're a very interesting man."

"My friends call me Flix."

"And may I? Call you Flix, that is?" she inquired, batting her eyes at him.

"It would please me very much," he admitted cautiously.

"I can do that too," she flirted.

"What?"

"Please you very much."

Blushing, Flix struggled to control his emotions. "Maybe we should try to tackle this project before my mind wanders any further afield."

"Suit yourself," she responded, not missing a beat, "but my offer stands."

Clearing his throat, Flix directed, "Let's tap back into that database of yours and run a search for any documents containing these four words: term, limitation, presidential, and election. Then, to narrow it even further, limit your search to the two hundred year period from say, 1787 to 1987."

Typing in his instructions as fast as he uttered them, she announced, "There are 12,829 separate entries which contain all four of those words at least once. May I suggest eliminating any documents under one page in length and including only those with two or more uses of each of our key words?"

"You can do that? Okay, let's try it."

"Now, that's better," she commented, seeing the sharply reduced number of entries remaining.

"Very good," he agreed. "Now arrange them in chronological order, and print them out in hard copy, oldest first," he spelled out authoritatively.

"That's still gonna be quite a stack," she emphasized, brushing his shoulder with her hand. "What say I print them out for you this afternoon and bring the box by your place tonight? Say, around eight o'clock?" As she spoke, she touched Flix's leg above the knee.

Recoiling for an instant as if he had been bitten by a snake, he admitted, "I can tell you in all honesty, Miss Nikki, that a man my age would relish having a girl like you, if only for an hour. Nevertheless, decorum prevents me from accepting your offer. For God's-sake, I haven't been with a woman in eight years!"

"Flix, darling, don't be embarrassed," she purred like a cat in heat. "If you don't want me to come by your place tonight because you think someone might notice, we can do it right here on the floor, right now. We won't be disturbed; hardly anyone ever comes down here at all."

"What are you suggesting?" he panted breathlessly, his loins warming to the occasion.

"General, what I'm suggesting is sex," she dramatized, unbuttoning her blouse. "Pure, unadulterated, sex. "I've never had a General before; surely you won't deny me this privilege? And don't worry if you haven't done it in over eight years, it's like riding a bicycle—you never forget how. Never."

9

DEBATE

Senate Office Building, District of Columbia

When he was troubled, like today, the wrinkles around Flix's eyes looked especially deep. He had only just returned from a weekend in Maine with Nikki where he had discovered a gun missing from his collection. Though the house showed no signs of a break-in, if the gun hadn't been stolen, he could not imagine where it had gone to. Thinking that perhaps he had brought it down to Washington with him on an earlier trip, or that he had left it at the gun club where he and Nate had gone to practice shooting, Flix had turned both his locker at the gun club and his apartment upside down looking for it, but to no avail. He couldn't find it anywhere.

When he reached Nate's office intending to tell him what had happened, the Senator was on the comm with Musette. From what Flix was able to gather from his side of the conversation, Nate's son Frankie wasn't getting along so well with his aunt and his uncle, and he was beginning to be a problem at school. But since Nate didn't wanted to talk about it when he hung up the comm, they moved directly to the topic of the day—term limitations. Using the materials he and Miss Nikki had dug out of the library, Flix was endeavoring to prepare his protégé for the upcoming Senate debate. The discussion quickly turned into less of a talk and more of a lesson, less of a conversation and more of a lecture.

The old man was in the middle of a thought. "Almost from the beginning of our history, there has been an inordinate fear that a President might wish to establish himself as a monarch or a dictator. Beginning with George Washington, critics of every strong President have accused them of usurping powers belonging to the Congress, or to the Judiciary, or reserved to the people."

"Yet, it was all so much nervous talk," the Senator challenged, his mind still distracted by what Musette had told him about Frankie's behavior at school. "No such thing ever happened."

"It almost did, Nate. And some say it is happening right now."

"Aren't you exaggerating just a tad?" Nate countered.

"Yes, maybe just a little," Flix admitted, struggling to find a comfortable position in his chair. "But the precedent of a President holding office for only two terms was established centuries ago by George Washington himself, and was observed by Thomas Jefferson, Andrew Jackson, and several others who, like Washington, would have been elected to a third term had they sought it. The second Roosevelt, however—the one who was confined to a wheelchair—broke the unwritten law by winning election to a third and then an unheard of, *fourth* term. Revulsion against his shattering of the two-term tradition led—in the middle of the 20th century—to passage of the twenty-second amendment, an amendment which limited a President to two four-year terms."

"*And*," Nate interrupted reflectively, "it prevented several good men from running a third time. Like Kemp and Fitzgerald."

"Don't forget Reagan. And Goldstein," Flix reminded the younger man.

"Yes, of course," Nate agreed. "But if I remember my American history correctly, there was a political upheaval in the middle of the 21st century which brought with it all kinds of legislative changes including *repeal* of the twenty- second amendment."

Chuckling as he shook his head, Flix remarked, "You're referring, I should imagine, to that pack of fools calling themselves the Laborites. The repeal of twenty-two wasn't the half of it, but it *was* on their platform. Since then, there have been three runs of six-term Presidents, counting the current egomaniac, of course."

"Which is why we are again faced with a movement to limit Presidential terms," Nate summarized neatly as he paced about his cluttered office. Since being elected he had never quite gotten used to the hustle and the bustle of D.C. life. Compared to the quiet little backwater town where he had grown up, Washington was like living in a fishbowl. Without his loving wife at his side, and without his girlfriend there to console him, he found himself increasingly lonely.

"That is a contributing factor to be sure. Still, Nolan himself has alienated a lot of people, and he'll be lucky if not running again is the worst thing that ever happens to him."

Not picking up on the deeper meaning in Flix's comment, Nate continued with his cross-examination. "So, give me some ammunition to fight this thing in the Senate," he pleaded. "Over the years Congress has weakened the Executive Branch to such a degree that if this issue goes before the people in the next plebiscite, I fear it will pass."

"Maybe it should," Flix responded philosophically as he stroked his cane.

"That's *not* what I want to hear!" Matthews scolded.

"Sorry, Nate, but it has been a lively issue since the Republic was founded, and I am not sure you are going to like everything we have uncovered.

"*We?*" Nate asked, an astonished look on his face.

"That cute law student I told you about, informs me that in the hundred and forty year period from 1810 to 1950, Congress made no less than two hundred and ten separate attempts to fix the length of Presidential tenure. She found some interesting archives dating to the very birth of our nation. Here, read this," Flix instructed as he handed Nate a sheaf of papers. "Out loud, if you please."

"Yes, boss, whatever you say," Nate smiled as he began to read. "The tenure of the Presidential office under the proposed new Constitution..."

"*Proposed*?" Nate blurted out loud, interrupting himself. "Did you say 'proposed'?" Shocked by what he had just read, he fumbled for words, "What the...?"

"Read, for God's-sake, read!" Flix ordered, pleased no end with Nate's reaction.

Matthews continued, "Presidential tenure under the pro-posed new Constitution is one of the most difficult and perplexing problems to come before our Convention. How long should the term of the President be? Should he be eligible for reelection? It was not until the closing days of the Convention that a decision was reached, and then only in the final report of the Committee of Revision, submitted on September 12, 1787..."

"Seventeen eighty-seven?!" Nate exclaimed, interrupting himself again. "Where did you *get* this stuff, Flix? It is more than five hundred years old!"

"Read, boy, read," the elder man insisted, his straight white teeth gleaming.

"In that report, provision was made for the term of four years and election by the electoral college...What in the heck was the electoral college?" Nate asked, puzzled by the strange sounding phrase.

Answering hesitantly, Flix explained, "The electoral col-lege was a sort of temporary legislature convened for the sole purpose of electing the President based on the popular vote he garnered on a state by state basis. It too was eliminated by the Laborites."

"I see," Nate replied even though he didn't. "You must tell me more about these Laborites."

"In due course, I promise to, but *do* go on reading," he instructed, growing increasingly impatient.

"In the plan submitted by Mr. Randolph on May 29, 1787, however, the term of years was left blank, as was also the case in later resolutions. A proposal for a tenure of seven years, accompanied by a provision of ineligibility for a second term, appeared in the series of resolutions referred to the Committee of Detail on July 23 and again in a draft from the Committee of Five on August 6, but throughout the debates the matter recurred constantly without decision. The report of the Committee of Eleven filed on September 4, 1787 provided for a four-year term without reference to reeligibility, and that provision appeared in the revised and final draft.

"This is good stuff, Flix," Nate complimented warmly. "The Founding Fathers were right about not limiting Presidential terms."

"Perhaps," the senior man replied. "Perhaps, the currently proposed 108th amendment—like the ancient twenty-second—will one day place the American people in jeopardy. It is a limitation on the people's right to choose and it could leave the nation in a straitjacket. Leadership is the big issue, and the determination of a second term President might be the driving force necessary to guide our country to victory in its darkest hour. His going out of office in the middle of such a struggle could be the difference between triumph and defeat."

"Spoken like a true General," Senator Matthews asserted mischievously.

Angered by Nate's flippant tone, Flix shot back, "For God's-sake, Senator, we must not shackle the future! Unless someone shoots him first, every President should have the opportunity to serve for as long as the voters want to keep him in office!"

"Easy, my friend, easy," Nate consoled. "You know I agree with you, but remember: they are pushing for a single term of either six or seven years. If I'm not to make a fool of myself in the upcoming debate, I must examine *both* sides of the argument."

"Devil's Advocate, eh?" Flix verified, understanding better what the Senator was driving at.

"Yes, something like that. Senator Duncan and his crowd argue that the chance for reelection detracts from the office; that the incumbent President has his eyes fixed only upon the forthcoming election; that all acts of the current term are affected by his ambitions for the *next* term; and that the fourth year is consumed solely by campaigning," Nate reeled off, summarizing the views of his chief opponent. "How would you rebut these charges, General?"

"Simple," Flix replied, his dark eyes focusing intently. "All of what you have said is true. And yet it is truer still for Congresspersons; they are up for election every *two* years! I would rebut the Honorable Mister Duncan this way: in a democracy, campaigning is the lifeblood of our freedoms. To be responsive, elected officials should be voted upon each and every day."

"Nice," Nate responded, thoughtfully rubbing his chin, "very nice. I like your style, Flix. To paraphrase then: Being restricted to a single term can undermine and cripple a President, especially as his period in office nears its end."

"Yes, that is the essence of the philosophical argument," Flix concurred, "but you had better prepare yourself for the historical arguments as well."

"Like what?" Senator Matthews probed, disenchanted by the worrisome look in his advisor's eye.

"Like, Thomas Jefferson, for instance."

10

CANNONBALL

"Did 'ole Tommie have an opinion on *everything*?" Nate inquired as their meeting wore on. Even as he spoke, he peeked out his office window to see a flock of tourists gathering outside for a tour of the ornate Senate Office Building. Whenever the weather was agreeable, like today, visitors would fill the cherry tree-lined walks along Basin Drive.

"Just about," Flix returned as he read from his notes. "In 1805 he said—and I quote—'the President of the United States should have been elected for seven years, and be forever ineligible afterward.'"

"Geez," Nate redirected incredulously, "Jefferson said *that*?"

"Yep, 'fraid so," Flix confirmed dejectedly. "I gave you fair warning earlier that you would not enjoy everything we uncovered."

"Do you think Duncan and his cronies know this as well?" Nate questioned naively.

"For God's-sake, boy!" Flix boomed, the medals on his uniform swaying as he waved his cane around wildly. "If our pixy of a law-clerk found it, Duncan's people will too."

"Then we're sunk," Matthews declared sullenly.

"You haven't heard all of it yet, Nate. There's more."

"More? What more could there be?" he queried in a

depressed tone, figuring the battle was lost before it began.

"In 1834, Andrew Jackson said that Presidential terms should be limited to a single period of either four or six years. Rutherford Hayes recommended an amendment setting a term of six years—and forbidding reelection. William Taft wrote in 1915 that it would have been wiser to make the term of the President six or seven years, rendering him ineligible thereafter. Even Wiggins—one of our most popular multi-term Presidents—said that appointments made by a President who cannot succeed himself, would be less likely to be political. Then there was…"

"Enough already, I get the point!" Nate urged emphatically. "Some of our most cherished leaders have favored a single—though somewhat longer—term for Presidents." Pausing sadly, he added, "And our present-day political adversaries are going to invoke history to carry the day, aren't they?"

"Oh yes," Flix agreed, his swarthy skin peeking out from his neck-tight military-style shirt, "but I think the trouble we are facing is much worse than you suspect. Don't forget, this is both an election year *and* a census year. That means a national plebiscite will be held as well."

"To this day, I have never been very clear how that all came about—the plebiscite I mean. I have read the Constitution over many, many times," Nate reported, stepping back from the window, "and the original provisions made it a very difficult document to amend. Yet, nowadays it's so damn easy. How did this all change?"

"Look in your file, Nate. I believe it's Appendix III. Nikki, that honey of a law-clerk, prepared a wonderful account of the amendment process, which is must reading."

"Honey of a law-clerk? Pixy of a law-clerk?" Nate cross-examined, astonished to hear a man of Flix's age speak that way about a woman. "Aren't you just a tad old to be thinking of such things?"

"Since when did *age* have anything to do with it?" the General countered. "Anyhow, I am not old; I am 'seasoned', remember? And don't be fooled by this cane—all my *other* body parts work just fine."

"Flix, you are a dirty old man."

"Give me that report," Flix demanded testily as he grabbed the sheaf of papers from the Senator. "I'll read you the important parts myself. And, for your information, Nikki and I share certain common interests," he justified proudly.

"You *are* incorrigible. When am I going to meet her?"

Ignoring his protégé's gentle taunts, Flix commenced reading excerpts from Nikki's report, "It might be argued that America's current troubles date to the administration of President John F. Kennedy circa 1960. In those days, the Soviets and the Americans were the principal protagonists in a race to be the first into space. Interestingly enough, each nation built their fledgling space programs on the shoulders of the V-2 rocket technicians they captured after that century's second battle for domination of the continent between the xenophobic tribes of Germany and the sturdy, if naive, armies of Britain.

"Although the underlying principle was elementary, building a rocket powerful enough and reliable enough to lift humans into space was in fact a prodigiously complicated business. Yet, it was a business in which the Russians bested the Americans, an outcome which did not sit well with the then U.S. President. Indeed, Mr. Kennedy was so enraged by the Soviets attaining orbit first, he committed America to landing a man on the moon before them. At the start, the U.S. space program rode to the heavens on boosters originally designed to carry nuclear warheads, and astronauts began as little more than brave passengers strapped to ballistic missiles. And although Kennedy never lived to witness the fulfillment of his dream, in time the Americans *did* prevail.

"As ventures into space became ever more confident, orbital missions which were once measured in hours, stretched into days, and eventually to weeks; primitive capsules gave way to more sophisticated and spacious craft as pilots controlled ever more complicated maneuvers. Although national pride guided America to the moon, the realization of that ambition left the country bored with space and before long, the exploration program quickly wound down. No one even revisited the moon for decades and on *that* occasion, the entire Japanese crew perished.

"Early in the next century the American Smelting & Refining Company discovered that..."

"Isn't that the same company my wife Darna owned so much stock in?" Nate interrupted curiously.

"Yes, one and the same," Flix answered curtly. "Now shush so I can finish reading this...Where was I? Oh, yes... ASARCO learned that a hitherto undiscovered field of meteorite craters were shot full with a commercial grade of silver-ore even while other newly-discovered fields were home to strategic metals previously found only in the Republic of Byelorussia or in South Africa. Shortly thereafter, ASARCO landed..."

"Geez, Flix," Nate interrupted again, this time exasperated. "What the heck does all this have to do with constitutional law?"

"I'm not adrift, son. Give me five more minutes and you'll understand," Flix implored, his dark eyes flashing with excitement.

"Okay," Nate sulked, again sinking into one of his overstuffed chairs, "but sometimes your stories are so ..."

"Well, nevertheless," Flix continued, "shortly after making this momentous finding, ASARCO landed a civilian crew on the moon and inaugurated mining operations. The humongous quarrying machines mashed the rocks—along with the occasional miner—into rubble, then the gravel was cooked in giant smelters until the pure ore oozed out. Next, the hot metal was poured into molds to form enormous 'cannonballs' which were then accelerated to escape velocity by rail-guns and launched back towards the Earth for further processing.

"Positioned high above the planet in several carefully selected orbits were a number of spherical receptacles woven from high-gauge steel cable. These oval-shaped pouches were euphemistically referred to as 'catcher's mitts'. Once an ore-laden cannonball was caught in the mesh of an orbiting mitt, it was transferred to a waiting skyhook for aerial drop to a surface factory. After a time, the extraction and delivery process ran so efficiently that silver foil became cheap and plentiful, dislodging its aluminum counterpart from most homes in short order. ASARCO stock soared, making many farsighted investors wealthy."

"So *that's* how Darna's family became so rich!" Nate remarked, never having been told of this before.

"As if you didn't know," Flix charged, gently tugging at the man's sensibilities.

"Honest to God," the Senator claimed sincerely. "I never knew and I never cared."

"In that event, you probably don't know what I'm about to tell you either."

"What's that?"

"Right from the word go, the exploitation of the moon had many obstacles to overcome, not the least of which were the naysayers back at home," Flix explained diligently. "Environmentalists on Earth wanted ASARCO's 'cannonball express' shut down. Claiming that it was only a matter of time before one of the cannonballs missed its intended mitt and crashed to Earth slaughtering thousands, perhaps millions, these alarmists spread fear throughout the land.

"With the two sides arguing incessantly, the dispute eventually vaulted into the press. ASARCO countered the environmentalists' assertions by claiming that in the unlikely event one of its ore-cannonballs actually swept through space without being gloved in one of their orbiting mitts, it would melt harmlessly into vapor as it spun through the atmosphere. As is often the case, the quarrel finally made its way to the Supreme Court which ruled, after its own time, that the jurisdiction of U.S. law extended only as far as the rooftops of buildings anchored firmly to American soil. Therefore, any mining activities conducted on the moon, or any commercial activities conducted in orbit above the Earth, were subject to the much less restrictive international canons. That meant that

ASARCO was free to operate its orbiting mitts without fear of reprisal from the anti-business environmentalists."

"I still don't get where you're going with this," Nate pointed out.

Undeterred, Flix barreled on, "The event which linked the exploitation of space to our present constitutional crisis was the accident of 2020. In that year, one of the cannonballs missed its intended mitt by a wide margin. It was probably pushed off course by a small meteor. Contrary to ASARCO's assurances, however, it did *not* melt down to an innocuous blob upon reentry. Instead, the molten ball of silver came down outside Kingston—the capital of what was then our 52nd state—where it skewered a drunken peasant-farmer asleep in his field.

"News of the incident was brazenly suppressed because the President of the United States at that time owned more than 60,000 shares of ASARCO in his not-so-blind trust. Shrewdly realizing that the negative publicity could be explosively damaging to his career, not to mention devastating to his pocketbook, he successfully buried the truth for four years while he slowly unloaded his holdings."

"Oh my God," Nate sighed, digesting what a scandal it must have caused; might *still* cause.

"When the sobering facts were finally revealed, the disclosure enraged the public, igniting a political firestorm which swept the Laborites to power in the next general election. The backlash was so fierce, so anti-science, so anti-anything American, that enormous stupidities were committed in the name of protecting the environment.

"Among other blunders, the Laborites set back the cause of medical research for decades by agreeing to cancel the funding for the human genome-mapping project. And if that weren't enough, they instituted a confiscatory 100 percent tax on capital gains, a tax which played no small role in the intense recession of '29. Yet, the worst and the most enduring stupidity—the blunder for which we are still paying three hundred years later—was the damage they did to Article V of the

Constitution."

"Article V? That's the amendment article, isn't it?" Nate questioned, racking his brain to remember his civics lessons.

"Precisely," Flix replied. "The Founding Fathers allowed two methods for amending the Constitution. The first was upon a vote of two-thirds of both houses of Congress. The second was upon application of the legislatures of two-thirds of the states. In either case, the amendment had to then be ratified by the legislatures of three-fourths of the states. Because both methods were cumbersome and time-consuming, amendments were few in number."

"At least up until the time of the Laborites, I take it," Nate chimed in.

"You take it right," Flix nodded. "The Laborites devised yet a *third* way to amend the Constitution—one which was more in keeping with the tumultuous times. At the time of the census, once each decade, a national plebiscite was to be held to decide various issues. Ratifying a proposition required the approval of two-thirds of the eligible voters from just two-thirds of the eligible states, all of which were defined in such a way that it became far easier to approve amendments than ever before. Catering to a rash of narrowly defined interests, the nation was soon enfeebled by the accumulating burden of a crazy quilt of legislative agendas. Paralyzed, it wasn't long before the nation retreated into the stagnation and isolation we face today."

"How do we get out of this cul-de-sac?" Nate wondered openly.

"I'm not sure we *can* get out. My best guess is that a weakened America invites aggressors. Someday, the wolves will gather at the door," Flix lamented, his eyes drawing tighter. "Thank God I won't be around long enough to witness it."

11

LOBSTER BAKE

Mount Desert Island, Maine

Even now, at this late stage in life, Flix loved to hike. And when, on a crisp April day like today, he got one of those rare chances to get off the beaten path, his cane was more of a help than a hindrance. Using his trusty staff as a walking stick to negotiate along the twisting mountain paths, he could have easily kept up with a man twenty years his junior. With the possible exception of studying military strategy and tactics, nothing made him happier than to set out in the morning from his estate near Bar Harbor and try to once again conquer one of the island's many peaks.

The south ridge trail up to the top of Cadillac Mountain began just below the entrance to the Blackwoods Campground and wound for nearly eight miles up into the forest. Although the National Park Service rated it as strenuous with many steep grades and many steady climbs, that didn't faze him a bit because today he had a fiery young companion with him who made the whole trek worthwhile. She had been working at his side round-the-clock to prime Senator Matthews for the term limitations debate, but after yesterday's successful filibuster, it was clear that Nate's forces had won. With that out of the way, Flix and Nikki could safely escape town for a couple of days.

The two lovebirds had flown up last evening from D.C. in

Whetstone's private airchop, then taken out after dawn this morning by gcar, stopping first at Thunder Hole to marvel at the spray of the ocean as the waves exploded through the underwater cave and up into the air, and then again at Otter Point to watch the shiny mammals as they danced and played on the wet boulders. Later, as they rounded Hunters Head— the cry of a loon splitting the silence overhead—she had caught sight of the telltale discharge from the spouts of two humpback whales frolicking in the bay. Only in the protected waters surrounding Acadia National Park could the giant cetaceans still be found within sight of land.

Though the island's name suggested that it was a barren desert, it was anything but. Indeed, the locals aptly pro- nounced it "dessert" as the wind-swept island was sweet with the smell of balsam fir, sea breezes, and old money. In fact, Mount Desert Island, and Bar Harbor in particular, was a summer playground for the privileged class, a status General Felix Wenger had attained only recently after many years of public service, and yet a status in which he always found himself a tad uncomfortable. For a simple man like Flix, a lobster bake and a corn on the cob was more fitting than a state dinner or a formal ceremony paying homage to the latest nameless diplomat or ambassador.

As he and Nikki entered onto the first set of switchbacks at the base of Cadillac Mountain, his muscular legs warming to the effort, Flix hungrily replayed the mouth-watering pageant he had attended time and time again out here on the island. The roadside chef would fill a string bag with a live lobster, a couple handfuls of long-necked steamer clams, and an ear of unshucked corn. Opening one of the steaming, concrete-encased kettle drums, he would lower the bag into the boiling water. Though Flix knew the answer, he would ritualistically ask the bearded man, "Do you fill the drum with seawater or tapwater?" And the owner would explain in Maine's classic r-less brogue, "Makes the seafood taste betta to boil it in seawata." Then, without waiting for Flix to ask how a successful sea captain had come to run a roadside lobster bake, the genial chef would point out that, "The fish have gotten scahce, and the lobstuh have gotten plentiful."

When Flix's dinner was ready, the weather-beaten man would fish his bag out of the drum, dump its hot, luscious contents on a plate beside a cup of melted butter, and hand it to him with a flourish. Eager to get started, Flix would find a seat at one of the outside picnic tables and begin the feast with nothing more than a stack of napkins, a wooden fork, and a pair of strong hands. Afterwards, if it wasn't too dark, and if the tide was still out, he would wade out to the sandbar which gave the town its name. Oh, such simple pleasures!

Smacking his lips as he shook off his daydream, Flix reached out to touch her hand. Lifting it to her lips, Nikki licked his fingers in a way that could only be described as obscene.

"Stop that," he scolded, but there was no ferocity to his voice. He hadn't felt this good or this young in years, and she was to blame. To her credit, in a matter of a couple weeks she had taken him from a preoccupied, self-pitying old man to an energetic spring chicken. And, in the course of those twenty or so days, she had exercised his loins in a way he never would have guessed was possible. Indeed, after having spent so much time huffing and puffing in the bedroom, it felt good to be out-of-doors.

The weather was cool and a delicate fog hung over the bay. In other words, it was a perfect day for a climb such as this. As the two of them slowly ascended the mountain, leaving the thicker air at sea level behind, they each fell silent to reckon with their private thoughts.

Even as Nikki wrestled uncomfortably with her reservations about the dangerous game Vice President Whetstone was asking her to play, Flix thought back to that long, desperate hike he and Tiger had taken across the Saudi desert so many years ago. How, in order not to wind the stallion, he had slung his unconscious friend over its back even as he stumbled along at its side; how, as the cool night air had washed over them, Tiger had finally come to; how, by the end of the next day, the two of them had been propping each other up with each step; and how, dehydrated and delirious, they had found their way first to a fishing village on the coast, and then on to the U.S. embassy in Qatar. Considering all that they had been through, they should have returned home to a hero's welcome. Instead—to avoid a reprisal from one of Rontana's allies—the Pentagon had suppressed any news of their accomplishment. That they were denied the public acclaim they so richly deserved still made Flix seethe with anger to this day.

"Honey," Nikki began sweetly, interrupting his recollections, "you seem lost in thought. Come back to Earth, will you?"

"Why would a luscious young thing like yourself be interested in an old duffer like me?" he asked, remembering how curious it had been that no one had questioned her presence when they had first boarded the Vice President's airchop to come up here. It was almost as if the pilot and the crew had met her once before. And if that wasn't enough to make him suspicious, she had been asking more and more pointed questions about what he did, and how he did them. On one occasion, he actually thought she knew about the secret cipher book he had hidden in his wall safe, but he put his fears aside as she plied him with her charms.

"Old duffer?" she objected, without answering his question. "You're not *that* old."

"Be serious now," Flix insisted, stopping on the trail to catch his breath. "I know why I'm infatuated with *you*."

"And why is that?" she purred, rubbing herself against his leg.

"I haven't had sex *this* great in twenty years!" he exclaimed boyishly. "Your body's so firm and you're so …eager. But I ask you again, why are you attracted to *me*? I have no money to speak of, and I certainly have no perks to offer you, so why?"

"You're an interesting man," she replied.

"Lots of men are interesting," he returned. "You'll have to do better than that."

"Well, if you want to know the truth, I'll tell you the truth, but the answer's kinda corny," she confessed sheepishly, her auburn hair bouncing off her shoulders.

"I want to know," he replied firmly.

"My father died when I was real young," she lied convincingly, "and my mother, bless her soul, never remarried. I never had a father, don't you see?" she sniffled at the edge of tears. "And you took me under your wing so…"

"There, there, please don't cry," he consoled, patting her on the head. "I didn't mean to judge you harshly or dredge up bad memories—I just needed to be sure, that's all," Flix pointed out sympathetically. "I'm an old war-horse, and I guess I'm just suspicious of everyone and everything."

"I understand," she nodded, rubbing the tears from her eyes. "Why don't we sit down for a spell and take a rest—we've been walking for hours. And then, when you're all rested, I have a little surprise for you," she revealed. Even as she spoke, she unbuttoned her blouse two notches. "Just the thought of doing it with you right here in the grass where someone might catch us has got me all hot and bothered," she teased, successfully side-tracking his suspicions with her offer of yet more sex.

"Why you little vixen," he panted, anticipating what was to come next.

12

HONEST MEN

Vice President's Mansion, Arlington, Virginia

"How was your trip north?" Whetstone probed, an evil smirk smeared across his hollow-cheeked face. "I understand from my airchop pilot that you took a guest along with you up to Maine."

"Not that it's any of your concern," Flix snapped, "but yes, the girl you recommended I hire to help me research term limitations, accompanied me up to my cottage. After working so hard to prepare Nate for the Senate filibuster, we both deserved a little rest and relaxation."

"And did you get any?" the Vice President quizzed, knowing full well from Nikki's report that he had not.

Rather than bite on Silas' taunt, General Wenger just glared. It was the kind of look which, had he been carrying a side-arm, might well have been followed by a discharged weapon.

"Which reminds me," Whetstone continued, his lanky arms hanging limply at his sides, "how do you think it went with Matthews last week?"

"Good, very good," Flix answered, proud of the mentor-student relationship which was developing between himself and Nate. "He has been handling himself like a pro in the debates. You should have seen him last Friday—Nate really put Duncan in his place. Who knows, we may win this round yet."

"At this juncture, I couldn't care less," Whetstone retorted callously. "It's apt to be a moot point before long."

"Don't be a *fool*," Flix squawked, his dark eyes emphatic. "Just because you murder Chester and succeed to the Presidency doesn't mean the debate on term limits will end. In fact, it may gather steam. I don't see how we can avoid it being on the plebiscite no matter *what* we do."

"Perhaps you are right," the Vice President acknowledged, wanting to quit this subject and get on to a topic of greater importance. "Let's get back to Senator Matthews, shall we? When the dirty deed is done, I will have to appoint the right man to fill out the rest of my term. It seems to me that a wholesome midwestern Senator would be the perfect choice. What do you think?"

"But you've only just appointed him to replace McDonald as Chairman of the Military Oversight Committee. Don't you think making him your Vice President would be a little premature?"

"If I were confident enough of his ability to handle the M.O.C., couldn't I also be expected to trust him as my Vice President?" Whetstone reasoned logically. "He's immensely popular you know. Tell me what you think. Would our Nate make a good pick or not?"

"He doesn't seem the type," Flix pointed out, hoping to derail Silas in another direction. "I fear he's too much of a...Boy Scout."

"You can't cheat an honest man, is that it?" the tall man rebutted philosophically.

"Well, for your information, that statement is as wrong as the old saying, 'Crime doesn't pay'," the General countered. "Of *course* crime pays; that's why there is so much of it. And it goes without saying that honest men like Nate are defrauded every day. The expression ought to be, 'You can't *con* an honest man'."

"What's the difference?" Whetsone quizzed as he nervously crossed and uncrossed his long legs.

"I guess it shouldn't surprise me that you wouldn't know the difference between conning someone and cheating them," the older man answered caustically as he assumed the air of a theology professor at a seminary. All too often lately he had found himself in the position of teacher, instructing others on principles which he believed in deeply.

"Let me put it to you this way," Flix continued professorially. "You can misrepresent yourself to an honest man; promise to perform a service for a fair price, then renege; or purposely fail to deliver a truckload of goods, then take off with his money; but in both of these instances you have committed a fraud. You have cheated him, but you have *not* conned him. To con a man you have to appeal to his greed; you have to convince him that it is *he* who is doing the cheating. *That* is a con!" Flix summarized with a flourish.

"Okay, old man," Whetstone patronized, "I suppose what you're trying to tell me in your long-winded fashion is that Matthews won't play ball. But consider the alternative; consider what *Nolan* is doing. With this Hawaii deal of his, he's trying to con the entire nation! I see no way around it—he *must* be eliminated!"

"Sy, you know I don't need convincing," Flix confirmed, his closely-cropped, black hair falling across his forehead. "I fully agree that we can't permit the treaty with Ambassador Ling to be signed under any circumstances. My only objection at this point is waiting until the Council of Nations dinner to finish it. By then, word of the treaty will have leaked out and the Hawaiians may very well have declared themselves a free state on their own. Like a snowball avalanching downhill, once talk of cutting Hawaii loose begins to spread, we won't be able to stop it. I say we kill him now!"

"Whoa, slow down, old friend," Whetstone admonished. Let's not forget who is in charge here, shall we? I call the shots, remember? Anyway, weren't *you* the one who wanted this to be a very *public* assassination?"

"Well...yes," the General stammered, embarrassed to be tripped up by his own words.

"Well then, let's stay with the original plan," the gaunt man suggested, knowing he had Flix right where he wanted him. "I already promised to reinstate you as Chairman of the Joint Chiefs, didn't I? What else do you *want* from me?"

"Don't be an idiot!" Flix exploded, his row of medals shaking with fury. "You know the Chinese can't be trusted! Remember your history for God's-sake! Think back to what happened in the twentieth century when the Brits first turned Hong Kong over to those heathens. After promising to guarantee their civil liberties, the shameless bastards burned the city to the ground!"

"Que sera, sera," Whetstone dramatized with a wave of his bony arm. "That's old news, my friend. In any event, I can't change our plans at this late date. The assassin has already been hired, and the timing has already been set."

"What do you mean the assassin has already been hired?! I thought we agreed not to take that step until I gave it my final stamp of approval?" Flix reminded Silas bitterly.

"But I gave you the dossier *weeks* ago. How long was I supposed to wait?"

"Sure you *gave* it to me, and I admit that I even read the damn thing, but since the name on the file was an alias, I never had the chance to check her out myself," Flix explained, his angry face beet red. "Plus—and you know this very well— I've been busy working on this term limitation thing, a job you yourself said was a top priority."

"It can't be helped now—plans have been made and fees have been paid."

"Don't you think I ought to at least know who the killer is?" Flix questioned, a hint of panic in his voice. "For God's-sake, Silas, without a name or a number how am I supposed to communicate with the perp and tell her about the escape route I have worked out?"

"But you've already *met* our assassin," Whetstone reported fiendishly, a mysterious look plastered across his gaunt face.

"No, you must be mistaken," Flix replied, reflecting back

on all their earlier discussions to see if he had forgotten something. "Perhaps you introduced the killer to someone else; I've never met the woman."

"Nikki," he answered matter-of-factly. "Nikki is the assassin."

"You have *got* to be kidding!" Flix yelped incredulously, his blood beginning to boil. "*That* sweet girl? You hired *her* to do this?!" he screamed, as he got to his feet. "You set me up, you bastard!"

"Yes, Flix, I suppose I did," Whetstone declared as the General's heart sank. "And now it's up to you to save her pretty little butt."

"I won't do it," Flix snapped without thinking it through.

"Oh, I think you will," Whetstone retorted haughtily.

"What makes you so sure?"

"Weren't you the one who just got finished lecturing me on the difference between conning a man and cheating him?"

"And am I supposed to assume from that comment that I'm next on your hit list?" Flix hypothesized as he digested just how evil Silas had become. Even as he waited for Whetstone's answer, General Wenger again thought of the automatic that had been stolen from his collection last month. A shiver ran down his spine as he realized the fix he would be in if a gun belonging to him were implicated in the assassination. Now, he not only had to save Nikki, he had to save himself.

"Don't be silly," Whetstone coaxed. "Why would I want to eliminate *you*?"

"Because I know the truth…the truth about everything," Flix pointed out calmly. "The truth about the plot to kill Nolan; the truth about how we have been hiding much of our military spending in the budgets of other departments; the truth about the viruses we have been developing at the biowarfare lab in Fort Detrick, Maryland. You see? I know it all."

"And who would believe you?" the Vice President probed, his tone almost that of a dare.

"People love conspiracies, Sy," Flix replied, fingering the trigger in the crook of his cane. "Fact is *always* stranger than fiction."

13

TRIPLE PLAY

Chevy Chase, Maryland

She was perched atop a bar stool in her fashionable apartment sipping a glass of tortan and listening to the gentle April rain outside her window, when the comm rang. Chester was expected shortly, and for an instant, she thought he might be calling to cancel. Under the circumstances, that would be a devastating turn of events, and as she lifted the receiver from its holder, she prayed it wasn't him.

"Well, little one, I'm glad I found you at home," the fatherly voice began.

"Just making some last minute preparations," she replied, slipping the lethal weapon he had given her into her handbag to be sure it fit. In the pocket next to it sat two clips of durbinium-tipped shells. Instead of blunting on contact like a normal bullet would, the metal casing of a durbinium shell peeled back into a star pattern, penetrating soft tissue like a throwing star. Very nasty and very effective. When she was done here today she would slip into the Goldstein Center disguised as a maid and tape both her gun and her ammo beneath her assigned table in front of the podium.

"Daughter, I have told him today that you would be doing the hit," Whetstone made clear, his gaunt face revealing the stress of the last few days. Though victory was now close at hand, he was getting increasingly nervous that events might spin out of control.

"Is that so?" Nikki replied without a hint of surprise. "And how did the old geezer react?"

"Like all military men, our Flix is nothing if not predict-able," her father remarked as he paced the room, speaking into the remote comm perched upon his desk. "You must have made quite an impression on the General, little one."

"And did you tell the General that I was your daughter?" she asked as she readied herself for her guest's imminent arrival. The President was expected at her doorstep within the quarter-hour and unless she had on just the right perfume and just the right amount of make-up, he was sure to complain. She already had on his favorite nightie.

"You must be kidding!" her father yelped, his tinny voice booming into the comm. "Why would I tell him our little secret? That is something we must both carry to the grave."

"Yours or mine?"

"Now, honey, don't get down in the mouth," he petitioned in a condescending tone. "You *know* how it upsets your mother so."

"Yes, and how is the family lunatic?" Nikki inquired with obvious disdain.

"So long as reporters from the Guild provide me with regular photo-ops, I see her twice a month," the Vice President declared coldly. "Institutionalizing her was one of the *shrewd-est* moves I have ever made."

Studying her graceful face in the mirror as she delicately applied her eye-liner, the assassin tingled inside with satisfac-tion. Silently congratulating herself on how well she had used her exquisite good-looks to compromise both Flix and Chester, she looked forward with relish to the completion of this job.

"Ever the politician, eh dad?" Nikki chimed in, fully aware of what a lowlife her father could be and how he had used her mother's condition to his advantage.

"Never miss a chance if I can help it," he acknowledged impassively. "Which reminds me: will you see him tonight?"

"Who? Chester?"

"Who else?"

"Yes, daddy, I expect him at any minute," Nikki patiently explained. "He's very agitated, and he uses me as a source of relief."

"Is that what they call it now?" Whetstone responded, frustrated by the sexual void in his own life.

But before she could fashion an answer, the sound of a firm rap on her apartment door told her that her guest had arrived. "Gotta go, dad," she whispered into the comm even as she fipped on the evening news to cover the sound of her voice.

"Is that you, Chet?" she hollered, adjusting her negligee in the mirror as she went to answer the door. "I'll be right there."

"For crying out loud, do hurry up," he anxiously whined from the hallway. "I'm on a tight schedule."

"Where have you been, loverboy?" Nikki complained as she threw open the door. "I thought you would *never* come," she panted, flinging her arms around his neck and winking naughtily at the two secret service agents standing in the wings.

"I'm sorry I'm late," Nolan apologized unconvincingly, "but there were some last minute wording changes in the treaty which I had to go over before the signing ceremony tomorrow evening. I can't stay long," he admitted as he loosened his tie and took off his shoes, "but I needed to see you."

"Well, here I am," she announced proudly, strutting her stuff in front of his face like an eager teenager.

"Is everything okay?" he inquired as the teevee droned on quietly in the background.

"Of course, everything's okay," she reported, suddenly afraid that he was on to her. "Why do you ask?"

"For crying out loud, I tried to call you all weekend long and all I got was your machine."

"How sweet of you to be concerned," she replied tenderly, "but you needn't have worried."

"Where *were* you?" he asked distrustingly.

"A friend of mine fell ill, so I went to her place for the

weekend to help her out with the new baby," Nikki lied as she stared blankly at the teevee set, watching, but not hearing the news. Even as she spoke, the comm suddenly jangled to life in the other room.

"Now who could *that* be?" Nolan wondered peevishly. "Don't answer it," he urged as she got up off the bed. "Just let it ring."

"I have to," she justified, hoping the disruption would end his line of questioning, "my girlfiriend might need my help again later this evening."

As she picked up the comm, he bellowed to her from the bedroom, "Don't make any plans for tomorrow night—I want you at the banquet."

"I won't honey, I promise," she yelled back, as she momentarily cupped her hand over the receiver so as not to shout into the caller's ear.

"Hello, you have reached 692-2402," she began cautiously. "How may I help you?"

"Is he there?" Flix growled in obvious reference to her visitor.

"Even as we speak," she answered, suppressing her astonishment at hearing his voice.

"Then just listen for God's-sake," he urged in a serious tone.

Nodding her head as he said his piece, she listened intently to every word he uttered. "I assume you'll be doing him with the gun that was stolen from my place, so once the job is complete, drop it and stay low. One of my men will pick it up. As soon as I see the gun hit the floor, the lights will go out, and there will be an explosion at the north exitway from the auditorium. Everyone seated in that area will undoubtedly scramble *away* from the blast; you are to proceed directly *toward* it. I know it will be dark, but two men dressed as D.C. cops will meet you in the hallway and arrest you. Go with them willingly. It's your only chance to come out of this alive. Say 'yes' if you understand my instructions."

"Yes, I won't be late for my hair appointment," she

commented, figuring that the ever-suspicious Nolan might be eavesdropping on her side of the conversation, "and thanks so much for calling."

"And, Nikki," Flix whispered into the comm before he hung up, "despite your subterfuge, I want you to know, I appreciated every moment of affection that you gave me. I've never had better sex in my life."

"We'll have to do it again one day," she smiled wryly as she broke the contact.

"Who was that?" Chester quizzed irritably, dismayed that she hadn't been concentrating all her attentions on him.

"My hairdresser," she lied again. "You want me to look nice for your dinner party tomorrow night, don't you? Now where were we?" she reviewed as she provocatively slipped off her panties and draped them over his head. "Did I hear you say something about missing me?"

Now it was his turn to put *her* off. "Shush!" he directed as his eye unexpectedly caught something newsworthy on the teevee. "Turn up the set—I want to hear what they're saying."

"But, honey, I've been waiting all day for Little Chester!" she objected as she stood between him and the teevee, slowly disrobing.

"For crying out loud, woman, be quiet! I tell you, this is important," he snapped as he reached for the knob himself.

"...today there were again violent demonstrations in the streets of Honolulu and in Kona. Separatists demanding that Hawaii secede from the Union confronted police armed with water cannons and stun-guns. Apparently, now that word has leaked out of President Nolan's secret negotiations to sell the islands, the locals intend to declare themselves a free state instead. We will have another update on the tense situation here in the Aloha state on the 11 o'clock news. Until then, this is Wendy Batchelder reporting for K-SUN news..."

"Damn reporters," Chester swore, his usually boyish grin turning somber. "How in the world did they get ahold of this already?"

Knowing that the circle of confidantes who had been

informed as to the treaty's progress was small, Nolan shook
his head angrily. "I see Silas' hand in this," he murmured,
obviously seething with fury.

"Oh, Chester," Nikki dramatized in her soap-opera fashion, "you're going to sell *Hawaii*? I've been saving up for
months so that I could afford to go there over the holidays."

"You silly twit!" he boomed as he pushed her away.
"We're *selling* Hawaii, not sinking it. You'll still be able to
vacation there whenever you please."

"But why, Chester?" she questioned, maintaining her
dumb-blonde profile. "Have they done something wrong?"

"This is not what I came here for," he detailed savagely.
"*That* is what I came here for," he made clear, pointing to her
naked body. "That is what I *always* come here for," he
explained, his tone becoming more gentle as he reached out to
her.

"There, there, it's okay," she purred, nuzzling his head
against her breasts. "Soon I'll make everything better," she
murmured, the irony in her words obvious only to herself.

Bethesda Medical Center, Maryland

"Senator Duncan ta see ya, mam," the orderly announced
as they entered Clara Whetstone's private room together.
Judging by the young man's Elvis Presley style haircut and his
down-home drawl, the male nurse was from Kentucky or
perhaps West Virginia.

"She don't say much," the affable fellow whispered to the
Senator. "Been here two years maself, and ah don't think ah
heard a complete sentence outta her yet."

"For Chrissake, you have got to be joking!" Duncan
exclaimed, not believing his ears. "She hasn't spoken in two
years! I find that very hard to believe."

"That's not what ah said," the orderly objected in a nasal
tone. "What ah meant was, ah maself have never heard her say
much. Some of the female nurses, on the udder hand, have
gabbed with her at great length. Ah gass she don't like men too

well. That's the theory anywho."

"Is she coherent?" Senator Duncan asked, afraid his trip over here would be for naught. Ever since Chester had asked him to do this favor, one thing after another had prevented it. Only now, with the debates over and done with, could he afford to take the time.

"See for yaself," the hillbilly offered with a stupid grin on his face. "Ya got one hour 'tils ah serve lunch."

"Thank you," Duncan responded, turning his attention to the woman who sat across the room from him peering impassively out the window. In all the time he and the male nurse had spent talking to one another, she had never flinched or even turned her head once to see who was there. Either she didn't care, or she didn't hear, or else it didn't matter. Duncan didn't know which, nor did he know where to begin. Twice he started to speak and twice he caught himself mid-sentence. As he stood there crippled, he regretted having ever let Chester talk him into doing this; he wasn't equipped mentally for such a clandestine activity. Deciding to drop the whole thing after all, he started for the door.

Much to his surprise, she suddenly addressed him in a clear, firm voice, "Why don't you have a seat, Senator, and tell me what's on your mind."

Shocked by her authoritative tone, he swung his head around wildly to see whether there was someone else in the room with him besides her—but there was not. Fumbling for words, he began, "I…"

"Yes?"

"I…don't mind if I do," he croaked, pulling up a chair to be near her.

"Well?" she insisted in an impatient tone as if she had to rush off to an important staff meeting at any moment.

"Actually, President Nolan sent me," Duncan revealed, figuring that he couldn't fabricate a story as unbelievable as the truth. "Your husband is his Vice…"

"Just how *stupid* do you think I am? What exactly have you been told about me? Have you been led to believe that I'm both deaf *and* dumb?" she exploded indignantly, her beautiful eyes flashing. "I can read, you son-of-a-bitch; I can listen to the radio; I can watch teevee. Don't you think I know that my Silas is Chester's Vice President?"

Stunned by the vitality and the strength in her tone, he sank back into his chair, searching his mind for the correct approach. "So why, pray tell, are you here?" he asked, his words blunter than he had intended.

"Because it's safer," she explained as if the answer should be obvious.

"Safer? Safer than *what*?" he questioned, searching his soul for the right words. "Forgive me, but I don't understand."

"He beat me mercilessly," she confessed without tears. "Day after terrible day."

"Why for Chrissake?" he gasped, wondering what such an attractive woman could have done to deserve such treatment.

"For starters, because I gave him a daughter instead of a son," she asserted without flinching.

"So it's true then," he ratified, recalling the file Chester had shown him in his private chambers.

"Whatever you've heard...and more."

"Am I to understand that you voluntarily *consented* to be put in this hospital—this *place*—to avoid being beat up?" he queried, astonished by the scenario.

"Yes."

"Why didn't you divorce the bastard?" Duncan pressed. "The man's a monster—why didn't you *leave* him?"

"I tried once or twice, but he always tracked me down. And then, when he would bring me back home again, he would beat me even worse than before."

"Why didn't you go to the police?"

"I did, but he had too many friends in too many high places. Bethesda was the only solution he would accept," she described, waving her hand in deference to the stark hospital room they were sitting in.

"And you *agreed* to this?" the Senator exclaimed. "You're caged here like an animal!"

"I'm alive," she groaned. "And I intend to stay that way. Now what do you want?"

"To bring him down."

"I can't help you," she replied matter-of-factly.

"Or won't?"

"Yes, that's right," she confessed. "Can't and won't."

"There must be some way I can persuade you to change your mind."

"Bring me a gun," she responded icily. It was the coldest tone he had ever heard in his life.

"Pardon me?"

"You heard me, Duncan. Bring me a gun, and the next time the son-of-a-bitch shows up here with his reporters and his teevee crews, I'll blow out his fucking brains on national television!"

"You're crazy."

"Yes, I am. Wouldn't you be?"

"Look, I share your frustration—I really do—but bringing you a gun will only land *me* in jail," Senator Duncan pointed out soberly.

"In that case, I can't help you. Please leave," she ordered.

"I'll leave now if you wish me to," he answered, getting to his feet, "but I'll be back. There's a Council of Nations dinner I must attend, but after that we'll talk again."

14

PEACE IN OUR TIME

On a night as important as this, the Goldstein Convention Center was lit up like a birthday cake, its incandescent brightness reflecting off the Potomac in a dazzling array of color. Easily visible across the river was the white-marbled splendor of the Jefferson Memorial, its spherical dome preserved under the glass of its protective bubble. And in the distance, the illuminated memorial to George Washington shone down upon the city. The tallest of the three giant obelisks gracing the Mall, Washington's Memorial was flanked on the south by the bronze-colored column the Laborites had constructed to honor themselves, and on the north by the rust-colored shrine erected after the bloody annexation of Mexico in '01.

Blocking the circle driveway of the Goldstein Center, scores of black embassy limousines were lined up as dignitaries from all the Pacific basin countries, plus most of the European Community and substantially all of the Andean Coalition queued up to hear what the President had to say on this, the one hundredth anniversary of the founding of the Council of Nations. This U.N.-style organization which had been patterned after its twentieth century namesake was headquartered in the old Pentagon building, and President Nolan—as chief executive of the largest C.N. member—had the honor of hosting this evening's centennial event. Rumors concerning the reputed treaty with China had been flying in the press all week long, and he had promised to make an announcement in his address tonight.

Franklin Hall was nearly half the size of a football field, and this evening it was crammed full with dozens of round dining tables, each large enough to seat twelve VIP's. To mark the momentous occasion, each table was decked out with the finest silver, the most exquisite china, and the most expensive lavender tablecloths money could buy, all courtesy of the estate of former President Goldstein.

Running nearly the full length of the east wall, and covered with a single handmade tablecloth, a series of sturdy, rectangular platforms doubled as the head table. After the introductory pomp and circumstance was concluded, President Nolan and his wife were to be seated near the rostrum in the center of the forty foot-long table, while his department heads, his bureau chiefs, and his key House and Senate supporters flanked him on either side. Both Senator Matthews and Senator Duncan would have places of honor on the platform.

Secret Service agents and their FBI counterparts were highly visible participants in the gala affair as they patrolled the aisles and framed the doorways, the sensitivity of their detecting devices turned up so high nearly every patron had to empty his or her pockets before entering.

As the throng slowly filtered into the auditorium, Nikki waited patiently in line for her turn to pass through the security checkpoint. The female assassin didn't flinch at the sight of Flix giving orders to the uniformed patrols, because she knew that if something were to go wrong now, he wouldn't be the one to turn her in. Not only was he in this too deep himself, the General wanted this messy business cleaned up as badly as she did. Even so, she crossed her fingers. If everything had gone as planned, her fowling piece was still securely taped to the underside of the table, its furtive presence hidden by the oversized tablecloth. Otherwise, things were about to get dicey.

As the blonde-headed killer glided dispassionately past

one ambassador after another, and past one teevee crew after the next, she considered how she would react, what she would do, what she would say, if perchance her gun and her ammo had been discovered since she had taped them in place last night. Aware that no excuse could possibly bail her out of this trouble if she got caught, Nikki swallowed hard as she approached her prescribed seat and donned her elegant evening gloves. At Chester's request, she had been assigned to the table directly in front of him, an ironic twist of fate which would make her job of killing him a good deal easier.

More than fifteen minutes passed before the emcee shushed the gathering to their seats, and another five minutes passed before the applause died down and everyone settled into their chairs. Spreading her napkin in her lap, Nikki reached under the table with one hand. The lethal bundle was hanging there just where she had left it, its sinister contours easily recognizable to her practiced fingers. With the lights dimmed and the audience's attention directed at the podium as the emcee made his introductory remarks, she quietly tore the weapon loose from its moorings and dropped it in into her lap. Wrapping it in her napkin, she next grabbed for the two magazines of durbinium-tipped shells and silently snapped one of the clips into place. Now she was ready.

"President Chester Nolan is a man who needs no introductions," the emcee explained to the assembly as Nikki scanned the head table for her father's gaunt face. "He has been our nation's chief executive for twenty-one years and as our leader he has earned the trust and the respect of every American. Tonight, on the eve of a century of peace-keeping efforts by the Council of Nations, he is here to tell us of a momentous treaty which will preserve peace into the next century. So, without any further ado, I give you the leader of the free world, President Chester Nolan."

As everyone in the assembly hall sprang jubilantly to their feet, clapping their hands in wild pandemonium, Nikki surreptitiously slipped the loaded automatic into her empty handbag along with the extra magazine of shells. She had to pick her moment, and this wasn't it.

"Friends...supporters...allies," Nolan shouted, trying to be heard over the noise of the rabble even as he winked playfully at Nikki in the first row. "I appreciate your applause, really I do, but the waiters are eager to serve us our dinner, so please take your seats so we can get on with the business of the evening."

As the sound of chairs scratching against the hardwood floor slowly subsided and as order gradually returned to the room, Chester began speaking in his Kennedyesque fashion, "For as long as I can remember, America has been living beyond her means, accumulating debts which have become increasingly harder and harder to pay. At the same time, the balance of power in the world has been progressively changing as the Kingdom of China has steadily expanded its sphere of influence to include the Philippines, Japan, and most recently, the Korean peninsula.

"Quite honestly, given our budgetary constraints, we can no longer afford to defend all of our far-flung territories, and rather than invite war by exposing one of our outlying states to an aggressive foreign power, I have chosen a bolder path, a path which should significantly lessen the tensions between our two great nations. Not long ago it occurred to me that perhaps there was a way I could solve *both* of our problems at once—reduce our foreign debt and, at the same time, reduce the risk of armed conflict with our powerful Pacific neighbor. Thus, with these two objectives in mind, I entered into secret negotiations with the ambassador from China to sell them the eight islands in the archipelago of Hawaii. Of course, this treaty must still be approved by an affirmative vote of the Senate, but its successful conclusion will guarantee us peace in our time."

An uncomfortable hush fell over the crowd as the rumors which had been circulating for weeks were confirmed. At first it seemed as if the news had fallen on deaf ears, but then a lukewarm applause broke out in the back of the room. Before long it engulfed the entire auditorium in a tepid show of support. As the audience got to their feet in an obligatory fashion, Nikki reached into her pocketbook. What she held in the smooth grip of her hand was an odd-looking gun—an advanced weapon Flix himself had designed—bulky, but not large. The perforated cylinder that was the silencer snapped pneumatically onto the barrel, reducing the decibel count of a gunshot to no more than a loud spit, and yet it was engineered to such perfection it had no effect on the accuracy at close range. The clips released and inserted at the base of the handle in a matter of seconds. It had the firepower of a .357 Magnum in a gun half the size and weight of a Colt .45.

Letting the clutch drop to the floor so that she could steady the revolver with both hands, she pumped the entire magazine of lethal hollow-point rounds into the unsuspecting President, splattering his brains and his torso all over the podium and the wall behind him.

At first, camouflaged by the din, no one even noticed from where the shots had originated. But then, as Nolan slumped forward, and as the spray of blood sullied the head table, screams broke out from the VIP's seated there.

Even as the Secret Service scurried to identify the assailant, she wrapped the gun in her napkin and let it fall to the floor next to her handbag according to Flix's instructions. Suddenly, when someone in the crowd pointed in her direction yelling, "Assassin! Assassin!", time stood still. But before anyone could react, the explosion Flix had promised ripped through the north wall of the auditorium scattering the guests in every direction.

As pandemonium enveloped the convention center, she scooped up her handbag and her gun, and moved swiftly toward the exit. Good to his word, two of Flix's D.C. cops grabbed her in the hall and placed her under arrest. Whisking her from the building and out to a waiting squad gcar, they shoved her into the backseat with unnecessary roughness. When she got up off the floor, she found herself sitting next to a somber General Wenger. Flix didn't acknowledge her presence. His eyes were cold as he listened sphinx-like to the live radio coverage of the proceedings inside the auditorium as her father took the rostrum.

"Please remain calm," Whetstone urged as a gaggle of aides swarmed over Nolan's lifeless body. "Please don't panic!" he yelled into the mike. "Make way—make way! Let the doctors through! Oh my Lord this is terrible…just terrible."

Even as Flix rapped the hilt of his cane against the roof of the gcar and ordered his underlings to get moving, Silas' voice could be heard booming across the radio as he uttered the words he had been rehearsing all week, "Under the terms of Section One of the Twenty-Fifth Amendment, I am assuming control as Chief Executive and Commander-in-Chief until such time as a determination can be made as to President Nolan's condition."

15

FUGITIVE

With official vehicles of all sorts converging on the convention hall, no one paid much attention to the D.C. police gcar as it pulled away from the curb, its klaxon wailing. Disappearing into the late night traffic, the squad gcar shot out onto the beltline highway at high speed. Dousing its siren and pulling off to the side of the road a mile or so up the expressway, Flix and Nikki quickly transferred to a waiting taxi. Two miles further on, they switched gcars again, this time boarding an executive limo which took them both to the airchop pad at the edge of the city. Not until they got safely into the air did either of them say a word, and not until they had landed in Maine and arrived at his house without incident, did they begin to breath a sigh of relief.

Propping himself up in front of the teevee set, Flix found the night to be a short, fitful one without sleep. As bulletin after bulletin trickled out of Washington concerning the assassination and the midnight swearing in of Silas Whetstone as President, Flix grew increasingly anxious as there were also scattered reports of a police gcar which had raced from the scene of the crime, and of a widening manhunt for the shooter and her aged accomplice. And if the news reports weren't enough to upset a man in his situation, he was knowingly—even willingly—harboring a fugitive in his home, a fugitive who was as likely to blow his brains out as she was to drop her drawers and have sex with him.

As he sat there trying to figure out what to do next, he even thought of escaping out through the root cellar in his basement, never to be heard from again. It occurred to him that life and death were but two spokes on the same wheel; two cloverleafs on the same highway. In that sense, he and Nikki were both but shadowy reflections of the same demon. Like obedient soldiers blindly doing their jobs, each of them had committed murder at their own time and in their own way; only Nikki, unlike Flix, had never really taken the time to understand the reasons why. And whereas they each had done their assassinations for God and for country, only Flix could distinguish between the two; only he could tell the difference between good and evil.

Instinctively, Flix knew that this would be his last trip to Desert Island with her. He was confident that sooner, rather than later, she would try to kill him, and that one way or the other he would have to defend himself against her. So sure was he of this outcome that when he turned off the teevee and retired to bed for the night, he kept his cane loaded and close at hand. Not even her amorous advances could change his mind about sleeping alone that night.

By morning's light he was so agitated over the prospect of having to confront her in his own home, he couldn't wait to get out of the house and onto the trail. When she insisted on coming along, he readily agreed figuring that out in the open at least he had an even chance.

For the first mile or so they were both quiet. But when they stopped to catch their breath after a series of steep switchbacks, he finally broke the silence. "Why didn't you just tell me the truth from the start?" he asked in an accusatory tone. "Why did you have to lead me on?"

"That's how Silas wanted it," she replied matter-of-factly, her muscular arms tightening as she spoke. "And if I'm going to pay the rent, I have to follow the orders I am given."

"A soldier just like me, eh?" he clarified, wishing there were some other way.

"In a manner of speaking," she confirmed grimly.

"And was seducing me a part of your orders?" he cross-examined, his voice cracking with disappointment. Not only had *she* let him down, not only had Whetstone let him down, he had let himself down as well. By thinking with his Johnson rather than with his mind, he had trapped himself.

"You should know me better than that," she smiled bewitchingly.

"You're right," he agreed, nodding his head. "I should know you better…I should have checked you out more closely before getting involved, but I didn't," he reported, holding tight to his walking stick, his closely-cropped hair rustling in the breeze.

"Well then, let's start over," she suggested, her ripe breasts bulging beneath her sweater. "Hi, my name is Nikki—Nikki Patterson," she asserted, proffering him her hand. "How can I be of help, General Wenger?"

"My friends call me Flix," he recommended, introducing himself to her as if they had just met. "Tell me, Miss Nikki, how did you get into this grisly business? What kind of hold does the Vice President…I mean, the President …have over you that you are willing to go to bed with me just to do your job?"

"Mr. Whetstone has always been like a father to me," she explained earnestly.

"Is that so?" Flix shot back in a disbelieving voice. "I know for a fact that Silas Whetstone treated his *own* wife and daughter so badly, they *both* had to be institutionalized."

"I wouldn't know about that," she answered, squirming uncomfortably.

"Indeed, now that I think about it," Flix reminisced as they both edged apprehensively along the trail, "he had a daughter who would be just about your age by now. Pretty girl as I recall, but it's been at least ten years since I last met her and my memory's not what it used to be."

"I don't see what my da…I mean, I don't see what Mr. Whetstone's personal life has got to do with me," she objected as if she were taking Flix's comments personally.

"It's only that I never thought of him as being fatherly," he returned with a flash of his straight white teeth. Silhouetted against his tan skin, Flix's satisfied smirk looked wider than ever. Though he had not recognized the resemblance earlier, he found himself wondering whether Nikki was in fact Silas' misfit daughter. A little bit of plastic surgery and a nose job might have been all that was required to change her appearance.

"Perhaps you just don't know him like I do," she returned, her blonde hair bobbing against her shoulders as they meandered further up the trail.

"Perhaps," Flix answered doubtfully, hesitating to ask the obvious question. "So what's next? I imagine that just as I was given instructions to whisk you up here and out of harm's way, you were given instructions as well."

"Yes, I was," she confirmed in a menacing tone. "Only I had planned on letting you die a happy man. You see, for an older fellow you're not a half-bad lover. I thought I'd let you do me one more time before I killed you."

"Oh is *that* what you thought?" Felix snapped haughtily as he stopped on the trail to get his breath. Stepping back a few paces, he continued, "Well, I'm sorry to disappoint you, missy, but I'm going to die a happy man with or without your help. So get on with it, won't you?"

"Just like that?" she asked, surprised at his willingness to die.

"Just like that," he replied firmly, putting all his weight on his right foot as he deliberately lifted the tip of his cane a matter of inches from the ground.

"Suit yourself," she declared, reaching into her handbag for the gun she had used to shoot the President. Deftly popping the extra magazine of durbinium-tipped shells into the stock, she calmly leveled the weapon at Flix's abdomen.

"My, my, aren't you the sly one," he commended in an approving tone without flinching. "I didn't even see you pick it back up off the ballroom floor last night. Very clever," he complimented tersely as he gently raised his cane higher and noiselessly cocked the trigger hidden in its crook.

"Thank you," she acknowledged arrogantly, performing a curtsy for his viewing pleasure.

"That gun is from my collection, you know," he pointed out candidly. "There's not another one like it in the world."

"So I'm told," she replied impassively. "Now, you wouldn't want to make this go easier on yourself and hand over the code book you've been keeping, would you?"

"No, I'm afraid I can't do that," he answered, realizing what Whetstone had been after all along.

"I thought not," she acknowledged. "Too bad."

"Let me see if I have this straight," he elaborated, pointing his cane accusingly at her. "You waste me with the same gun that was used to assassinate Nolan, and what, leave it on my person so that it looks like a *suicide*? And I suppose before you go, you will type a note on my Smith Corona—something to the affect that, distraught over what I had done, I decided to take my own life?"

"Works for me," Nikki taunted as she drew closer, her automatic still aimed at his chest. But before she could utter another syllable, he acted.

Pressing his forefinger against the trigger, a single, high-velocity bullet bolted out through the rifled barrel of the hollow cane. Vaulting the short distance across to where she stood, it blew a messy, gaping hole between her breasts.

As she flew backwards from the impact of the large calibre shell, her arms flailed outward in a jerky motion and her muscular legs stiffened like rigid poles. Whistling out from between her lips, a sickening final gasp of air issued from her lungs. As her sphincter muscles relaxed, a line of pee dribbled down her leg. It was a horrible finish for a despicable woman.

Quivering from the dilatory effects of the adrenaline surge, Flix slumped to the ground exhausted. He lay there motionless for a long time. Not until a hawk screamed at him from above did he snap out of his trance. As he got shakily to his feet, it dawned on him that just because Nikki was dead

didn't mean it was over. There would be other assassins—
Whetstone would see to that!

Scrambling down the trail, his mind racing as he went, Flix
began sketching out a plan. What he needed now more than
anything else in the world was somewhere safe to hide; a place
that even Silas Whetstone wouldn't think of, a safe harbor far
enough away from the eye of the hurricane that he could
perhaps find some moments of peace.

Flix had to find a way to reach the one person he could trust
more than anyone else in the whole world—the one person
who owed him his very life—his old friend Tiger Matthews.

16

TIGER

Farmington, Missouri was like so many of those little towns dotting the American landscape—a long ways from nowhere and close to nothing. With its white picket fences, wide boulevards, and wooden rocking chairs guarding every porch, it was the kind of place which was great to be from— and even greater to return to.

Still—fearing for his life and hoping to shake any tails who might be pursuing him—Flix had followed the most circuitous of routes in getting there. Traveling cross-country incognito, he had taken the better part of three days to make the trip from Bar Harbor, going first by coal-burner out of Bangor, then by rental gcar from Buffalo, then by paddlewheeler down the Ohio from Pittsburgh, and then again by coal-burner from Paducah. Though he hadn't heard any newscasts since before leaving Maine, he figured that by the time he arrived in town, Chester Nolan had almost certainly been given a decent burial in Arlington Cemetery.

As had been the custom for half a millennium, important dignitaries were normally accorded a traditional twenty-one gun salute. The firing of a gun salute dates to the early days of the British navy. At that time, deck-guns could not be loaded quickly, so the act of firing one in salute indicated that the saluter had disarmed himself in deference to the person or ship he was saluting. The greater the number of guns fired, the greater the degree of disarmament. Since, at that time, there were twenty-one guns on one side of the larger ships of the line, firing all of them became the highest mark of respect a captain could pay. When the United States adopted the custom in the 1800's, the twenty-one gun salute became America's highest military honor, an honor typically reserved only for heads of state. Surely Chester Nolan, a six-term President, respected—if not loved—by many, deserved such recognition.

Although it seemed like a thousand years had passed since Flix's last visit to Farmington, it really hadn't been all that long. In fact, his most recent trip here had been five months ago when—after the election—Nate had invited him to be on his staff. On that occasion, Flix hadn't taken the time to see Tiger, and the truth be known, he had been putting it off for years. Back in the days when Nathanial Sr. was Governor of Missouri, the two of them had had a falling out over the closing of a military base on the outskirts of St. Louis, and Flix had never gotten around to telling him how sorry he was. Hence, it was with some trepidation that he stumbled up the dark porch steps to Tiger's house tonight and knocked on the front door.

There was an uncommonly long delay before the porch light came on, but finally the door creaked open.

"Well ah'll be cornswoggled," Tiger confessed in his Missouri drawl as he studied the face of his uninvited guest. "Ah never expected you to come *here* of all places. Isn't that kinda dangerous?"

"Dangerous?" Flix exclaimed, glancing nervously over his shoulder. "Dangerous in what way?"

"Why, yer a wanted man," the elder Matthews explained. "There's a price on yer head, ma boy."

"A price?" Flix repeated, genuinely alarmed. "Whatever do you mean?"

"Come on in already," Tiger demanded, hurriedly switching off the porch light to hide Flix's presence from any curious neighbors. Though his leisurely manner of speaking often made him sound dumb or even uneducated, Tiger was as sharp as a tack and as straight as an arrow.

"You got yer nerve comin' here!" he boomed once they were both inside.

"I don't understand what you're so upset about," Flix sighed, exhausted after his long trek.

"Yer a fugitive! Yer picture has been all over the teevee...*and* the newspaper," Tiger emphasized, tossing him the front page of the *St. Louis Herald*.

"My God," Felix shrieked, his face turning white as he scanned the headlines. "They think *I* killed the President?"

"Found your 'complice on a mountainside not far from your estate," Tiger elaborated as he sat down in one of his living room chairs. "The FBI identified the slug in her as being of the same calibre as that fired by that nasty ole cane of yers, and the gun found beside her body has been positively identified, not only as yers, but also as the weapon used to murder Nolan. Lordy, Flix, where have you *bin* the past three days?" he inquired motioning his guest to a seat. "Why did ya do it?"

"Do you have a spare room?" Flix asked anxiously, avoiding his friend's questions. Even as he spoke, he kicked himself for the blunder he had made. In his haste to get off the mountain that day after he killed Nikki, he had neglected to dispose of her gun—his gun.

"Were ya followed?" Tiger retorted just as anxiously.

"I'm not sure, but I don't think so."

"Listen," Tiger began coolly, "you can stay here 'cause I owe ya one, but I can't say as I'm real happy about the prospect."

Nodding somberly, Flix relaxed and settled into the overstuffed chair. The living room, though tidy in a freshly-vacuumed sense, was a jumble of magazines and trinkets. Unlike the methodical habits of his son Nate, Nathanial Sr. was clearly an eclectic mixture of professor and politician, teacher and administrator. His home looked as if he had never once completed any housekeeping chore he had started.

"Ah understand from Nate that ma son hired ya to be his

advisor," the crusty old man began, picking up where he had left off.

"In a manner of speaking," Flix shot back harshly, "but what's it to *you*?"

"Did ya drag ma boy into this nasty affair too?" Tiger questioned, almost afraid of the answer.

"Give me a *little* credit, won't you?" the General responded, not looking so official since he dumped his uniform back in Bar Harbor, adopting a civilian guise instead. "I know you must take me for some sort of a megalomaniac but..."

"Can't we be friends?" Tiger pleaded, the lines in his face revealing his age. "We were so close once. You saved ma life," he reminded Flix.

"That was a long, long time ago."

"So it was," Tiger agreed. "And since then, ar' paths have followed different—and sometimes conflicting—routes, with you taking the one which led to the pinnacle of the Armed Forces, while ah took the one which led to the Governor's chair. But damnit, man, think back!" the elder Matthews implored, dredging up old memories. "Think back to the days at Camp Na-Cha-Tan. We were mates even then."

Flix smiled wryly, "We *did* have fun together that summer, didn't we?"

"We *always* had fun together," Tiger replied, a faraway look welling up into his eyes as his mind cascaded back to the less troubled days of his youth, back to the days before he was even called Tiger.

"Remember the canoe race?" Flix quizzed, smiling widely.

"How could ah forget?"

"And afterwards, did you make it with that girl you were hiding in your cabin?" Flix asked with a lecherous grin on his face.

"Nah, I chickened out," Tiger admitted sheepishly, "but listen, let's get back to you. Nate should know that yer okay; he should know that yer ready to give yerself up."

"Are you crazy?!" Flix burst out loud. "I'm not giving myself up! Whetstone is behind the whole thing!"

"Are you tryin' to tell me that the Vice President killed the President just so *he* could be President?" Tiger cross-examined incredulously. "That's preposterous!" he charged, jumping to his feet and drifting toward the kitchen as he spoke.

"It gets worse," the General assured, following his friend to the pantry. "I have reason to believe the shooter was Whetstone's daughter no less. She was supposed to kill me too, only I got her first."

"You have got to tell all a this to Nate," Matthews insisted, "he'll know what to do."

"I can't," Flix dramatized, his voice cracking. "I feel so ashamed...he won't understand why I agreed to help Silas in the first place."

"Nor do I," Nathanial murmured. "Why did you?"

Knowing that his friend deserved some answers, Flix cleared his throat to break the silent tension between them. "Why did I do it, you ask? Perhaps I can explain. Do you remember Rontana?"

"How could ah forget?"

"Remember what Patterson told us about men like Rontana and what it would take to snuff out a man like that? Remember what we were told about the paradox? The paradox of power, or something like that?"

"Vaguely," Tiger replied, racking his brain to recall the details.

"How, in order to stop an ugly man, an opponent had to take risks well beyond those of a rational man?" Flix spelled out, retelling the lecture their death-squad was given a half century ago. "That's why I did it."

"Ah see. And was it worth it?"

"I don't know yet, but I can tell you one thing for sure."

"What's that?"

"Our country's a mess."

"And murdering the President was supposed to *help*?"

"Nolan was going to sell Hawaii to the Chinese," Flix pointed out.

"At least that way we woulda gotten *somethin'* for ar'

trouble," Tiger countered. "This way we get nothin'!"

"Whatever do you mean?" Flix implored as he accepted the cup of java Tiger had poured.

"Hawaii has declared itself a free state," Tiger explained. "They have confiscated the fleet at Pearl and commandeered the airbase at Lihue."

"When did *that* happen?" Flix wondered, realizing he hadn't heard the news in days.

"The mornin' after the assassination. But there's more."

"What more could there possibly be?"

"Though it hasn't made the papers yet, Nate tells me the Chinese have given our new President an ultimatum. If he doesn't immediately sign the treaty Chester negotiated, an' if he doesn't submit it promptly to Congress for approval, they are threatenin' to take by force what they woulda gotten by treaty. Though no shots have actually bin fired yet," Matthews elaborated, a note of sadness creeping into his voice, "we are technically already in a state of war."

"God's-sakes," Flix sighed as he slumped into the nearest chair. "What have I done?"

17

BLACKMAIL

The subcommittee's closed-door session had been under-way in Senator Matthews' private office for more than an hour, and Nate was growing increasingly irritated by the proceedings. It had only been a matter of days since the assassination, and he had yet to recover from the shock of what had happened or who had been implicated in the incident. And as if learning that Flix had been involved hadn't been enough of a blow to his confidence, Chester's body wasn't even cold when an altogether different challenge had presented itself, a challenge he was trying to deal with now.

"Geez," Nate murmured under his breath yet another time, "this amounts to blackmail." Senator Matthews was no scien-tist, but according to the man he had recruited to temporarily fill Flix's slot on his staff, state-of-the-art genetic experimen-tation had now made it possible for biowarfare-engineers to precisely tailor lethal toxins and then to mass produce them in nearly limitless quantities. With the Chinese just itching for an excuse to invade Hawaii, and with Overlord Mao's bio-geneticists having supposedly made a viral breakthrough with the potential to further upset the military balance of power, Nate's committee had no choice but to take their threat seriously. Extending the long Oriental tradition of tinkering with the natural order of things by engendering unusual carp and breeding peculiar-looking canines, they had now plainly gone to the heart of the matter by altering the genetic make-up of a common virus and transforming it into a deadly killer.

"May I remind you that our work is merely a natural outgrowth of the research *your* scientists began long ago," the Overlord's representative continued, his double chin quivering. Like a pudgy Buddha, the Ambassador had fat hands, a bald head, and a bulging belly. As he spoke he fiddled with a grasshopper-shaped amber amulet which hung on a necklace from his thick neck.

Remembering his earlier briefing, Nate guessed the obese man was alluding to the human genome project launched by the United States back in the twentieth century. This gargantuan undertaking which spawned a multitude of spin-offs ranging from the nonsensical "Designer Gene" craze to the remarkable solutions for a host of genetic diseases, and from the genocidal nightmare of Rontana to the establishment of a gene-storage facility on Mars, could only be described as ponderous. Its completion changed the course of human history.

"This is preposterous," Nate interjected glumly as he struggled to focus his attention on what the man was saying.

"Although American biologists taught the world how to repair faulty genes," Ambassador Ling continued, unfazed by Nate's remark, "the subsequent advancements bordered on the miraculous. Tampering with normal genes and modifying them according to mankind's whims meant innovative researchers could now accomplish feats from engineering low-fat milk-cows, to correcting the eating habits of diabetics, to even shifting the migratory patterns of Canadian geese!" the sweaty Oriental announced proudly. "The step we took next was all but inevitable."

"I'm still not clear just what it is you *have* done," Senator Benson blurted, warily eyeing the humungous man who had accompanied Ambassador Ling to this meeting. The beefy guard, introduced to them only as Chang, had the bulging arms and sloping forehead so typical of a lowland gorilla.

"Yes, for Chrissake, do boil it down to its essence,"

Senator Duncan implored, impatiently looking over at Nate to see if he agreed.

The Overlord's lackey nodded his bald head and smiled, his slanted eyes shifting mischievously. "Gentlemen. In Nature, molecules are found to spiral to the left or to the right. And even though amino acids generally come in both left and right spirals, all of the proteins used by living things are made exclusively from just the L-amino acids."

"I suppose L is for 'left' and R is for 'right'?" Senator Duncan speculated, attempting to demonstrate his keen intellect to the other two committeemen.

"Actually, Senator," the speaker chuckled contemptuously, glancing over at Chang, "L is for 'levo' which—in Latin—*did* mean left. However, right-handed amino acids are not referred to as R-amino acids, but rather as, D-amino acids, the D standing for 'dextro' which was the Latin for right."

Angered by the rebuke, Duncan shot back nastily, "This is boiled *down*, for Chrissake?"

"Geez, Dunc, be patient," Nate instructed brusquely. Even as he spoke, Nate wrote himself a reminder that he had to call home today. Ever since his wife Darna had died from that terrible fever, and he had left his son Frankie with the boy's aunt and uncle, relations between Nate and Frankie had been strained; Nate would never forgive himself if he neglected a day as important as this. Not only was this Frankie's 13th birthday, there had been a message on his desk since yesterday to call his dad.

"Matthews, the late, great Chester Nolan may have made you *Chairman* of this committee, but that does not give you the right to shut me up!" Senator Duncan exhorted, his face getting red with anger. "You succeeded in doing that to me before—in the term limitation debates—but I'll not stand for it again."

Ignoring Duncan's temper tantrum, Nate directed the Overlord's man, "Sir, please continue."

"Thank you," he replied. "Whereas the body runs on proteins built solely from L-amino acids, our DNA is fashioned exclusively from D-sugars, giving it its well-known right-handed helix. This opposing 'handedness' of DNA versus its constituent proteins is what makes the proliferation of life possible."

"Is there a point to all this?" Senator Benson inquired politely. Of the three Americans in attendance, he was the oldest and the most refined, his trim mustache giving him an air of civility. "Of what importance is this matter of twirl to the common man?"

"Hear, hear," Duncan agreed. "For Chrissake, isn't all this left and right crap nothing more than a boring backwater in biology?"

"Boring?" the fat man repeated. "No, not at all. Human chemistry is quite sensitive to the handedness of the molecules it encounters. For instance, the molecule 'limonene' swirled one way creates the scent of a lemon, yet when it is spiraled the other way, it leads one's nose to smell the scent of an orange."

"Big deal!" Duncan roared, getting to his feet. "Lemons or limes—who the hell cares? I've had enough of this," he made clear as he headed for the door. Chang didn't budge to let him pass.

"Sit down, Duncan!" Benson ordered harshly, not wanting a confrontation.

Ignoring the heated exchange, the Oriental pressed on, "Back in the twentieth century, you Westerners learned an unfortunate lesson in left and right. Swirled one way, the molecule 'thalidomide' cures morning sickness, but when it is swirled the other way, it causes horrible birth defects. Our scientists relied heavily on this spiral sensitivity in defining the objectives of our research," the Ambassador concluded ominously.

Senator Duncan swallowed hard as he began to digest what Nate had suspected from the start: they were about to be intimidated with blackmail.

"My friends," the visitor announced triumphantly, "our technicians have developed a virus which enters the host body through the mouth; in its food, say, or in its drink, or even via an exchange of saliva with another, as with a kiss. This virus is capable of bringing about a subtle— albeit lethal—modification in the host's mitochondrial RNA, a change which induces the cell's RNA to produce a 'D' version of a particularly essential L-protein. After a time, the toxicity of the D-protein accumulates in the nastiest of places, producing symptoms reminiscent of viral pneumonia, like high fever and dementia. Only it won't respond to the standard treatments. Within 48 hours of exposure, the host body…"

"The *host* body?" Nate exploded furiously, his gray eyes flashing with anger. "The *host* body? You bastard! You are talking about people as if they were fucking guinea pigs!"

"My friend, there is no need for cursing; no cause for anger," the Chinaman consoled softly, even as he motioned Chang to remain calm.

"I am not your friend," Nate shot back as Duncan nodded his head in agreement. "And there is a very good reason for anger," he added as he rose to his full height, his light, hair shifting gracefully with his movements. "Just what the *hell* do you want from us anyhow?"

"Money," the yellow-skinned diplomat replied matter-of-factly.

"Money?" Duncan repeated incredulously. "Chrissake! You're here asking us for *money*?"

"Compensation actually," Ambassador Ling clarified. "Compensation to reimburse us for the time and the trouble we will now have to expend in order to subdue Hawaii. We hadn't really intended to market this killer virus, but because of your President's refusal to turn the islands over to us, we are now prepared to put this batch up for general auction. That is, unless of course, you wish to purchase it from us instead."

"Geez, now I see what this is all about," Matthews confirmed thoughtfully, doing his best to digest the terrible truth. "It's so very thoughtful of you to give us this opportunity," he added viciously. "And how long do we have before we must submit our bid?"

"One week," the fat Chinaman declared with a satisfied

grin on his round face.

"And if we miss the deadline?" Benson probed, suppressing his indignation.

The question went unanswered as the pudgy Oriental politely bowed and exited the Senate chambers with the hulking Chang close on his heels.

As soon as the door closed behind him, Senator Matthews sprang into action! Reaching across his desk for the comm, Nate depressed the first two contacts. A distressingly familiar voice immediately sounded in his ear.

"Yes, Senator," the man at the other end of the line reported gruffly. "This is Dirk, speaking." Though the security man was posted only a few feet away in Nate's outer office, his voice sounded distant and detached.

"Dirk, Ambassador Ling and his bodyguard just left my chambers. I want an open surveillance placed on him, and I want regular reports as to the Ambassador's movements. Is that understood?" Nate asked, not expecting an argument.

"But, sir," the guard whined, preferring not to have to exert himself today, "I need authorization before..."

"Need I remind you," Nate began in an intimidating tone even as Senator Duncan excused himself, "that the Senate has opened public hearings on whether or not to hire a private security firm to guard the Senate Office Building rather than to continue dealing with cantankerous civil servants like yourself?"

Allowing the unveiled threat a moment to sink into the dullard's brain, Matthews shouted into the comm, "Now follow the man, or else consider yourself on report!"

Even before Dirk could reply, "Yes, sir," Nate had broken the contact and encoded another call. In the time it took for the electronic signal to race through the fiber-optic network to its destination, he twisted his head to address Senator Benson who was still standing dumbfounded in the room with him. "Ben, you had better meet with Hampton from Internal Intelligence—we need as much background as he can provide on this Ambassador Ling fellow and on that monkey of his,

Chang. And Ben," Nate added, his mind racing, "see if you can't get Hampton to provide us with a list of all our under- cover operatives in mainland ..."

As the comm came alive, Nate interrupted himself. The voice at the other end of the line commented dispassionately, "I'm listening."

"Mr. President," Nate recited urgently, the faint cleft in his chin seeming deeper than it actually was, "the bloody Chinese have just gone and declared war on us."

"Yes, I gathered as much," the President interjected in his comical tone. "A parcel arrived here within the hour and it describes in written form what I presume was related orally to your committee in its face-to-face meeting with Ling."

"What do you suggest we do, Mr. President?" Nate quizzed politely without actually expecting an answer. In his jaded opinion, the nation's newest Chief Executive was an incom- petent who had vaulted undeservedly to the White House upon the assassination of his popular predecessor, Chester Nolan. Nate feared that President Whetstone would buckle under the pressure of the present crisis with China.

"If we agree to this blackmail," Whetstone expounded, his spindly legs and long, thin fingers giving him the look of a cartoon character, "the nation will be enslaved forever."

"Good opening to the inevitable televised speech," Nate let slip caustically, "but not good enough."

Ignoring the jibe, the President declared, "I have called a meeting of the Joint Chiefs in one hour, and I expect you to be there as well."

Cringing at the thought of having to sit through another meeting with this idiot, Senator Matthews nervously ques- tioned the President, "And what do you intend to propose to the Joint Chiefs?"

"As Chester always did in the past, I will solicit their learned counsel," Whetstone assured, his gaunt face swelling hideously, "but I plan to strongly recommend we seek out and destroy the Overlord's biowarfare research facility. The Chi- nese understand nothing if not bombs."

"Silas, with all due respect, you can not *bomb* every research laboratory in China!" Nate objected strenuously, practically shouting into the comm. "The genetic instructions for manufacturing this damn virus could be stored on a fiche, and the fiche could be hidden anywhere!"

"Well then, I'll have Hampton's people hunt down and murder every scientist connected with the project," Whetstone offered, a note of desperation creeping into his tinny voice.

"Geez, Silas, can't you be serious? I don't see how your silly ideas are going to help us."

"Que sera, sera; what will be, will be," the President chanted psychotically. "Although you're probably not aware of this, America has an ace up its *own* sleeve."

"Oh yeah? And what's that?" Nate interrogated, hoping to smother the sarcasm in his voice.

"We have viruses of our own, you know," Silas revealed, shocking the Senator into silence.

Before Nate could choke out a "No, I didn't know," the President directed, "Be here in my office in one hour Matthews—and don't be late." Then Whetstone broke the contact and the comm went silent, leaving Nate to contemplate their conversation alone.

As much as anything else could have in the last few, turbulent days, Whetstone's revelation stunned him. At first he reckoned that Silas had finally lost it completely; but then, on further reflection, he decided that the man must be bluffing. America had no biological weapons of her own, and even if she did, he—Nate Matthews, the Chairman of the Military Oversight Committee—would have known about the existence of such an arsenal. Therefore, it couldn't possibly exist. Or could it?

The more he deliberated about the possibility, however, the angrier he became. If *he* wasn't privy to such information, how could a distracted, bungling man like Silas Whetstone be expected to be? Inasmuch as the new President simply didn't seem bright enough to lie about such matters, what if he *were* telling the truth? What if the United States actually *did* possess such weapons? And if all of this were true, what *else* wasn't Nate aware of?

Shivering involuntarily and suddenly feeling very much alone, young Senator Matthews wished Flix had been there to guide him through these perilous waters. Even now, he couldn't quite bring himself to believe that a man he respected so much, a man his father had respected so much, could have been involved in something as nefarious as the assassination of a sitting President. If only he knew where Flix was, if only he could talk with him, Nate could finally get some straight answers.

18

MESSENGER

By the time they called it quits for the day, not one of the Joint Chiefs had submitted an acceptable plan to the President on how to compel the Hawaiians to come back into the fold, nor had they settled on the best way to handle the biowarfare threat posed by Ambassador Ling. Dismayed by the unproductive meeting, Senator Matthews was eager to get back to his office, only the President held him back, another agenda clearly on his mind.

"Nate," Whetstone initiated once the room had been cleared of the herd of pathetic generals and the flock of weak-kneed admirals, "as a personal favor to me, I would like you to hand deliver my reply to Overlord Mao."

"Geez, Silas, you can't be serious," the Senator objected.

"I've made up my mind."

"Mr. President, Mao is liable to take out his anger on me personally. You know—shoot the messenger to avoid hearing the message? For heaven's sake, we're practically at war! I'll not do it," Nate vowed, digging in his heels.

"Senator," Whetstone interjected calmly, determined to un-make-up the man's mind, "I'll see to it that you are protected at all times; my Secret Service men will be at your side constantly. Not only that, you will ride back and forth to Beijing in the comfort of my own personal suborb."

"Secret Service, my ass," Nate yelped as he paced nervously around the President's ready-room suddenly remembering the Luger Flix had given him for protection, the very same Luger he had left behind today in his desk drawer. Promising himself never to make that same mistake again, he charged forward, "Was the Secret Service able to protect Nolan? How are they going to be able to protect *me*? You've never met Mr. Chang; he could snap my spine like a twig! In any case, it's a moot point—we have operatives for this kind of work. In fact, I've already asked Hampton for a list..."

"Forget about Hampton—I need you," Silas insisted as he followed the Senator across the room. Standing side by side, the two men were a study in contrasts. Although Nate was a tall and muscular man, the President was at least a head taller. And whereas Nate was a picture of health, Whetstone was a caricature of deformity. At times, his hollow cheeks and gawky walk made him look as if he were dying from consumption. Even so, his quiet determination spoke of an inner strength which couldn't be easily compromised.

"I need you to do this for me," Whetstone clamored. "Unless my reply is delivered in person, Overlord Mao will not take it seriously, and I doubt whether he will give an audience to anyone of lower rank than you."

"*Rank?*" Nate retorted in a perplexed tone. "What are you saying? I have no rank! I am an elected politician, not a duke."

"Indeed, but I would like to appoint you to the recently vacated office of the Vice Presidency."

Unsure how to react, Nate stammered, "Well...I don't know what to say, Silas. I'll need some days to think about it."

"Take all the time you want, but you must make this trip for me. Consider this, Senator," Whetstone justified as his tone turned more formal, "if I go to China, that will be seen by Mao as a sign of weakness. But if the Chairman of the Military Oversight Committee goes, the future Vice President of the United States goes, that will be seen by him as a sign of strength. Don't forget, it was *your* committee that the Ambassador chose as a forum for his face-to-face presentation. I'm begging you now, please do this one thing for me."

Still not convinced, Nate rejoined, "Why should I? Since Nolan was assassinated and you assumed the Presidency, I have stood behind you every inch of the way. Moreover, when you were Vice President and when I was a Congressman, I faithfully supported even your most hare-brained schemes in the House and yet…"

"Damnit, Nate," Whetstone interrupted furiously, "haven't you figured it out yet?"

"What, Sy?" the Senator groaned impatiently. "What haven't I figured out yet?"

"It's just an act!" the President explained, retiring to a chair. "The public image I have cultivated of being the bungling incompetent is just an act."

"Sure, Sy, sure," Nate dramatized, chuckling under his breath. "Well, act or no act, I will support your programs in the future, just as I supported Chester's initiatives in the past. And yet, on the very same day you ask me to be your Vice President, on the very same day you ask me to go to China on your behalf, I come to find out that you have been intentionally keeping me in the dark as to some of our most precious military secrets. Damnit, Silas, I am the Chairman of the most powerful committee in the Senate—a position *you* recommended me for—how *dare* you?"

"No made-up explanation I can offer will make you happy, so I will tell you the painful truth."

"In other words," Nate summarized caustically, "if you could conjure up a good lie, you'd just as soon feed me that line instead?"

"Something like that," Whetstone admitted hesitantly. "Now, my soon-to-be Vice President, do you want to know the truth or not?"

"Sure," Nate replied, expecting to be told a whopper of a lie.

"Americans lost their stomach for war long ago, and as a consequence, over the past generation our military prepared-ness has been skillfully and deliberately gutted by the liberals. That includes, by the way, the two co-conspirators on *your* committee—Senators Benson and Duncan. Because of this, we have…"

"We?" Nate probed curiously. "Who is 'we'?"

"People like Daniels and Robertson and me and…"

"Flix?" Nate verified, swallowing hard. "Was Flix in on this too?"

Whetstone nodded without speaking.

"I can't believe that Flix, of all people, could have been involved in such a scheme."

"Son, it is about time you grew up and dropped this Missouri naiveté of yours. Yes, of course, Flix was in on it," Whetstone acknowledged, confident that he would now have Nate's full and undivided attention. "Only now he's gone AWOL, and I'm not even sure if he hasn't defected to the other side."

"Defected? What do you mean 'defected'?"

"I haven't heard from him in days," Whetstone explained. "Have you?"

"No, I haven't either," Nate answered sullenly. "Do go on with your story, however," he urged, his voice barely a whisper, his gray eyes belying his disappointment.

Taking a deep breath, Whetstone tipped his head in agreement and began to reveal his long-held secrets. "No one actually *reads* the budget anymore; it runs for thousands upon thousands of pages. So, in an attempt to combat the liberals and the isolationists, Flix found a hundred different ways to hide our most essential military spending, one more ingenious than the next. Hell, half of them I don't even know myself, but I understand that Flix kept track of them in a little black book he always carried. Agricultural price-supports paid for biowarfare research; medical grants to big-city hospitals paid for laser-guided weapons; surveys for updating road-maps hid satellite reconnaissance; budgets for inner-city youth centers were used to train Green Berets; park ranger fire-fighting schools were in fact…"

"Enough already!" Nate shouted angrily. "I get the picture! Under the guise of being an imbecile, and to prevent anyone outside your circle from suspecting what you were up to, you and your...*buddies*...lied to the public. I cannot—I will not!—believe that Flix would have intentionally withheld this information from me. And as for you—*you* should be impeached!"

"Have you no sense?" Whetstone retorted in a cocky tone Nate had never heard him use before. "We're fucking heroes! Don't you realize the pickle America would be in right about now if we hadn't done what we did? Nolan didn't have the inclination, the appetite really, so..."

"Am I to understand that you, as Vice President, and who else—Flix?—plotted to have Nolan assassinated just so that you could take over and save us from ourselves?" Nate questioned with a stunned look on his face. "And now you want me to condone this insane act by agreeing to become your Vice President?"

"Believe what you will, Nate, but if we had not camouflaged America's most controversial—her most strategic—military programs, the entire nation would now be a hostage to their ransom demands. Instead," Silas announced proudly, "we have the means to turn this thing around—to call their bluff."

"Indeed, you *are* mad!" the Senator pointed out, slamming his fist on the table. "You think the Overlord is bluffing?"

"Of course not," Whetstone replied calmly, "but you are going to inform him that I think he *is* bluffing. More to the point, you are going to tell him that we have such a huge stockpile of equally awesome poisons that if even one of his loathsome parasites so much as *farts* in American airspace, we will blanket the Chinese mainland with tons of this putrid crap. He will end up being the absolute ruler of absolutely nothing 'cept a continent of dead bodies. Oh, and one last thing," the lunatic added, chuckling lightly, "you tell him to keep his mitts off of Hawaii, or I will consider it an act of war."

"Given *their* military strength, and given *your* carefully cultivated image as a fool, why should he heed your threats?"

"Two reasons," Whetstone elaborated, seeming particularly pleased with himself. "Inasmuch as everyone knows that

I am an imbecile, they would not consider me bright enough to make up a story of this magnitude. Therefore, they must regard my threats as being real. And in the second place, *you* will be the one delivering my message. Your reputation for telling the truth is so far above reproach, no one would even entertain the thought that you might be the bearer of a lie."

"Is it?"

"Is it what?"

"A lie?"

"Of course not," the President asserted, smiling thinly. "You'd be amazed by what we have developed in our biowarfare labs."

"Face is everything to the Chinese," Nate declared firmly. "If you don't offer the Overlord a face-saving means for backing down, then reasserting his honor will be the foremost thing on his mind. He will take out his anger on you...and on me...and perhaps on the country as a whole. And if Mao himself cannot regain face, the debt of revenge will fall to his son, Ambassador Ling."

But Silas would not be deterred; in fact, he became insistent. "Nate, you take my suborb to Beijing, and you tell Mao what I have said. You tell him I can no more afford a public disclosure of what I have done behind the nation's back, than *he* can afford the public embarrassment of not being able to intimidate a weak-kneed, imbecile of a President. You tell him there will be no reporters, there will be no loss of face, and there will be no blackmail. Period. End of discussion."

19

DIRK

Shutting the heavy wooden door to his office and settling into his armchair for the first time since Ambassador Ling had left there this morning, Nate directed his attention to the keypad on his comm. Encoding the number he knew by heart, he let it ring until the familiar voice of his father came on the line.

"How's it going, dad?" Nate opened, his voice revealing the stress he was under.

"How's it goin' with you?" Nate's father echoed in his slow, Missouri drawl, relieved that his busy son had finally taken the time to return his call. Like Nate, Nathanial was a tall, good-looking man built from rugged, northern European stock. And like Nate, Nathanial also had a lot on his mind.

"I guess things are going as good as can be expected considering the circumstances," Nate admitted, sighing heavily. "Sorry about not calling home sooner, but with the assassination and the funeral, and with today's developments, things have been a little nuts around here. I got your messages though—what's on your mind?"

"Before ah git to that, there's someone here who wants to talk at you," Nathanial explained patiently. "Do ya have the time to talk to Frankie?"

"Of course," Nate snapped indignantly. "I was planning on calling him myself later—after I talked with Musette.

What's he doing at *your* place?"

"Let me put 'im on," the elder Matthews offered, "he kin tell you hisself."

"Hi, son," Nate began apprehensively. "Happy birthday! Did you get my card? I've been meaning to call you all day but this was the first chance I got. How come you're at grandpa's house instead of at Uncle Tommy's?"

"I don't like them, and they don't like me," Frankie answered in a whiny voice. "Why can't I come out and be with you?"

"Not until school's out, Frank," Nate explained, a tinge of guilt in his voice. "Anyhow, there's only a couple more weeks left. I want you to finish up eighth grade right there in Farmington with your friends. This coming fall you can start high school out here in D.C."

"Promise?" Frankie asked, desperate to be with his father again. Ever since his mother had died, he had been lonely in the extreme.

"I promise," Nate assured him even as a knock came to his office door. "Come in," he yelped, cupping his hand over the receiver. "Frankie," he said, again speaking into the comm, "please put grandpa back on. And don't forget," he added as he motioned his visitor to a chair, "even though we're not together right now doesn't mean I don't love you."

"Sit down, Dirk," he whispered to the brawny man from Security. "I'll be with you in a moment."

"Take your time, Senator," Dirk whispered back, yawning loudly as if he were already bored.

"Lordy, Nate," his father began once he was back on the line, "as much as ah like Frankie, ah'm not sure it was such a good idea to leave 'im here with yer brother and that wife of his. Thangs aren't goin' so well over there."

"Geez, Dad, we have been through this before," the Senator made clear in an exasperated tone. "The November election was right smack in the middle of the school year, and I wanted him to stay there until May. I would never have been able to set up my office out here *and* watch out for a teenage boy at the same time. It isn't easy for a single father to raise a child all by himself."

"Son, I know ya miss 'er, but this is yore *boy* we're talkin' about," Nathanial asserted dramatically. "He's gitting in trouble at school. Can't ya see the boy needs a mother?"

"Surely that's not what you called me about," Nate responded, impatient to get on with what was left of his day.

"No, it isn't," Nathanial replied resignedly. "Ah got someone *else* here who needs to speak at you."

"Fine, dad, put him on, but I'm in a bit of a hurry," he snapped, glancing nervously across the room at Dirk who was busily clipping his fingernails onto the Senator's freshly vacuumed carpet.

"Here, *you* talk to him," Nate heard his dad say in a disgusted tone as he handed the comm to his house guest.

When the new voice came on the line, the man spoke with military precision. "Do not say my name," Flix ordered sternly, "just listen carefully."

"Oh, it's you…Uncle Tommy," Nate stammered, muttering the first name that popped into his mind and wishing that he didn't have a visitor sitting there staring at him.

"Shut up and listen, you fool!" Flix roared severely. "Your comm is most assuredly tapped. Don't use it again. And don't tell anyone you've spoken with me. Call me back tomorrow morning at 9:00 a.m. from a pay comm and then we'll arrange to meet. Now hang up, and try to get a good night's sleep— you'll need it."

Before Nate could say anything further, the line went dead.

As he sat there white-faced and shaking, Senator Matthews kicked himself for neglecting to tell Flix of Ling's threat against the United States or of Whetstone's offer of the Vice Presidency. Somehow his mind was all jumbled up and clouded by the day's events.

"Senator?" Dirk questioned, jerking Nate back to reality.

Turning to face the man who was still perched in the armchair on the other side of his sprawling desk, Nate asked,

"What brings you here *this* time of night?"

"You told me to report back in, didn't you?" the simple-minded fellow countered, irritated that he had missed his favorite, late night teevee show on account of this meeting. "Are you okay, Senator? You look as if you have just seen a ghost."

"Yes, I'm fine," Nate barked, struggling to regain his composure. "Just some problems I have to deal with back at home. So tell me, Dirk, what have you learned?"

"Not a great deal," the security guard summarized nonchalantly, his bushy eyebrows creasing. "I followed the Ambassador just as you asked, and after he left here, his bodyguard drove him across town to his apartment in Embassy Row. Maybe an hour later, the two of them left in his limo again and headed for the airport. According to the manifest, they hopped a suborb back to Beijing. Sorry, Senator, but that's all there is to report."

Nate nodded his head approvingly, but said nothing. Preoccupied with the flood of questions he intended to ask Flix when they met, he acted as if Dirk wasn't there.

"May I go home now, sir?" Dirk brusquely asked, antsy to get out of there.

"Uh…yes…of course," Nate answered, rising to his feet. "And thank you very much for coming around."

"My pleasure," Dirk claimed as he made a bee-line for the elevator. He had one more stop to make before settling down for the evening.

"You should have seen his face," Dirk explained discretely to the President as they strolled along Pennsylvania Avenue, their voices hushed. Directly in front of them were two secret service agents; two more hung a stride behind. All four men carried their sidearms prominently, their muscular hands at the ready.

"I can imagine," Whetstone snickered wickedly. "I just listened to the recording. He's supposed to call Farmington again tomorrow morning from a pay comm, so be at his home early, and tail him. Use a radio listening device and let's see if we can't pick up both sides of that conversation. I imagine the good General is staying with the Governor."

"Will do," Dirk replied obediently, shivering in the cool night air. He cursed his stupidity for not bringing along a windbreaker.

"Oh, and one more thing," Whetstone added in a firm voice before sending his snitch on his way, "I want Flix taken alive. Not only did he kill someone very dear to me, he possesses a book which contains some vital national secrets, a book which must be recovered at all costs. He's no good to me dead, capisce?"

"I'll do my best."

"Damnit!" Whetstone exploded, giving his guards a start. "Considering what I am paying you, you had better do *better* than your best."

20

RECONCILIATION

To say that their reunion was strained would have been an understatement. Not only had the circumstances compelled them to observe the most stringent of precautions to avoid being seen as they proceeded to their rendezvous point, once they arrived there, the two men had to deliberately keep their voices low as they warily mixed in with the capacity crowd. Although the third floor of the Indianapolis Children's Museum was as unlikely a place to meet as Flix could have chosen, amidst the raucous atmosphere of hundreds of children taking advantage of the May Day holiday from school, they did what they could to work out their differences. With Flix struggling to justify his actions even as Nate vocalized his objections, the icy air between them remained chilly until Nate told him of the deal Whetstone had tried to strike with him in the aftermath of Ambassador Ling's visit. Only then did they find some common ground on which to agree.

"As an inducement to get me to travel to China on his behalf, your buddy Silas, offered me the Vice Presidency," Nate began, breaking the ice.

"Don't do it!" Flix boomed without a moment's hesitation.

"Go to China?"

"No—be his veep."

"Why not?"

"If you give him half a chance, he'll compromise you and your good name in every way imaginable."

"And what about China?"

"You should definitely go. But this is too dangerous a mission to undertake alone," Flix emphasized as the two men wandered aimlessly from exhibit to exhibit, "I must go with you."

"That's out of the question," Nate countered as they ventured into a room full of model trains. "You're a wanted man; you'd be arrested even before we left the country."

"Look, I'm a master of disguises, plus I have plenty of friends left in the intelligence community. It shouldn't be any problem at all for me to come up with forged papers. Trust me, I'll just adopt a false identity for the trip; no one will even notice me. Anyhow, I can't hide out forever," the General explained matter-of-factly as he rapped his cane against the museum floor for emphasis.

"I agree—you *can't* hide out forever," Nate acknowledged, nodding his bushy mop. "Sooner or later you will have to turn yourself in."

"I don't think you understand," Flix advised passionately. "Though I didn't know it at the time, Nolan's assassin was Silas' daughter."

"His daughter?!" Nate cross-examined incredulously, a troubled look plastered across his face. "Geez, I thought you told me his daughter had been institutionalized?"

"I was so completely and utterly taken in by Nikki that my passion blinded my…"

"Did you say *Nikki*? The researcher you hired?! *She* was Silas' daughter?! *She* was the killer?" Nate declared tensely. "Why you old fool."

"For God's-sake, Nate, you've got to believe me when I say I didn't know it at the time. That's why he wants me so badly now."

"Which only buttresses my argument that much more: unless you're ready to give yourself up, we can't risk having you come out of hiding," Nate explained sensibly as a dozen third grade girls went zooming by, their pig-tails bouncing. Watching them laugh and twirl, he wished for an instant that Darna had given him a daughter as well as a son. Perhaps he'd have a second chance with Musette.

"Don't be silly," Flix exhorted. "By this time he has already figured out where I have been holed up, and rather than endangering your dad further, we would all be better off if I kept on moving. Besides, I wouldn't want to miss this showdown with Mao for the world. I have faced death before, and I'm not afraid to face it again."

"My, aren't *you* the brave one," Nate retorted sarcastically.

"A great philosopher once defined heroism as when the needs of the many outweighed the needs of the few—or even the one. Saving America might cost me my life, but save her, I will," Flix summarized defiantly. "You still have that Luger I gave you?"

Nate nodded, patting the pocket of his overcoat.

"You'll want to keep it closer to you than ever before. Things may get a little dicey before long."

"I know America has had her share of problems, Flix, but was killing Chester really the right thing to do? Was it worth the price you paid?"

"Let me ask you something, young Matthews. Do you know what America is actually all about?"

"Well...I...what do you *mean*?"

"Here you are," Flix scolded in a condescending tone, "a U.S. Senator from the great state of Missouri, a contender to be the Vice President of the United States, and you don't even know what America is all about?"

"Well, of course, I do," Nate shot back indignantly. "Capitalism and freedom and the right of assembly and ..."

"I'm afraid that somewhere along the line you missed the point."

"I take that personally."

"And well you should," Flix pointed out as he sat down at a bench to rest. "If someone of *your* status doesn't understand what America is about, how the hell can you expect the man in the street to?"

"So tell me, mister assassinator of Presidents and hider of state secrets, what *is* America all about?"

"Persecution," Flix explained patiently as if he were a Rabbi ministering to his flock. "Actually, the avoidance of persecution. That's why people came here to begin with and that's what originally made America great. The history of democracy, of freedom, has always been one of crafting systems of law to prevent the ruling elites from stomping down and enslaving their subjects. The Founders drew not only on the lessons of the Magna Carta and on the prototype democracies of ancient Greece, but also on the Iroquois Great Law of Peace."

"The Iroquois *what*?" Nate implored, never ceasing to be amazed by how much history Flix knew.

"Historians have long attributed the central tenets of the Constitution to the likes of Thomas Jefferson and Benjamin Franklin, but few realize that the League of the Iroquois greatly influenced the colonial Founders as well. The Great Law of the Iroquois not only embraced the basic ideas of democracy and federalism, it also gave an equal voice to each of the tribes comprising the League. It included a guarantee of religious expression, a mechanism for the impeachment of top leaders, and a formula for amending the centuries' old constitution. Benjamin Franklin in particular saw the Iroquois system as a model on which to base the Union."

"If this is true, how come more people aren't aware of it?" the Senator quizzed.

"The nature of racism is to never give credit where credit is due."

"You began your dissertation by berating me for not understanding what America was all about," Nate interjected, tiring of Flix's lecture. "Is there a point out here somewhere that you wish to make?"

"Only this: unlike the democracies of ancient Greece, slavery did not exist in the Iroquois nation."

"So?"

"So, each time democracy has been reinvented, it has built in a new layer of protection for its citizens."

"That is, I suppose, until now," Nate cut in, not liking the direction the conversation was going. "Is that what you're trying to say?"

"Yes. Ever since the Laborites made it easy to amend the Constitution, we have been backsliding further and further into a deeper and deeper hole," Flix asserted dramatically. "By granting every splinter group, every fringe element, every angry mother who dredges up two others who agree with her, the unfettered right to assemble and speak their mind, these invaluable franchises have been needlessly squandered and diluted to such a degree that no one has the right to say *anything* for fear of offending *someone*. There are no universal truths if every trifle is given a voice."

"Eloquently put, but where do we go from here?" the Senator inquired as the two of them moved on, pushing ever deeper into the bowels of the museum.

"No matter what the odds, no matter what the methods, no matter who must die, it is a warrior's duty to fight. Whenever there is a battle to be fought, the warrior's duty is clear—the battle must be won, and won at all costs. If America is not to slide off the same slippery precipice as every democracy before her, if America is not to careen down a slope made slick by the damnable grease of bread and circuses, we must make a stand and we must make it now! Left to his own devices, Nolan would have sold off the Union piecemeal; we must do what it takes to patch her back together. To appease the people, he callously bargained away more and more of our military strength; we must do whatever it takes to rebalance the scales. If Whetstone wants us to go to China and stare down the Overlord, we go to China and stare down the Overlord."

President's Ready Room, The New White House
The tube ride into downtown D.C. from out in Bethesda

had taken only a few minutes' time, but it had been long enough for Senator Duncan to eliminate any lingering doubts he may have had from his mind. He had called the President shortly before leaving Maryland and, despite the scant notice, Silas had agreed to meet with him early that afternoon. Now, as he passed through the inner security gate of the Chief Executive's mansion, and up the front steps of the great white building, he girded his loins for what he knew would be a messy confrontation. He wasted no time coming to the point.

"I mean to bring you down," Senator Duncan opened once they had gotten past the niceties and onto the test of wills.

"Them's fighting words, boy," Whetstone responded, talking down to the older man in his usual haughty manner. "I thought we were friends."

"Friends? Hah!" Duncan answered, a bead of sweat rolling off his bald head and onto the tip of his nose. "That'll be the day."

"I don't recall having ever done anything to hurt you," Whetstone retorted, watching his accuser tremble.

"And for that I will always be grateful. Nonetheless, I am in pain, and you are the name of my pain."

"Enough games already," Whetstone snapped, "I have a country to run. Now tell me what's on your mind and who it is I have supposedly hurt, or else get the hell out of here."

Nodding his head as his eyes glanced around the room, Duncan dug in his heels and started through his list of allegations. As he spoke, he noticed that not a stitch of furniture had been moved since he was last here speaking with Nolan. The desk was where it had been and so was the U-shaped ring of couches. "Let's begin with Chester Nolan, God rest his soul. You killed him," Senator Duncan accused.

"That's ridiculous!" Whetstone retorted, not sure how much Duncan actually knew. "I was sitting right next to the man when it happened."

"What I meant was, you *had* him killed," Duncan clarified as he corrected himself.

"That's equally ridiculous," the President contended, figuring that Duncan was just on a fishing trip. "Why would I do such a thing?"

"So you could be President, for Chrissake; so you could reverse the course of Chester's foreign policy and prevent Hawaii from being sold to the Chinese."

"Senator, you've been popping too many pills. Who gave you all these crazy ideas?"

"Chester did," Duncan replied candidly. "Before he was shot, he persuaded me to conduct an investigation and to compile a dossier on your clandestine activities. This I have done."

"I see, and what *else* did the late, pathetic, Chester Nolan tell you?" Silas cross-examined, debating whether or not Duncan was on to something.

"He told me about Clara, and so I went to talk to her ...twice. To be perfectly honest, I have just come from the hospital today," he explained, hoping to see Silas fidget.

"I see," the thin man noted without flinching. At times like these, his gawkiness took on an evil aspect. "And what did the old bird tell you?"

"Enough," he answered without elaboration.

"In other words, *nothing!*" Whetstone taunted, positive that Duncan had no hard evidence.

"She has convinced me that you were responsible for masterminding the whole thing."

"Is that so? She's certifiable you know," the President explained, already devising a line of defense in the event Clara decided to go public with her allegations. "Besides making me out to be the bogeyman, what else did you two lunatics conjure up?"

"She is going to spill the beans, Silas. I persuaded her to come forward and tell the world what a lowlife you really are."

"Que sera, sera. No one will believe her," Whetstone contended arrogantly. "I tell you, she's certifiable. If they put her on the stand, she'll go to pieces."

"It doesn't matter," the Senator countered, enjoying the spectacle as his opponent wriggled. "The truth will come out and you will be ruined. You'll have to resign."

"You have no idea what you're doing," Whetstone emphasized, regretting ever having agreed to this meeting.

"Not only do I know what I'm doing, I mean to run against you in the primary. The national plebiscite is almost upon us, and with the memory of Chester's assassination so fresh in everyone's mind, I intend to campaign for the repeal of the second amendment, the right-to-bear arms amendment."

"You can't be serious," Silas yelped apprehensively. "You'll bring down the whole Bill of Rights! Most constitutional lawyers agree that since the first ten amendments were passed as a package, repealing *one* is tantamount to repealing them *all*."

"I'll do whatever it takes to rid the world of you."

"Get out of my sight!" the President boomed, pointing to the door even as he nearly tripped over one of the couches in his haste.

"I'm in your face," Duncan sneered, as he got up to leave. "And whether you like it or not, I'm going to stay there until this is over."

"You're a dead man," Whetstone promised, his voice hissing like a snake, his eyes glaring fiercely.

As the Senator slunk down the hall with his tail tucked between his legs, Silas made up his mind. Something had to be done about Clara—and about Duncan—before this got out of hand.

21

CONFRONTATION

The short hop up through the clouds and out across the globe had been unremarkable not only in its duration but also in its distractions. Air Force One, the President's personal suborbital transport, was so luxurious, and so plush in its appointments, that both of her passengers found themselves awed by its quiet splendor. Though both Nate and Flix had ridden in their share of suborbs before, neither of them had ever been in a ship this fine.

Because Nate's assignment was maximum-classified, no one even paid any attention to the distinguished-looking gentleman who accompanied him onboard. Introduced to the skeleton crew only as an interpreter, without his uniform General Felix Wenger had passed easily for the level eight diplomat pictured on his phony identicard. With tensions running high in the Pacific, the Air Force Colonel piloting the suborb had been instructed to take the longer, but safer, route east leaving from National Airport on the outskirts of D.C., instead of from one of the three gateway cities on the west coast normally used by suborbs headed for Asia and the Pacific Basin.

Ninety minutes later they were met at Beijing International by the Overlord's limousine and driven to the Imperial Palace. After being led through a sumptuous garden and past a placid pool stocked with dozens of colorful koi, Flix and

Nate were escorted along a winding path lined with stands of manicured yew. After passing through yet another courtyard, they found themselves standing in front of the Overlord's not-so-modest home. Chang's bulk filled the doorway. Without exchanging a word, the big man frisked them swiftly and thoroughly. Not until he was satisfied that they were unarmed, did he admit them to the ornate lobby.

"Senator Matthews," Overlord Mao Tsui began in a scratchy voice, "I bid you welcome. Turning to Flix and dipping his head courteously, Mao observed, "I don't think I've ever had the pleasure."

"Nor I," Flix returned without introducing himself.

Extending his scrawny hand to Nate, Mao declared matter-of-factly, "You have met both my sons."

Squinting his eyes, Nate recognized in the shadows at the far corner of the room, the fat and distasteful man who had made the threatening presentation before his committee. To the Ambassador's left stood Chang, immobile like a mountain. A banner emblazoned with the likeness of a giant grasshopper framed the wall behind them.

"I didn't realize Mister Chang was *also* your son," Nate stammered as he stole a nervous glance in Flix's direction.

Delighted to see that he had gotten the Senator off balance, Mao ministered, "I suppose not."

Unlike either of his two sons, Mao was a thin and wiry man with a flowing mustache, Considering how fat Ling was, and what a monster of a man Chang was, Flix pictured Mao's wife as being anything but petite.

Continuing in typical Chinese understatement, the Overlord added, "Judging by my reports of how the two of you got along in your meeting, I suppose it is safe to say that you, Senator Matthews, and my son Ling are not yet the best of friends."

Nate smiled, but said nothing.

"My son informs me that you were not impressed with the successes of our genetic engineers," the Overlord suggested from a mouth formed by restless suspicion. But before Nate had a chance to respond, Mao abruptly changed subjects. "Have either of you two fine gentlemen ever visited our humble country before?" he inquired in a disinterested tone.

Answering for both of them, Flix interjected, "Unfortunately, we have never had the opportunity."

"Well then," Mao graciously offered, "I must arrange for a private tour once we have concluded our business. China is a…"

"I think not," Nate interrupted curtly as he warily eyed the two brothers standing watch at the outer door. "Affairs of state require our immediate return to the capital."

"I see," the Overlord remarked thoughtfully in impeccable English. "Then am I to conclude you are the bearer of bad news?"

"For us both, I fear," Nate admitted, wondering whether he and Flix were going to make it out of this alive.

"Your President doubts my word then?" Overlord Mao Tsui asked in a disappointed voice. "He doubts our determination to have Hawaii? He doubts we have developed the viruses my son spoke of in his meeting with you? What a silly man! How could such an imbecile be elected President of such a powerful nation?"

"Actually, he wasn't elected…" Nate pointed out even as Flix crinched uneasily.

"Yet, didn't my son explain to your war-making committee—so very patiently I might add—all about our virus and its terrible, even gruesome, effects? Is your President a fool after all? Perhaps he wishes for us to provide you with a demonstration?" Mao intimidated as he motioned for Ling to approach.

"NO!" Nate retorted sternly, growling at the wiry Overlord and at his pudgy son. "On all counts, no! My President is *not* a fool; in fact, he is a very dangerous man, and he generously offers *you* a demonstration of our *own* genetic concoctions if this feeble attempt at intimidation persists."

"Feeble?" Ling repeated, enraged by the charge. "Father, allow me and my brother Chang to tear these two dullards apart."

Waving his son off with the back of his hand, Mao challenged, "Are you trying to suggest that America *also* has such a virus in her arsenal? Laughable!"

"Why so?" Flix chipped in, waving his cane in a menacing fashion.

"In the first place—little man with no name—you Americans are too soft—too meek—too moral—to develop such nasty weapons. And in the second place, you Americans can't keep a secret! If your scientists *had* discovered a microorganism as foul as this one, they would have blabbed it to the world—*everyone* would know of it by now."

"There are some things not even the Pentagon knows about," Flix countered in a know-it-all tone. "At our biowarfare labs in Maryland we have some nasties from the past stored in cryogenic freeze—the Zairean strain of the Ebola virus, the anthrax bacterium, the Yersinia pestis— better known to you as the bubonic plague, the variola virus for smallpox…"

"The *what*?" Nate gasped, stunned by Flix's revelation.

"The *what*?" Mao echoed, caught off guard for the first time. "The virus for smallpox was supposed to have been incinerated nearly three hundred years ago!"

"That's what the world was led to believe, but in fact …"

Shaking his head pitifully as he defiantly crossed his arms, the Overlord exclaimed, "No, it is a hoax…and you are bluffing. I do not believe either of you," he concluded in an arrogant tone.

"I do not believe us either," Nate admitted cautiously, studying Flix's face to see whether he was speaking the truth, "but what my friend here is telling you is neither a boast nor a hoax. This information was kept secret from me, as well as from the rest of the world. Even so, Silas, I mean the President, *assures* me that…"

"Lies! All lies!" Mao exploded. "I will hold you both as my hostages until the ransom is paid," he spat viciously. "I will not be made out to be a fool!"

Looking the Overlord directly in the eye, Nate responded as calmly as he could with the answer he had rehearsed on the flight over here, "I am but a messenger, sir. You can no more hold me hostage in the hopes of changing the President's mind, than you can imprison a carrier pigeon for the purpose of altering the message already banded to his foot."

"Perhaps I should point out, Senator, I *eat* pigeons for lunch," Mao declared as his son suppressed a wicked giggle. "Then again, maybe you are right. Unlike your Mr. Whetstone, you have a keen intellect. Perhaps you and your friend here would like to come work for me? At least I pay well."

"Not in this lifetime!" Nate shot back without hesitation.

"You spurn me so easily, but you have no idea of the power I..."

"With all due respect, it is not power that I seek," Nate forged ahead resolutely.

"If not power, then what?" Mao cross-examined. "Money? Sex?"

"Truth," Nate answered simply.

"Truth?!" the Overlord parroted incredulously even as Ling chuckled softly in the background. "And I suppose justice too?" he added sarcastically. "Truth and justice *are* the American way, aren't they? Part of your folklore, really. Well, Senator, maybe you're not as smart as I first thought."

"Well maybe I'm not," Nate confessed bravely, "but frankly, neither are you. If you were as smart as everyone says you are, you would not force the President's hand. I recommend you use your head and withdraw your demands."

Unsure whether to explode in a fit of rage or whether to make peace with the determined Senator, the Overlord nodded his head and smiled a sinister smile. "Because I am unwilling to call the bluff of a man who seeks the truth before all else, I see that I must permit you to go in peace today. But be forewarned: although I am allowing you and your President to win this round, I will *not* withdraw my demands; I *will* exact my pound of flesh. It will be a lesson you won't quickly forget."

With that, Overlord Mao turned and walked abruptly from the room, his overweight son Ling following closely behind.

Chang remained at his post beside the door, a glare of unquenched hostility painted across his wide face.

Fidgeting nervously in his seat, Frankie waited impatiently for the cadence of the final bell to signal the close of yet another school week. He had big plans for the weekend. Not only had the weather turned milder, but to make the night complete, his teachers had been unwittingly cooperative by not assigning any homework for Monday. He would walk home, gulp down dinner, and—if he could avoid another argument with his aunt—he would fire up his new moped for an evening of cruising the streets in search of yet another place to rob. In the past month, he had successfully done several homes in the neighborhood, and despite a suspicious glance from Chief Munson the other morning at church, Frankie was sure the Chief didn't have so much as a clue who was responsible for the rash of burglaries.

Franklin Matthews had never been a dependable child, yet until Darna's death from that unstoppable pneumonia last October, his strong-willed mother had usually been able to keep him on the straight and narrow. Now, however, with her gone, things had changed. If coming from a long line of successful men wasn't enough of a burden for a thirteen year-old to bear, when his father stuck him with his nebbish uncle and his tyrannical aunt, Frankie was like a ship deprived of its rudder, like a kite detached from its tail. Without his mother there to keep him pointed in the right direction, Frankie gladly welcomed every chance to be impossible. Consciously striking back at his father for having left him behind in tiny Farmington while he went off to the big city to play Senator, the troubled boy had turned to burglary to satisfy his irresponsible and rebellious nature.

When the school bell finally sounded, Franklin was swept along by the throng of students rushing merrily from the building. As he absentmindedly strolled up Locust Street humming a curious tune, he kept his eyes on the ground even as he entertained himself with a mindless sidewalk game. Having no reason to rush, Franklin strained to space his steps so that neither foot would fall upon a crack or a seam in the concrete walkway. Completely oblivious of the thin, bespectacled gentleman approaching him on a collision course from the left, a man whose own hands were full with a large box and whose own eyes were fixed on a van parked at the curb, young Matthews plowed headlong into the stranger.

The impact of the collision nearly knocked the poor fellow over, and as both males struggled desperately to prevent the box he was carrying from crashing to the sidewalk, Frankie distinctly heard the rattle of glass from within the carton.

The skin between the man's freckles became red with rage as he swore vehemently at the boy, "You stupid dolt! Why don't you look where the hell you are going?" he shrieked even as his horned-rim glasses clung to the end of his nose.

Because the man wore a white lab-coat over his street clothes, and because the rattling glass sounded like rows of test-tubes pigeonholed in a series of metal racks, Frankie's first impression was that he was some sort of a scientist. When he helped the man to his feet, he was more certain than ever that he had drawn the correct conclusion. Not only did Frankie recognize the EPA logo emblazoned on the side of the box and on the side panel of the van, he remembered his uncle telling him how government inspectors would be in town this month testing the city's wells for contaminants.

But before Frankie could apologize for his blunder, the thin fellow pushed him away. "Mindless idiot!" he roared. "Small towns do breed such small brains, don't they?" he spat with contempt, cursing at the boy under his breath.

Angered and belittled by the scientist's remarks, Franklin vowed to target this house for a visit after dark tonight. Taking note of the address, he pressed forward up Locust before turning west onto Main. His aunt and uncle lived out beyond the edge of town, a walk which took him nearly 20 minutes.

He entered the yard to the roar of his surrogate mother and his stand-in father engaged in yet another heated debate. Ever since his real mother had passed away and his real father had dumped him here, Franklin had become the topic for most of these vociferous fights. Tiptoeing across the front porch, he hoped to avoid the squeaky plank just in front of the door.

"And I don't like it, Thomas," his repulsive aunt was shouting. "He's out almost every night doing Lord knows what, and he doesn't come home until Lord knows when. I tell you," she squawked shrilly, "he's gonna get himself into trouble and Nate's gonna hold *us* accountable."

"But darling…" the flustered husband tried to interrupt.

"Tonight is the last time I want him to go cruising on that stupid moped his father bought him. And I mean to tell him so when he comes home," she boomed like a police sergeant. "Where th'hell is that boy anyway? He should be home from school by now."

"Now dear…" the henpecked man tried again.

"Don't you 'now dear' me! When that boy…"

"That *boy*, as you call me, *is* home," Franklin began in a caustic tone as he burst through the door, "and I have heard everything you just said. I understand that this is to be my last night of cruisin' and maybe it will be. But that will be *my* decision, not yours, so why don't you just drop the whole thing? You're not my mother, and nothing you can do or say is going to change that!"

"Smart-aleck kid! What do *you* know of life?" she challenged like a bull-dog. "Your nephew needs a whipping, Thomas," she pointed out as she turned to her husband. "Would you like to do the honors?"

Much to Franklin's relief, his uncle did not budge. Instead, he rolled his eyes to the ceiling in a way that only Frankie could see.

The boy grinned a "thank you" in his uncle's direction, as he eased himself back toward the door.

Seeing him smile, his aunt started in on him again, more poisonous than before, "Frankie, if my husband were half a man, he'd bust ya one right in the chops. But he's not. To think that his *father* is 'Tiger' Matthews, hero and former Governor, and that his brother is *Senator* Matthews, soon to be Vice President. What has become of the vaunted Matthews' line?"

Pouncing on her husband like a wildcat, she insisted belligerently, "Thomas, *do* something! This bum thinks that just 'cause his daddy is a hot-shot Senator, he can get away with anything. We never should've agreed to babysit this little shit!"

"Now dear, the boy is..."

"Don't you 'now dear' me! That boy..."

"That *boy*," Franklin interrupted, at the end of his rope, "is outta here!"

With that, Frankie stomped from the front room and burst from the house muttering, "Whipping indeed! Why did my dad leave me with these people? I hate him for that. I just hate 'im. Except for my grandpa, I hate 'em all!"

Swallowing hard as the tears came to his eyes, he wondered for the umpteenth time why his mom had to get sick. "Is there no God?" he questioned as he ran out into the temperate night air. "No God at all?"

Unable to exorcise his wrath upon his aunt, and still unable to accept the death of his mother, he forgot about his moped and set out on foot. The lonely walk back into town only served to remind him of a better target for his ire—the rented house where the EPA scientist had sworn at him this afternoon!

GESCHICK

Part of the fun of breaking-in had been the *fear* of getting caught; that it could actually happen had never occurred to him. When the room lights flashed on and a gruff voice behind him instructed, "Hold it right there!", Franklin's heart sank. He had been caught red-handed and now all that remained was trying to talk his way out of it. He knew that with Chief Munson in charge of the investigation, that would not be an easy task.

"Raise your arms, chump," the big man ordered sternly, not wanting any trouble.

Reluctantly, Frankie did as he was told.

"Now real slow-like," the Chief clamored anxiously, "turn around to where I can see your face. But no sudden movements. And keep your arms up! Capisce?"

"I understand," Franklin replied tentatively. As he cautiously swung around to face the Chief, he wondered how Munson could possibly have known that he had broken into this particular house. He had been real careful not to turn on any lights or to make any noise which would arouse the neighbors' suspicions, but apparently he had failed.

Upon seeing the young man's face in the stark light of the kitchen, Chief Munson exclaimed, "Matthews? Is that you? Frankie, of all people, you should have more sense than *this*. Are you the one who has committed all these burglaries?"

"No, don't answer that," the Chief countermanded, thinking better of the incriminating nature of his question. "You are going to need a lawyer, son, and I am going to need to get your father on the comm as soon as possible."

"Oh, yes, you do that," the teenager challenged disrespectfully. "As if the Senator could care."

"Believe me, boy, he cares," Chief Munson asserted, a sad look crossing his chubby face. "I know he cares."

"How would you characterize your trip?" Whetstone interviewed as he and the Senator sat down to dinner in the Lincoln Dining Room. Although it had only been two days since Ambassador Ling had stood in Nate's office and delivered his committee an ultimatum, it felt to him like a lifetime had passed. Nate was exhausted from the trip and he needed a good night's sleep.

"Did you convince Mao to back off?" the hollow-cheeked man asked between nibbles at his salad.

Lost in his own private deliberations, the Senator didn't answer. As Flix had warned, the wolf was finally at the door, only Nate had to face the demon alone. The Overlord's words had haunted him all the way home, and now they echoed over and over again through his tired brain, "It will be a lesson you won't quickly forget." As he sat there listening to Whetstone ramble on and on, Nate realized that the Overlord had marked both him and Flix for death, and that there would be no easy way out for either of them. He couldn't decide, however, who was the bigger threat to America—Silas Whetstone, her president; or Mao Tsui, her enemy. The choice was stark.

"Did you convince Mao to back off or *not?*" Whetstone repeated insistently, as he picked at the main course. It was a bland concoction of chicken and fish recommended by the White House physician for a man with his affliction.

"To be quite honest, Sy, I'm not entirely sure," Nate answered through drooping eyelids. Besides the two of them, the enormous dining room was empty. Only Dirk stood at attention guarding the swinging doors at the opposite end of the salon. "I'm wondering whether our talk wasn't a stop-gap measure. He means to have Hawaii, and I'm not sure there's a darn thing we can do to stop him from trying."

"You may be right," the gaunt man acknowledged as he coiled his long, slender fingers around the hilt of his soup spoon just as a snake might do around the body of its victim. "Our low-altitude recon flights confirm that the Chinese fleet has already sailed from Okinawa. It is undoubtedly headed for Pearl. Alas, we are but days from war," the President sighed in his tinny voice.

"Why can't we simply blockade the islands and force the Hawaiians to give up their declaration of secession?" Nate redirected, the cleft in his chin suddenly seeming deeper than usual.

"What in God's name would *that* accomplish?" Sy snapped, putting his utensils down and dabbing his face with the cloth serviette. "Our boys would only wind up in the middle with the Chinese pounding them on one flank while the Pearl Command attacked them on the other," he dramatized as he rose to his feet and began pacing the room on his spindly legs. Like a character from a Washington Irving story, this reincarnation of Ichabod Crane was gawky and Abraham Lincoln tall.

"So you're going to do *nothing*?" Nate probed in an exasperated tone.

"To the contrary," Silas retorted, "I'm going to let the Chinese and the Pearl Command duke it out until they've knocked each other senseless, then I am going to bring in the big guns from Alameda to mop up the leftovers."

"You cold-hearted bastard!"

"Flattery will get you nowhere."

"Millions could die while they're 'duking' it out, as you so blandly put it."

"Que sera, sera; what will be, will be," the President hummed nonchalantly. "Look, as my new Vice President, I appreciate your counsel, but…"

"I haven't agreed to that yet."

"Strange, all the newspapers are reporting that you have."

"Yes, so I've heard. I wonder where they got *that* idea from?"

"I wouldn't know," Whetstone lied. "By the way, Dirk here tells me that you didn't travel to Beijing alone."

"I...well...I took along an advisor," the Senator stammered as he glared menacingly in Dirk's direction, receiving only a smirk in return.

"Is that so?" Whetstone retorted. "Anyone I know?"

"I keep my own counsel," Nate maintained, angrily pushing himself away from the table.

"Do you?" the President taunted, knowing that he held all the cards. "Flix is a fugitive from the law. If you harbor a criminal, that makes you a criminal too."

"And what does having your daughter assassinate the President of the United States make *you*?" Nate snapped.

"A hero."

"Oh yes, I keep forgetting," the Senator rebutted rudely. "You and your cronies saved us all from ourselves. I don't think I have ever met a more arrogant man."

"Look here, Matthews," Whetstone roared, "like it or not, Flix did in fact murder my Nikki. You have him—and I want him."

"Even if I knew where he was—which I don't—I wouldn't turn him over to the likes of you," Nate declared defiantly.

"Don't be a fool," Whetstone yelped back. "Don't you think I know that Air Force One made a stop in Bangor on the way home?" he reported as Nate gulped diffidently. "Don't you think I'm smart enough to have posted a round-the-clock guard at his place in Bar Harbor?" Silas maintained as the color drained from Nate's face. "What can he possibly hope to gain by returning to the scene of the crime?"

What indeed? Nate wondered as he recollected his argument with Flix somewhere over the Arctic Circle. Nate had wanted to drop Flix at Lambert Field in St. Louis and call his dad to come pick him up, but Flix had been insistent on going to his house in Maine, saying only that he would catch up with the Senator in two days' time.

"Don't you think I can have him arrested any time I want?" Silas announced as Nate beat his brains trying to figure a way out of this.

"So why don't you?" Nate shot back more defiantly than ever.

"Because I'm not done with you yet," he justified ominously.

"But I've done everything you've asked," Nate pleaded, his voice cracking as if he were about to erupt into tears. "What more can you possibly want from me?"

"There's still the small matter of the upcoming national plebiscite," Whetstone explained.

"I thought we finished with that? My filibuster was successful. I already *led* the charge which narrowly turned the term limit initiative!" Nate objected, tired beyond comprehension.

"Indeed you did, and for that I will be forever grateful, but this latest effort is more insidious than ever. And to make matters worse, it has come at me completely out of left field."

"What are you talking about?"

"The entire nation watched Nolan get gunned down on national teevee and Senator Duncan has picked up on it as a campaign theme," Silas whined. "He's gonna run against me in the primary next month, if you can believe the gall of that man. The imbecile threatens to catapult the issue of gun control back to the forefront for the umpteenth time. I'm fearful that the right-to-bear-arms controversy will explode geometrically from a simple discussion of repealing the Second Amendment to a debate aimed at revoking the entire Bill of Rights. You did such a fine job derailing Duncan on the Presidential term limits thing, I need you to spearhead this project for me as well."

Seeing his opening at last, Nate plunged straight through it. "I can't do this alone," he made clear.

"I realize that," Silas admitted as if he had anticipated this sequence of events.

"To do this, I'll need Flix's expertise."

"I realize that as well," the President noted arrogantly.

"There is no such thing as a free lunch, Silas. If I agree to do this for you, and if Flix agrees to help me do it, you must promise that no harm will ever come to him."

"I promise."

"Why don't I believe you?"

"I couldn't say."

23

MUNSON

As Nate sped across the campus-like quad on the way from the White House to the marble covered Senate Office Building, the brisk night air felt good against his flush face. It was already dark, and except for the occasional couple strolling along hand-in-hand, the wide, graveled sidewalks were empty. Partially hidden by a patch of clouds, the moon hung like a lighthouse from the canopy overhead, a warning beacon put there by God to prevent any ships from foundering on the treacherous rocks below.

Though it had only been a matter of months since he had first come to Washington as a freshman Senator, he had never felt so pathetically alone before. Contemplating the future without Darna, Nate shook his head in despair. Though his feelings for her might never have been adequately described as "love", he still hadn't gotten over her death. Moreover, he still hadn't come to grips with his own, rather precarious situation. Without the patient counsel of his dad, or of Flix, he didn't know what his next move should be.

Pausing to study the triumvirate of obelisks in the hesitant moonlight, he noticed a figure recede into the shadows a dozen or more paces behind him. It didn't actually surprise him that he was being followed, only that the man keeping an eye on him was such an amateur. Nate had recognized early on that Silas couldn't be trusted, still the tail was so obvious, it was almost insulting. Considering for a moment whether or not to confront the stooge, Nate thought better of it, quickening his pace instead to make up for lost time.

When he arrived back at his office, there was a stack of messages piled neatly on his desk. Sorting through the missives, he separated them into three piles for tomorrow morning—must return, should return, and don't bother. There was one message, however, which sounded urgent enough to call back tonight. That one was from Newton Munson.

Stealing a glance at his desk chronometer, and reminding himself that Farmington was one hour behind DC, he took a chance on it not yet being too late to place the call. As the comm clicked energetically in his ear, indicating that the connection was being made, he wondered what else could possibly go wrong today.

"What d'ya want?" came the gruff reply from a man who had obviously already retired for the evening.

"Police Chief Munson?" Nate asked as politely as he could, embarrassed that he had woken the man.

"Yep, this is Munson," the burly man grumbled, half awake. "Who the hell is this?"

"Newt? Is that you, you 'ole foxhound?"

"Matthews? Are you crazy calling me this late at night?"

"Thanks, I'm fine, and you?" Nate kidded his old friend. Though Chief Munson was closer to his father's age than his own, Nate had always held him in the highest regard. Since his hometown's 500th anniversary was fast approaching, and since Nate was one of the town's leading citizens, he figured that Newt had called to try and talk him into making a personal appearance at the festivities.

"Don't tell me they put *you* up to bribing me to give a speech or something?" Nate teased, hoping to stay one step ahead of his sharp mentor.

"No, it's a tad more serious than that," the Chief answered gravely.

Suddenly fearing that something had happened to his dad or to Musette, he pressed, "What's wrong? You sound so down. Is my father okay?"

"It's your son, Nate," the Chief answered without elaboration. "It's Frankie."

Nate's pulse quickened as frantic thoughts started flashing through his head. He had barely begun to accept the loss of his wife; he wasn't sure he could handle it if something had now happened to his son. His voice cracked as he asked, "Franklin? Is he…hurt?"

"No, it isn't that simple, I'm afraid," Chief Munson explained as calmly as he could. "He's under arrest."

"What?!" Nate yelped incredulously. "Under *arrest*? For what?"

"Tripped the silent alarm breaking into the Sanders' house over on Locust."

"I don't understand…"

"Your boy's a suspect in six B'n E's committed since BeHolden Day."

"Newt, you gotta believe me," Nate implored, "I had no idea. Neither my brother Tommy nor his wife ever said a word. I mean, my responsibilities as a Senator have kept me away…"

"No one's *blaming* you, Nate, but I think you should come home," the Chief asserted firmly. "Soon."

"I will," he assured him. "In a few days—when this session of Congress adjourns."

"I'd come home sooner than that if I were you," Newt objected in a fatherly tone.

"I can't. I've got some serious problems here to contend with."

"You know best, Senator," Munson replied unconvincingly. "Or should I address you as Mr. Vice President now?"

"Newton, I want no special treatment here, but can he be charged as a juvenile? Frankie's only thirteen, you know."

"That I have done, my friend. That I have done."

"It might make a lasting impression on the boy if you held him a few days in your jail," Nate suggested, his mind racing ahead to judge the best way to handle this without causing himself any adverse publicity.

"I don't want to be a babysitter," the sheriff objected.

"Three days now might save us from three *years* later on," the Senator reasoned.

"Okay," the Chief consented reluctantly. "Three days, but no more. And when you get into town and sit down to talk with him, you agree to find out whether any other boys were involved."

"Agreed…and thanks," Nate acknowledged gratefully as he said good-bye and hunkered down into his chair for a nap.

No sooner had he hung up the comm, however, than someone rapped firmly on the outer door to his office. Exhausted by a day that seemingly would not end, he declined to answer it, thrusting his feet up on his majestic desk and closing his eyes instead.

"Come on, damnit," a familiar voice bellowed from out in the foyer. "Answer the door already, Matthews. Come on," he whined, "I know you're in there 'cause I followed you over here from the White House. Not only that, I just watched the comm light go out on your secretary's switchboard."

Irritated by the disruption, Nate dropped his heels back to the floor and—choking back a big yawn—hobbled over to the door. Upon seeing who it was, he immediately regretted his decision.

Senator Duncan burst into the room like a raving lunatic. "I want to know what is going on, for Chrissake," he barked icily. "I have figured out some of it, you see, but only enough to be dangerous. So you had better come clean and start explaining the whole thing to me right now."

"What exactly do you know?" Nate probed noncommittally, unsure what Duncan was alluding to.

"I know, for instance, that as a Congressman, Silas Whetstone beat and raped his own daughter," Duncan elaborated somberly. "I know that when his wife discovered what he had done, that he beat and raped her as well. I know that the beating was so severe the poor woman was left in a coma which lasted the better part of a year, and that she has been confined to an institution ever since. I know that, although his daughter eventually made a complete recovery, she became a virtual slave to his every whim, serving him most recently as a paid assassin. I know he only pays lip service to his cherished Bill of Rights and that he will do his best to scare the bejaises out of the whole country over my proposal to repeal the Second Amendment and replace it with something less generous."

"Geez, Dunc, you know...a lot," Nate interjected, shocked by the revelations. "Maybe too much. What...do you want...from me?"

"You have his ear, Nate. He trusts you. Find out what the man is up to," Senator Duncan implored. "For Chrissake, let's bring the bastard down before it's too late."

"Too late for what?"

"Now that the Hawaiians have apparently succeeded in pulling out of the Union, all sorts of *other* splinter groups will try as well. Already there's talk on the Navajo Reservation of the Amerinds declaring themselves free and independent nations. Where will it end?"

"It's still early in the game—Hawaii hasn't succeeded in pulling out yet," Nate replied, remembering Whetstone's strategy for grabbing victory from the jaws of defeat.

"Please think about what I have said," Duncan urged as he rose to leave. "I can't do this thing alone."

"I can't help you," Senator Matthews admitted without guilt, "but if you're going up against Silas—if you're planning on running against the man—you had better watch your back."

"Same to you," Duncan retorted as he left. "Same to you."

24

CLARA

Ditching the rental gcar on a side road about a half mile beyond the driveway to his house, Flix made his way back up along the beach under the cover of darkness. It was a cold and blustery night which, under any other circumstances would have made it miserable, but for what he had to do, the conditions were perfect. Not only would the howling wind mask the occasional tapping of his cane against the boulders dotting the shore, the inclement weather practically assured that the guards Whetstone had posted there would keep to the leeward side of the manor and out of the stiff breeze. At his age, Flix was no match for a couple of strapping studs armed with Uzis.

Still, guards or no guards, Flix had no choice. If he was to stay alive, he had to retrieve several items from his bedroom upstairs. What he was counting on was the sentries not knowing about the short tunnel which ran underground into the basement proper from the abandoned root cellar out back. So long as the old wooden door leading to the cellar could be kept from flapping in the wind, he ought to be able to enter the house undetected. Even so, he wasn't blind to the risk: if he got caught he would undoubtedly be shot on the spot; in all probability, the night watchmen had been given orders to shoot to kill.

With these hazards clearly in mind, Flix pressed his old

frame down against the ground as far as he possibly could. Passing noiselessly up the beach below his ocean-side estate, he swung along the northern edge of his property through the pine tree windbreak he himself had planted years before. It was at that point that he glimpsed the telltale flickers of a lit cigarette hanging from the shivering mouth of one of the two guards huddled next to one another beneath the canopy of his front porch. They were taking turns downing swigs from a leather-wrapped flask of tortan.

From where he stood at the fringe of the forest, Flix had an unobstructed view of the interior of his home through the enormous bay window which ran the width of his manor. The house was dark and quiet. Satisfied that no one was inside waiting to pounce on him, Flix worked himself around to the windward side of the building where the ancient root cellar was located. Reaching down to open the creaky door, he had his first disappointment of the evening—it was locked! Although he didn't remember having ever padlocked the aged door before, without a crowbar to pry the hinges loose now, he had no choice but to find another way in.

As he skulked up the back walk intending to slit a hole in his screened-in porch, he suddenly felt the unexpected pressure of a trip-wire against his leg. "Damn"! he swore under his breath, cursing his misfortune. But by the time he could react, it was already too late—the silent alarm had been triggered!

Stumbling backwards over himself, he retreated as swiftly as his old legs would carry him to the shelter of the forest, where he watched with amused fascination as the two muscle-bound lookouts swung into action trying to ferret him out. As luck would have it, before they could get too far in their search, an enormous raccoon lumbered by, evoking a laugh and a shoulder shrug from the two lugs as they dismissed the alarm to the careless habits of the nocturnal carnivore. Persuaded that there was nothing further for them to worry about, they returned to their post, the stench of alcohol trailing behind them.

Being more careful of the trip-wire on his second approach, Flix sliced easily through the screen with his blade and slipped quietly into the rear of his country home. The place was a shambles. Whetstone's men had turned the tidy house upside down searching for something; Flix prayed they hadn't found it. Closing his mind to the disarray, he slid silently upstairs; three of the four things he had come for, he had left stashed in the wall safe hidden behind a picture in his bedroom. The fourth item—an untraceable handgun from his private collection—he would have to do without; it was hopelessly buried in the mounds of debris strewn about his front room.

Feeling his way along the darkened walls of his bed chamber, Flix was relieved to find the picture undisturbed, and the safe behind it unopened. Somehow, in their haste to tear his place apart, the dimwitted burglars had overlooked his vault. Spinning the tumblers on the combination lock by rote, he retrieved a magazine of specially-manufactured shells for his cane, a stack of fake identicards he kept for just such an occasion, plus a slender book filled with dozens of ultra-sensitive addresses and an even greater number of secret codes. Slipping back outside by the route he had come in, it was only a matter of minutes before he was again on the windswept beach headed back toward the parked gcar. Once he was safely away from Bar Harbor, he pulled over to the side of the road to study the confidential address book under the glare of the car's overhead lamp.

Flipping past the pages of secret access codes, Flix fell upon the section of his compact folio listing the names, addresses, and comm numbers of certain high-level government officials, their wives, and their mistresses. For many years, as a BeHolden Day courtesy, a member of his staff had sent a basket of fruit to one Clara Whetstone, Silas' institutionalized wife. In all those years, however, Flix had never met the woman nor had he ever taken the time to commit her address to memory. Now, as he contemplated how to strike back at the renegade President, he decided he must see her. Scanning the entries one by one, he found her name sandwiched between

Dan Walker, Undersecretary of Transportation, and Homer Williams, Editor-in-Chief of the *New York Times*.

Pulling back onto the coast road with a determined look on his face, Flix pointed the rental gcar in the direction of the Bethesda Medical Center in Maryland. Months ago, in self defense, he had killed Clara's only daughter; now he wanted to explain to her what was at stake and why he still had to kill her husband.

When he arrived at the hospital's security gate shortly after noon the next day, he counted on his many years of intelligence work to see him through. As he expected, two humorless Marine corporals stood at the ready, diligently clearing each visitor past the checkpoint. Although many dozens of callers no doubt passed through the turnstiles each day, Flix surmised that few, if any, ever came to see the President's deranged wife. He figured that either he had better have a damn good excuse why he should be admitted to look in on her, or else he had better sign in to see another patient.

Having settled on the latter course of action during the long drive down from Maine last night, Flix had stopped along the way to call Tiger and—without considering the possibility that the call was being monitored—had asked his friend to make some inquiries on his behalf. When Flix checked with Tiger again at 9 o'clock this morning, Nathanial had given him the name of a current patient, the senior Congressman from upstate New York.

"Who are you here to see?" the tougher of the two Marines asked as Flix met his steely gaze.

"Benjamin Hancock," Flix replied, giving him the name Tiger had provided.

"And is the Congressman expecting you?" the uniformed man cross-examined, verifying the name against the patient roster.

"No, he is not, and I would appreciate it if you didn't warn him that I was on my way up," Flix explained in a jocular tone.

"It's a surprise."

"We don't like surprises here," the Marine declared flatly. "Please state your name for the record."

"I'm his brother-in-law, Willy."

"May I see some ID?"

"By all means," Flix asserted, fumbling in his pocket for the William James identicard he had copped last night from his own safe.

Studying the ID closely as if doing so would impart some special insight, the first Marine recorded Flix's fake name even as he signaled to the second sentry to raise the barrier. "Have a nice day, Mr. James," he suggested as Flix drove through.

"Same to you," Flix nodded as he spied a parking spot not far from the front door. Glancing first at Clara's room number in his address book, then counting the number of floors in the building, he reckoned that cubicle number 502 had to be on the top floor at the far end of the hall. Signing in at the front desk as Willy James, he asked the attendant which room Congressman Hancock was in.

"Shall I ring him, sir?" the perky candy striper inquired. Flix couldn't help but notice that her breasts were pressing firmly against the confines of her sweater.

"No thanks," Flix answered politely. "If it's all the same to you, I'd rather surprise Benjy."

"Benjy?" she probed in her adolescent tone, wiggling her chest in a provocative manner. "You two must be close."

"Married my sister," Flix explained, keeping up the charade.

Consulting the register, the girl asserted, "That's room 306. Elevator's thataway."

"May I take the stairs?" he inquired, moving away from the counter. "My doctor says I need the exercise."

"Suit yourself," she pouted, pointing down the corridor toward the EXIT sign posted above the two metal doors.

Taking his time and pausing at each floor to catch his breath, Flix resolutely climbed the five full flights of stairs, passing only one stern-looking Army man along the way.

Dipping his head so as not to be recognized by the officer, Flix wasn't aware that the stranger executed the same maneuver. When Flix reached the fifth landing, he poked his head into the hallway to check whether he could enter unseen, and upon seeing that the coast was clear, he swung swiftly into the corridor, locating room 502 in a matter of moments.

Although the heavy door was ajar—a sure sign of trouble in his opinion—he proceeded undeterred into the chamber. What he saw made him gasp.

An older, but nonetheless attractive, woman lay on the shiny floor in a widening pool of blood. Rushing to her side, he inquired, "Clara? Clara Whetstone?"

"Yes…" she replied, gasping for breath.

"God's-sakes, who did this to you?" he screamed as he pressed his finger to the call button next to her bed. "Who?"

"Said his name was…Wenger…Felix Wenger," she muttered, laboring for air. "Sends me a basket of fruit every year."

"Whaaat?" Flix screamed as a nurse burst into the room, a look of horror on her face.

"I was murdered by…by…General Felix Wenger," Clara sighed as she slipped into a final coma.

White-faced and trembling, Flix got to his feet and bolted down the hallway. He could feel the noose tightening around his neck.

25

THE DEVIL IS IN THE DETAILS

As Nate picked up the morning paper from the floor outside his office and passed through the reception area on the way to his desk, he found it curious that his security man, Dirk, wasn't already at his post in the outer lobby.Grumbling something to himself about lazy civil servants, he sat down in his easy chair to enjoy a few moments of peace and quiet with his newspaper before the day began in earnest. And that's when he saw it.

"WENGER STRIKES AGAIN!" the headline screamed, its bold, two inch tall letters jumping out at him.

Gripping the tabloid tightly in both hands, Nate began to read the lead article, but he was no more than a paragraph or two into it, when the comm rang, shattering the eerie silence. Nearly jumping out of his skin at the noise, he reached for the source of his discomfort, his hand shaking. It was his dad.

"Nate, is that you there?" the elder Matthews confirmed breathlessly. "Son?"

"Yea, dad, it's me—what's up?" he questioned, his voice trembling over what he had just read.

"What's up, you ask? Haven't ya heard the news?" Nathanial scolded, figuring that his son already knew what had happened. "Haven't ya even read the *paper*?"

"Just opened it," the Senator replied, wondering whether he was about to be ill.

"He called me early yesterday mornin'," Tiger explained without elaboration.

"Who?" Nate asked, not able to focus yet on what his dad was saying. "Who called you yesterday morning?"

"Flix, you dolt!" his dad rebuked in an uncharacteristic fashion. "Flix called the night before last from one of those roadside truck stops. It had to have bin 'bout 2 a.m. or there abouts."

"Geez, dad, what did he want?"

"The name of a patient at Bethesda, so ah made a couple a calls and found out that Benjamin Hancock checked in there a couple a days ago," Tiger explained in his slow Missouri drawl. "Flix was fixing to *see* Clara, not kill her."

"Guess he changed his mind," Nate rebutted, sick to his stomach over this turn of events.

"Not very damn likely!" Nathanial exploded. "Didn't ya read the *paper*?"

"Not yet, dad. I just got in. What does it say?"

"'cording to the *Herald*, she was killed at close range with a small calibre weapon."

"So?" Nate cross-examined, not getting his father's meaning.

"So," his dad retorted, "Flix's cane fars a massive shell."

"That doesn't make him innocent," Nate argued, playing the devil's advocate.

"Granted, not that fact alone, but consider this," Tiger elaborated, doing his best to convince his skeptical son of Flix's innocence, "both the Marines at the gate, and the attendant who spoke with 'im at the front desk, described the man who registered as General Felix Wenger as bean a much younger man than ar' Flix...and he didn't have a limp neither."

"You mean he didn't do it?"

"That's what I bin tryin' to say," Tiger declared irritably. "When he called me, he wanted to apologize to Clara for killing her daughter. Ah take it, he liked the gal."

"Who, Nikki?" Nate asked, remembering how easily Flix

had been taken in by the girl.

"Yep, that was her name."

"So, he was set up?" the Senator remarked, his voice sounding more hopeful as he made up his mind.

"Looks that way to me," Tiger summarized, satisfied that Nate had begun to see the light.

"He may show up here before too long," Nate explained, remembering Flix's promise when he dropped him off at the airport in Bangor.

"Be myty careful, son," the former governor warned. "He may be innocent, but he's still a marked man."

"I will," Nate declared, "I will. Listen, before I forget it, how is Frankie getting along with the Chief?"

"Stuck as he is in Munson's hoosegow, the boy's just fumin'. Just fumin'."

"It'll do him good."

"I shore hope yer right," Tiger pointed out. "Now be careful, and come home soon."

"Be sure to tell Newt I appreciate all his help and that I'll be in town the day after next at the latest."

"And in the meantime?" Nathanial speculated out loud.

"There is someone I must see," Nate answered, being intentionally vague as he heard Dirk rustling around in the outer office. "I really must go now—talk to you later."

Hustling past his tardy security man and down the palatial steps of the Senate Office Building, Nate wrapped his overcoat tight around himself to shut out the morning chill. As was not uncommon this early in May, spring had temporarily retreated in the face of a cold spell. Setting off across the lawn toward the New White House at high speed, Nate plotted to confront the President on his own terms. According to the newspaper, even though Clara's funeral wasn't to be held until the weekend, the President was receiving close friends and relatives this morning and this afternoon in the East Wing. Nate hoped to catch the man off-guard and force him to tell the truth about this whole affair.

After what Duncan had told him, and knowing Flix the

way he did, Nate doubted whether the media's account of Clara's murder was accurate. In all likelihood, it was Silas himself who had arranged to have his wife done away with in order to avoid an embarrassing disclosure. Not only that, it was undoubtedly Silas himself who had engineered to have Flix framed for the crime. And, in order for Whetstone to have known that Flix was on his way to the Bethesda Naval Hospital yesterday morning, it only made good sense that his dad's comm had to have been tapped. Likewise, it only seemed intuitive that for Whetstone to have had Clara killed after so many years of confinement, there had to be a reason— a very good reason. The way Nate figured it, the reason had to be that she was going to talk—perhaps already *had* talked— and that the truth concerning Nikki and Silas was about to come out. She had almost certainly spilled her guts to Duncan, and he was about to share what he knew with the world. So she had to die. Which meant Duncan was next!

Realizing that Senator Duncan had to be alerted to the danger as soon as possible, Nate changed his mind about confronting the President. To cover his tracks, Nate decided he would go down the Mall toward the White House, pay his respects, then double back on a side street to Duncan's office at the opposite end of the blocks' long Senate Office Building.

Matthews hadn't gone more than a hundred yards when he was accosted by a stooped, old beggar clamoring for money.

"Buddy, spare a five for a cup'a coffee?" he warbled in a squeaky voice.

"All I've got is a buck," Nate lied, wanting to be left alone.

"You cheap sonuvabitch," the disheveled panhandler squawked, raising his cane menacingly. "It's *cold* out here," he added, straightening up, the glint of his straight white teeth revealing his true identity.

"Pretend you don't know me," Flix warned before Nate could blow his cover. "I didn't do it; you have *got* to believe me."

"I do," Nate whispered back, his eyes searching his friend's troubled face. "But is there no *end* to this lunacy?"

"Not unless we kill him," Flix explained, his back again hunched over as a street person's might be.

"Are you crazy?!" Nate exploded, not caring who might hear him. "First you plot with Silas to bump off Nolan, then—when you realize the mistake you have made—you decide to plot *against* him?"

"Keep your voice down, damnit, or else you'll attract attention!"

"As if anyone could fall for such a dumb disguise," the Senator rebuked.

"You did!" Flix shot back.

"Okay, already," Nate relented. "We'll deal with Silas in due time, but first we have to warn Duncan."

"Duncan?! He's one of the *bad* guys!"

"Politically, maybe, but in this instance he's on our team," Matthews pointed out, knowing that Flix disliked Senator Duncan.

"Come again?"

"He knew the truth you weren't supposed to find out."

"What truth?" Flix inquired, wandering away from Nate as a pair of passersby approached.

"Clara wasn't out of her head after all," Nate elaborated. "She and Duncan were about to spill the beans on Whetstone."

"So *that's* why she was shot," Flix exclaimed. "Did Duncan tell you all this?"

"Most of it, yes."

"When...and where?"

"In my office. Two nights' ago, after I met with Silas."

"Then it must be bugged too," Flix reasoned, having already figured out for himself that Tiger's comm was tapped.

"Whaat?" Nate asked with bated breath.

"If your conversation with Duncan was monitored, that means you are in danger also," Flix explained with military precision.

"So what should I do?" the Senator probed, suddenly panicked. Even as he spoke he felt the comforting outline of the Luger Flix had given him in his coat pocket. "Should I leave town? I *am* needed back in Farmington; maybe I ought to go there today."

"Yes. Go there directly," Flix recommended. "I'll follow tomorrow, or perhaps the day after."

"Fine. Now, what about Duncan?"

"I'll find a way to contact him, and I'll ask him to join us at your father's house," he summarized as he again wandered further afield. "Oh, and thanks for the coffee money," he shouted, resuming his beggar's stance.

26

FRANKLIN

Nothing seemed different and yet everything had changed since he left here months ago to be Missouri's fresh young voice in Washington. Though his instincts were good and his intentions honorable, Nate was still a virgin in the ways of the world. Like an obedient puppy, he had done Whetstone's bidding and gone to China, accomplishing nothing more, in his estimation, than making a personal enemy out of the Overlord. Then, as if to add insult to injury, he had become enmeshed in a web of intrigue which promised to rock the nation to its very core when the truth ultimately came out. Not only had he knowingly covered up the whereabouts of a confessed conspirator in an assassination plot to kill President Nolan, now—as that same man contemplated still *another* assassination—Nate was keeping mum about that as well! And finally, as if all of that weren't enough for one man to bear, now he had to run home to deal with his troublemaking son. Feeling as if he were carrying the weight of the world around on his shoulders, Nate figured that the circumstances—if not the bad weather—excused his foul mood.

Well aware that he couldn't call his father to pick him up at the airport without alerting whomever was listening in on their conversations, Nate took a rental gcar from the terminal and drove himself. It was a lousy day to be on the road, what with the rain and all, so by the time he arrived at the outskirts of town, he had a blue disposition to match. On the surface, Farmington was just as he remembered it—the picket fences, the luxurious shade trees still devoid of their leaves on account of the season, the wide streets, the well-tended yards. And yet, just below the surface, something had changed, something that he couldn't quite put his finger on, and yet something which he would grow to fear in the days ahead.

Pulling up to the tiny courthouse and the even smaller police station next door, Nate put on the stern, father face he would need in order to deal with his son. Nothing about this was going to be easy.

Since Chief Munson was huddled behind closed doors with another officer when Nate arrived, he went straightaway to the lock-up where—after identifying himself to the guard as Franklin's father—he asked to be allowed to meet privately with the boy.

The air between them was thick with anxiety as Nate spoke first. "Geez, Franklin, what has gotten into you?" the father initiated as they each took a chair and sat in the cubicle next to the boy's cell. The lock-up was a drab and dreary affair, made even more so by the rain-cluttered skies outside.

"What's the sudden interest in my welfare, father-dear?" Franklin jeered cynically, his face looking ten years older than the last time Nate had seen him.

Angered by the insolent remark, Nate slapped Franklin hard across the cheek.

"Oh, you think punching me out is a smart strategy?" Frankie shot back, more indignantly than before. "Like leaving me in this fuckin' hole for three days?" he added in obvious reference to his short stay behind bars.

Working hard to regain his self-control, the father asked his son, "Franklin, I don't understand what you are up to. What exactly have you been stealing from these homes you have broken into?"

There was no reply.

"Answer me, damnit!" Nate shouted, again boiling over.

"Or what?" Frank scoffed. "You'll hit me again?"

"I might," Nate acknowledged, the cleft in his chin turning red. Although he was not rock hard muscular like he used to be, he was a big enough man to give a lad Frankie's size pause.

Unperturbed, Franklin stonewalled his father.

"What is it, son?" the Senator pressed. "Do you need money? Or are you just attempting to get my attention with these shenanigans? Is that it?"

Franklin looked away, unable to face the truth.

Forging ahead with his interrogation, his father asserted, "You believe—and with some justification, I might add—that I have ignored you, perhaps even rejected you. And as a consequence, you are striving to get even with me by getting yourself into serious trouble. Isn't that so?"

"Have I embarrassed the great Nate," Frankie retorted coolly, "the mightiest boot-licker of our time?"

"How did we grow so far apart?" Nate implored, his eyes searching his son's face for any signs of remorse.

"Dad, it's a thousand miles from Farmington to Washington," the boy replied, emphasizing the word "miles." "We couldn't *get* much further apart."

"I know, son," Nate acknowledged sadly before growing very quiet. "I know."

After a long silence in which the elder Matthews searched his soul for the right words to say, he picked up where he had left off, "If what you sought was my attention, by all means you have got it now. If what you wished was to embarrass me by your acts, you have accomplished that as well. But now—before you strip me of all my dignity—I want some answers."

"So, ask," the boy responded disaffectionately.

"To begin with, how many other boys were involved in these robberies?" he probed sternly, remembering the promise he had made to Chief Munson in exchange for his leniency. "Were you acting in concert with any other boys? Were you part of a gang?"

"A gang? In this jerkwater town?" Frankie chuckled, a wide smirk plastered across his adolescent face. "Sorry to disappoint you, daddy-oh, but I acted alone."

"What in the world were you *stealing* from these homes?"

"Small things, mainly: trinkets, pocket change, the occasional dessert."

"Food?!" Nate exclaimed astonished. "You were stealing food?"

"Yeh, like candy bars and stuff. Sometimes I would get hungry late at night," the boy pointed out as if every kid did it.

"But, Frankie, why steal at all? Weren't Uncle Tommy and Aunt…?"

"I was bored…and it was exciting," Frankie clarified proudly.

"Chief Munson wants to know how you selected your targets? He wants to know…"

"Lard butt wants to write a book on juvenile offenders?" Franklin mocked, making fun of the pudgy police chief.

"Don't be such a smart-ass!" Nate ordered, a fierce look in his eyes. "Just answer the damn question. How did you choose your targets?"

"Dad, it was completely random—I swear it! When I was in the mood I'd just go out and hit a place," Franklin confessed sincerely. "Unless, of course, I'd see some activity around the house, in which case I would go to the next dump and knock over that place instead. Like the night I got busted."

"Explain."

"Well, that afternoon when I was walking up Locust Street after school, I accidentally bumped into some water-survey velcroid from the EPA. Though I tried to apologize to him for nearly knocking him and his precious box of test tubes over, the jerk swore at me for being a clumsy oaf. Later that night, when I left Uncle Tommy's in a huff, I figured it would be cool to break into that guy's place to pay him back for treating me like such a kid. When I got there, the house looked quiet enough, but just to be sure, I got on my belly to peer through the lit basement window, and I saw several guys in lab-coats preparing petri dishes. Wanting to avoid a confrontation with the EPA, I went next door and hit the Sanders' place instead."

"Okay," Nate summarized, somewhat relieved, "I think I

get the picture. You didn't actually *stake* out the Sanders' home seeking a big score; rather, you went there more by chance so as to avoid the government scientists working in the basement next door."

Rubbing his chin thoughtfully, Nate continued, "The fact that you weren't armed and the fact that the burglary wasn't premeditated should help support your plea and soften the verdict, but much of this will be up to the good will of the Chief."

Signifying that he understood, Franklin nodded his head.

"Listen, son, I know it hasn't been easy this past year what with your mom dying and all. And I see now that my decision not to pull you out of Farmington Junior High to live with me in Washington was clearly a mistake. It was wrong for me to have left you here with your aunt and your uncle, and although I meant well, I see now that that has not worked. So," he clarified as he got to his feet and walked to the other side of the tiny room, "when we see what price the law demands you pay for your crimes, you will be returning to the capital with me."

"Really, sir!" Franklin let slip excitedly as a broad smile crossed his face. "I mean, if you insist," he added, struggling to contain his enthusiasm.

"I insist," the Senator confirmed, happy to see his son beam. "But don't think for one minute that this is over," he warned even as he patted Frankie lovingly on the head, "I still have to speak with Newt—I mean, Sheriff Munson—about what you have said."

"Thanks, dad," the boy acknowledged. "I understand, and I'll take what's coming to me."

"Dirk, my hat goes off to you," the President complimented, bowing and moving his hand to his brow as if he were tipping his cap to the burly fellow.

"Sir?" the security man queried as if he had no idea what his hollow-cheeked boss was talking about.

"My, aren't you the modest one," Whetstone remarked in

his usual tinny voice, putting aside the communique which had been troubling him so. "Your impersonation of my good friend General Wenger was so convincing, every police department in the country is looking for him in connection with the death of my darling wife."

"Just doing my job," Dirk replied, smugly appreciative of any compliment he could garner.

"But *we* know where to look for him, don't we?" the President suggested, a devious glimmer in his eye.

"Farmington?" Dirk volunteered.

"Almost certainly. I want you to establish a stakeout of the former Governor's house—Flix is bound to show up there again sooner or later."

"With all due respect, Mr. President, I don't think Flix is our biggest problem," the brawny man countered, his bushy eyebrows seemingly merging together into a single swatch of dark hair.

"No?" the taller man boomed. "Who then?"

"Duncan. With what he's learned about you from Clara, he can cause quite a stir."

"I think not," Whetstone countered, strutting about the room like a game hen. "With Nikki dead, and with Clara out of the picture—thanks to you—who is there left to substantiate his claims? Frankly, I have much more to fear from Flix. Of course," he added, reflecting pensively, "if Duncan should happen on the scene…feel free to take him out."

"Why would he, for goodness-sake?"

"Flix may be old," Whetstone explained patiently to his underling, "but he's not senile. By now he has figured out that the Governor's comm had to have been tapped and that Nate's office was also bugged. If he hasn't done so already, he will soon advise Duncan to get out of DC. Farmington is the logical place for them to meet."

"I understand," Dirk said as he rose to depart.

"Keep me posted," the President requested as he was left alone to wrestle again with his own thoughts, his suspicious eyes drawn once more to the communique sitting on his desk.

The ominous missive before him had been delivered to his office by a Chinese courier late yesterday afternoon. Picking it up now between his spindly fingers, his forehead creased deeply as he reread it for the umpteenth time:

> Let the games begin.
> It will be a lesson
> you won't quickly forget.
> O.M.T.

"What do you make of it?" he asked himself out loud as if he were a single actor playing both of the leading roles in a play.

"Sounds rather threatening to me," he told himself yet again.

"Who is 'O.M.T.'?" he asked himself once more, just to be sure he hadn't changed his mind.

"Overlord Mao Tsui, you dolt!" he answered confidently.

"What games?" he wondered, fearful of the truth.

"Is there to be a demonstration of their awesome viruses after all," his alter-ego questioned, remembering his debriefing of Senator Matthews following Nate's meeting with the Overlord.

Swirling dizzily as the questions pommelled him like jackhammers in a street, Silas slumped wearily into his uncomfortable chair. Confronted with this conundrum, it was more important than ever that Flix be found—and *not* for the purpose of arresting him as he had told Dirk. Now there was a much more vital reason. If the Chinese *were* planning a demonstration of their monstrous virus, only Flix would know how to authorize a retaliatory strike. Flix had ingeniously buried so much of the nation's military spending so deeply inside the budgets of so many other departments, that only *he* could find under which boulder he had camouflaged America's biological arsenal. It could be in the L.A. Police Department's drug rehabilitation project, or in the National Park Service's fire-safety program, or in Detroit's preschool vaccination initiative. It could be hidden *anywhere*, and only

Flix knew for sure!

As Silas Whetstone sat there, the sweat rolling off his anxious brow, he weighed whether—in exchange for being granted amnesty for the crimes he hadn't committed—Flix could be convinced to reveal the secret passwords necessary to deploy America's biowarfare arsenal against the Chinese. At this point, even the President had to admit the game was becoming exceedingly dangerous.

27

GRASSHOPPER

"Honestly, Nate," Chief Munson began, extending his hand in friendship as the Senator entered the privacy of Newt's modest office and took a seat, "it's darn good to see you."

"Thanks, Chief, it's been a while. You look a little frazzled."

"That boy of yours is quite the hooligan, Senator, and I really cannot take the time to rehabilitate him. As you can see," he declared, motioning to the mess on his desk, "I have my hands full with other matters just now."

"See here, Newt, I don't expect you to be the boy's mother, but in a town as small as this, the police chief has to wear many hats and I expect…"

"You *expect*?" Newt challenged angrily. "You expect?" he fumed, pounding his fist uncharacteristically on the desk. "Senator, you really *are* out of touch—just like the boy says. This is a vanishingly tiny police department, and as I told you before, I have no time for such shenanigans. I want Franklin out of my jail so I can concentrate on my more serious problems. For his transgressions, he will be ordered to pay a fine, plus spend one week cleaning bedpans at the old folks' home. If that's satisfactory, then we'll call it quits."

"Call it quits?" Nate cross-examined confusedly. "Geez, that doesn't sound like the Chief Munson I'm acquainted with. See here, Newt, I have known you for years—what's really the matter?"

Munson shook his head sadly before answering. "Old friend, take a peek at what I received in the mail yesterday," the Chief insisted from behind his swimmingly huge wooden desk.

Intrigued by Munson's comment and baffled by his dejected look, Nate did his best to imagine what article of importance could possibly have been delivered by the postman to the chief law enforcement officer in a municipality as inconsequential as Farmington.

Sliding open the bottom drawer of his bureau with one hand, even as he cleared an open spot on the desktop with the other, Chief Munson removed a large brown envelope and opened its clasp. Shaking it gently to reveal its contents, out fell a handwritten note, a stack of photographs bound together with a rubber band, and curiously enough, a dead specimen of a grasshopper. Seeing the enlarged hind legs of the insect, Nate was reminded of the conference he and Flix had had with Overlord Mao Tsui, and the tapestry which had hung against one wall of Mao's study that day. Trying now to concentrate on what Newt was doing and saying, Nate shoved the distasteful memory of that encounter back into the recesses of his mind.

As Nate watched with interest from his side of the room, the Chief spread the photographs out on the desk in front of him. There were ten snapshots in all, and they were numbered consecutively from 1 to 10 with an orange grease-pencil. Once he had arranged them in ascending order, with photo number 1 at his left and photo number 10 to his right, Munson grunted for the Senator to come and take a closer look.

Circling around the Chief's desk to scrutinize the photographs, Nate's face assumed a troubled frown as his eye caught on photo number 8. It pictured the farm-fresh face of a good-looking woman several years his junior, a woman he had been seeing off and on since before Franklin's mother unexpectedly died of pneumonia.

"What do these pictures represent?" Nate questioned nervously. "And why are they numbered like that?"

"I'm not sure myself," Newt exclaimed. "However, read this," he recommended, handing the Senator the communication which had accompanied the photos. "It won't shed much light on the mystery, but it does sound damn curious."

Sensing Nate's reluctance to take hold of the piece of paper, Newt added, "Don't worry about touching it; I've already dusted it for fingerprints. There were none."

"Mystery indeed!" Nate clamored, before taking the communique from him. "What in the world is the meaning of this grasshopper?" he asked, gently examining the preserved orthopterous insect.

"I haven't the foggiest," the Chief replied, his forehead furrowed. "I don't particularly like mysteries you know, and *this* one has already given me a headache."

Before coming to Farmington, Police Chief Newton Munson had been a beat cop in south Boston. After ten hopeless years struggling to combat drugs and murder and rape, he had thrown in the towel on that life and had set off in search of something better. Newt had been drawn to Farmington because it was an obscure village where muggings and robberies and rape were unheard of, where homes still had porch swings, and where front doors were rarely locked at night. Not only that, it was a place where his police revolver could remain unloaded and holstered for the balance of his career, and where the bullets he reluctantly carried to comply with the state regulations he abhorred, could be kept safely sequestered in his button-down breast pocket.

Nate read the menacing note once silently to himself, then out loud in a halting voice:

> Let the games begin.
> It will be a lesson
> you won't quickly forget.
> O.M.T.

"Oh my lord," Nate exclaimed, reaching for the edge of the desk as he felt his legs buckling beneath him. "This can't be happening!" he shrieked as the Overlord's ominous words came rushing back to him.

Chief Munson's eyes narrowed as his erupting migraine got underway in a big way. Between Franklin's burglaries and this terrorist's riddle, his quiet, serene world was being torn asunder.

Anxiously waving the two-line letter in his hand, his face white as a sheet, Nate croaked, "What do you make of this, Chief?"

"I'm certain this is a hoax," Munson lied as he struggled to mount a light laugh. Not wanting to alarm his guest, he thought it best not to tell Nate the truth, but instinctively, Newt knew better. He had had much too much experience dealing with urban nut-balls to think for a moment that this was merely some tasteless gag. It reeked of the sort of perverted psychopath Newt had confronted once too often on the back streets of Boston, the sort of sick lunatic he had hoped to escape by moving out here.

"You mean to tell me you aren't going to take this letter seriously?" Nate blurted out unhappily.

"What would you have me do, Senator? Warn the good people pictured here that I was sent a dead katydid? That some sort of vague threat has been made upon their lives?"

"Yes, damnit," Nate swore. "By all means."

"And as for *protecting* them, that is clearly an impossibility."

"Why so?" Nate petitioned, dissatisfied with that answer.

"Surely you, of all people, must know that my police force is a farce! It consists solely of me, plus my two volunteers. And as for calling in help from a neighboring community, that seems a bit farfetched as well—Springdale is forty miles away, and it is even smaller than our fair metropolis."

Nate smiled before frowning. "I hope you are right about this being a hoax, 'cause I have been fooling around with that one for quite some time," Nate explained, pointing to his wannabe girlfriend's picture on Munson's desk. "Her name is Musette."

"Yes, I know her name—you didn't exactly hide your affections over the years," Munson snapped disapprovingly. "She is quite attractive, I'll grant you that," the Chief remarked with a devilish twinkle in his eye. "But if I daresay myself, no one I ever met could match your Darna in the looks department."

"I appreciate what you're trying to say, Chief, but let's not get too far off the track," Nate redirected impatiently. "I have reason to believe that this thing is not a hoax," he explained, indicating the snapshots still spread out on the bureau.

"Oh? And why's that?"

"Because the initials O.M.T. may just stand for Overlord Mao Tsui."

"The emperor of China?" Newt retorted disbelievingly. "And what would Mao want with a podunk town like Farmington?"

"Me, perhaps," Nate pointed out, suddenly seeming much older than his years.

"But you're not even *on* this list!" Newt exploded, glancing at all the pictures again just to be sure.

"Granted, but this may just be his way of getting back at me," the Senator pointed out without explaining anything.

"For what?" Munson inquired analytically. "What did you do to him?"

"I can't tell you," Nate admitted reluctantly. "It's top-secret. But let me only say this: that grasshopper there is his calling card."

"Does this have something to do with the bastards wanting to take Hawaii away from us?" Munson interrogated, his nationalistic tone reflecting the rising anti-Chinese fervor in the country.

"I can't tell you," Nate repeated, "but I can assure you that his methods are brutal. I've met his son, Chang, and he's the size of a…"

Seeing that he wasn't getting anywhere, Newt hastily interrupted, changing the subject, "Speaking of sons, I take it you've spoken with yours? I think your boy misses his mom…and his dad. I think he's misbehaving just to get your attention."

Quietly nodding his agreement, Nate asserted, "Listen Chief, Frankie and I have spoken and you needn't worry about him any further. I'll see to my boy if you'll just agree to see to *them*," he urged, gesturing again to the row of photos. "Let's make sure that none of these fine townsfolk die."

"I'll do my best."

"I know you will, Newt, but like you said earlier, you're short on help around here. Why don't you just deputize me so that I can legally carry a sidearm and be of some assistance around here?" Nate suggested, thinking of the concealed weapon he was carting, the Luger Flix had given him. "I don't want Musette to die before…I mean, we're lovers…It's been months since we…"

"Whoa! Slowdown, old buddy," Newt ordered. "I don't want to know about your sex life. Anyhow, handing you a gun won't solve a thing. Hell, I don't even load mine," he announced, proudly patting the breast pocket of his uniform where he stashed his shells.

"Well, if you won't let me help you, I have an advisor on my staff—a former intelligence officer—who will be arriving in town shortly. He could easily be called in to lend us a hand," Nate suggested, reasoning that he would need a story to explain Flix's presence when he showed up.

"Enough already. If it turns out that this *isn't* a nasty gag, and if one of these nice people *does* show up dead, I'll reconsider your offer. But for now, I do not want the entire county up in arms. Capisce?"

"Geez, you want me to keep this whole thing quiet!" Nate asked, more than a little surprised. "From my dad too? What the hell are you trying to pull?"

"Listen, Nate, take Frankie home and let's forget about all this for tonight," the Chief instructed in an exasperated tone as he motioned Nate to the door. "I'll decide what needs to be done, and we'll talk again in the morning."

Imperial Palace, Beijing

A satisfied look smeared across his almond-eyed face, Overlord Mao glided impassively through the courtyard of his sumptuous garden and past an oddly-shaped pool churning with dozens of colorful koi. Following the winding path lined with stands of manicured yew, he bounded across the threshold into the Great Hall of the Imperial Palace. Instantly, he was flanked by two loyal officers of the Royal Guard as he moved deliberately down the length of the grand hallway. Life-size wax statues outfitted in full battle gear dotted the wide passageway at 20-foot intervals. These fearsome-looking mannequins commemorated ten dozen generations of Chinese prowess on the battlefield including every warrior of consequence from Genghis Khan to Emperor Hong Tsui, Mao's grandfather. Waiting for him at the end of the long hall like two obedient puppy dogs, his sons Ling and Chang paced impatiently back and forth, their drawn faces reflecting the fear and loathing they felt for their father.

"Sit with me, my sons," the elder Tsui demanded, motioning his heirs into the splendid meeting room. "Let us speak today of world affairs."

"You have news from the front?" Ling asked excitedly. Like a pudgy Buddha, the Ambassador had fat hands and a bulging belly. He spoke from a slit of a mouth which hung from his face beneath a pair of dark eyes and a bald head. "Has the he-devil Whetstone agreed to surrender the islands yet?"

"Even now as we speak, it happens," Mao declared, diabolically extending his scrawny hand in emphasis. A banner emblazoned with the likeness of a humongous grasshopper framed the wall behind him. "Even now we strike back at the heart of America."

"As you know, dear father," Ling praised in a contemptuous fashion, "I have the highest personal regard for you as a leader. Moreover, I have the utmost confidence in the success of your strategy," he continued, buttering-up his father as he went, "but why strike at Senator Matthews? And why strike at this grubby little town of his? It is but a dust-mite on the rump of a giant grasshopper."

"True," Overlord Mao admitted as he sucked on his flowing mustache, "but the grasshopper is our dynastic symbol, our standard actually, and Matthews is a dust-mite which has dug into *my* rump. Such a burrowing creature can cause a sore to fester and grow septic. We strike at Matthews because our spies tell us that he is to be the he-devil's Vice President. What happens to Matthews also happens to America."

"But he hasn't even been sworn in yet," Ambassador Ling objected even as his brother Chang grunted his accord. Chang was a beefy man of few words; he had bulging arms, a thick neck, and a sloped forehead.

"No matter," his wiry father pointed out. "Symbols are symbols."

"I thought our goal was to have Hawaii," Ling pressed in his nasal tone, not wanting to upset his maniacal father, but not wanting to lose sight of the prize either. "What do we care what becomes of the he-devil, Silas Whetstone?"

"We *will* have Hawaii," Mao boomed rabidly. "But Whetstone must first be made to pay for his affrontery. That he takes no action against our fleet means that he may be more devious than I first gave him credit for. Perhaps he has the biowarfare capability Matthews spoke of after all, or perhaps he expects us to square off against the Pearl Command and then, once our navy has been weakened by their guns, he plans to swoop down upon us with other forces we're not aware of. Either way, I won't oblige him."

"So what *will* you do?" Ling questioned, eager to have this meeting concluded.

"I am going to Farmington."

"Are you crazy?" Ling exploded, the disrespectful words escaping from his lips before he could stop them. "I mean, why do such a thing, father?"

"I want to see him suffer; I want to be there for the coup de grace."

"Do you think that is wise?"

"You mean to lecture me on wisdom?" Mao glared. "I think not. What you *can* do is alert your suborb-crew that you will be returning to the States within the hour. Your ship has diplomatic immunity and no one will raise a question if you drop off a passenger in St. Louis on the way back to Washington. Do I make myself clear?"

Recognizing that further argument was futile, Ambassador Ling nodded his head and excused himself from the room. His brother Chang followed closely behind. Without saying a word to each other they both entertained the same hateful thoughts. Someone had to stop their father before it was too late.

28

GUSTAV

On the short ride across town from the jail-house to Nate's shuttered residence, father and son exchanged only a few words. Nate had called his brother from Munson's office to tell him that Frankie would be coming home with him, but had ended up speaking with Thomas' repulsive ball-and-chain instead. The conversation with his sister-in-law hadn't gone well, so on top of all his other worries, he was now angry with her as well. Promising himself never to abandon Frankie to his pathetic brother and his domineering wife ever again, he shook his head in aggravation.

"What a bitch," he let slip, not quite under his breath. It was unusual for him to swear in front of his boy, but under the circumstances, he couldn't help himself.

"Who, dad?" Franklin asked, surprised to hear his father curse.

"Your aunt, that's who," Nate exclaimed, pressing his foot against the accelerator. As he sped down Locust Street, puddles of water left behind by the storm, splashed up against the side of the gcar, marking it with splotches of mud.

"Don't I know it," Franklin remarked without elaboration, nodding his head in agreement as the gcar lurched forward.

"Is this where it happened?" Nate asked as they passed the Sanders' house.

"Yes," Franklin grunted.

"All I can say is this: I'm truly sorry for what I've put you through."

Silently nodding in acceptance of his dad's apology, Frankie stared out the side window at the passing acres of farmland. Although night was fast approaching, it wasn't completely pitch-black yet. In the glow of the descending dusk he could still make out the tens of thousands of bright green shoots dotting the newly-sown fields. The ground in these parts was so fertile, farming was still a way of life as it had been for centuries. Though Frankie turned several times to engage his dad in small talk, Nate was a million miles away, his own mind hypnotized by the occasional swipe of the wiper blade.

Still tortured by the untimely death of his wife, and still traumatized by his own stupidity vis-à-vis his son, Nate was lost in troubled thought. As he contemplated the terrible mess he and Flix had gotten themselves into, his mind swung uncontrollably from one subject to the next. Though he tried to digest what life with Musette might be like—what life without Darna had become—he grew more and more depressed by the minute.

Then, suddenly and without warning, fear grasped at his bowels. As his overwrought imagination ran amok, Nate was terrorized by the image of the open package spilled across Munson's desk. Searching his mind for the common denominator which linked all these events together, he broke out into a cold sweat. This was no practical joke, of that he was sure; the Overlord was undoubtedly exacting the revenge he had promised. But what Nate didn't know—and what was haunting him now—was whether the yellow-skinned bastard had somehow had a hand in Darna's unexpected death as well. Shivering involuntarily, Nate buried the thought down deep as he pulled into the drive of his darkened house.

"Someone's sitting on the front porch," Frankie pointed out as the high beam of the headlights swept across the lawn.

"I wonder who *that* can be?" Nate queried out loud, thankful that in his agitated state he had a weapon to protect himself with.

"He looks pretty old to me," Frankie offered in the middle of a big yawn. "Maybe it's grandpa."

"Grandpa doesn't know I'm in town," Nate declared as he put the rental in park and dug in his pocket for his gun. "Please stay in the gcar while I find out," the Senator suggested, leaving the motor running as he opened the door and got out.

"Who's there?" Nate bellowed as he judiciously approached the porch, doing his best to stay in the shadows thrown by the headlights. The Luger Flix had given him was in the palm of his hand, yet carefully hidden from Frankie's view. Inasmuch as carrying a firearm without a license was illegal, Nate didn't want his son to know he was openly defying the law—at least not this soon after lecturing him on the merits of *obeying* the law!

"Well it's about time you showed up!" Flix chastised arrogantly. "I'm getting cold sitting out here on your front stoop." Seeing the gun in Nate's hand, he said, "Put that damn thing away before someone gets hurt around here."

"Geez, Flix, you scared me half to death!" Nate exclaimed, breathing a sigh of relief at seeing his trusted advisor. "What are you doing here?" he asked, slipping the Luger back into his coat. "I didn't expect you for days!"

"Nice to see you too," he retorted, not taking offense at the Senator's tone. "Is that your son waiting for you in the gcar? Why don't you introduce us already? I'm presently using the alias of Gustav Knapheide."

Chuckling, Nate interjected, "Sure, boss, whatever you say. It seems that I've been hanging around you too long."

"Whatever do you mean?" Flix verified.

"I'm even beginning to *think* like you," Nate clarified. "Expecting your imminent arrival, I have already provided you with a cover, *Gus*. Without giving him your name, I told the sheriff that you were on my staff and that you would be arriving soon to help with the investigation."

"Investigation? What investigation?" Flix exclaimed, lumbering to his feet with Nate's hand under one shoulder and his cane under the other.

"Who thinks up these aliases anyway?" Nate teased jovially as he went to the gcar, turned off the motor, and invited Frankie to join them.

"Gus Knapheide, this is my son Franklin. Frankie, meet my dear friend Gus."

After they shook hands and engaged in a couple minutes of idle chatter, Nate shooed Franklin off to bed and the two men stood on the front porch watching the stars rise in the night sky. Now that the storm had passed, it was a cool and crisp evening. Every once in a while the vapors of their breath fogged the air in front of their mouths.

"What investigation?" Flix asked again, picking up where he had left off before.

"A package arrived at the local police chief's office yesterday," Nate answered as he began to fill Flix in on all that had happened since they last spoke. By the time he was done with his story, the blood had drained from Flix's face.

"For God's-sake," Flix swore, "I can't believe Mao is doing this. He must be afraid of risking all out war with us, so instead he's cooked up this scheme to intimidate Whetstone into turning the islands over to him without a fight."

"How is this course of action supposed to intimidate *Whetstone*? The package with the pictures and the cryptic note was addressed to the police chief of Farmington, not the President of the United States! This isn't happening to Silas; this is happening to *me*!"

"That's where you're wrong," Gustav Knapheide née Felix Wenger clarified. "Our President has undoubtedly been apprised of the developments here in Farmington much as he was notified when Ambassador Ling made his presentation before your committee. And the Chinese will almost certainly keep him up to date in order to press their advantage and to get the most mileage out of their campaign of terror. Not only that, since you're the front-running candidate to be his Vice President, they have to assume that you'll use your influence to pressure him into relinquishing the islands. That's why they have chosen Musette as one of the targets—to get your attention."

"Bastards!" Nate swore. "But if you're right, and if Mao's afraid of risking an all out war with America, then that means he must have taken us seriously when you told him of the U.S.'s biowarfare capability. Knowing this, why doesn't Whetstone just stop this endless ratcheting up of brinkmanship and follow through with his pledge to retaliate in kind? Why doesn't he just pick a target and hit it with a viral demonstration of our own?" Nate interrogated sternly.

"Because he can't," Flix replied matter-of-factly as a cool evening breeze swept over them both eliciting a shiver from Nate.

"I thought you told me we *could* retaliate?" Nate exploded, fearing the bluff had been a lie all along.

"I didn't say *we* can't, I said *he* can't."

"I don't follow."

"Whetstone doesn't know the codes," Flix declared, pulling the confidential address book from deep inside the pocket of his suit coat.

"I still don't follow," Nate advised, his gray eyes getting darker with each passing moment.

"He isn't capable of activating a retaliation because he doesn't have the codes to do so. Only I have the codes. And, because I can't possibly remember them all, I've written them all down in the back of this little black book of mine."

Nate's jaw dropped as Flix continued his explanation.

"For each of the sensitive weapons programs we've buried from the public eye, I have the page number and the line number from the budget which lists the people in charge, their addresses, and their private comm numbers. It also reveals the passwords needed to access the particular weapons-system in question. The budget runs for some twenty-two thousand pages, and only I know which laboratories or which universities are the custodians of our biowarfare arsenal."

"Oh my Lord," Nate shrieked, burying his head in his hands. "And you're carrying the goddamn book *around* with you? It ought to be locked up! Hell, *you* ought to be locked up!"

29

DEHYDRATION

"Until we came back from China, it *was* locked up," Flix objected, referring to his enigmatic book of addresses and codes. "Whetstone's people tore my house in Maine apart searching for the damn thing, but after you dropped me off in Bangor, I snuck in there and grabbed it from my wall safe."

"So that's what you were after!" Nate exclaimed, rubbing his hands together to warm them as the two men sat across from one another on the porch steps. Though the rain had stopped for the moment, a flash of lightning in the distance suggested another front was rapidly approaching.

"Among other things, yes. And now I'm going to give it to you for safekeeping," he explained in a fatherly tone as he handed the top secret booklet to the Senator.

"Me?! Are you nuts?" Matthews bellowed, refusing to let his fingers touch the slender folio as if the cover were soiled.

"Sooner or later they'll come looking for me, and when they do, the only thing which will keep me among the living is that book. Hide the damn thing somewhere, and don't tell me—or anyone else—where you've hidden it," Flix implored, shoving the checkbook-sized sheaf of pages into Nate's coat pocket.

"On one condition," Nate bargained.

"Name it," Flix answered without faltering.

"If I agree to help you now, you must agree to help me in

return later."

"Anything," Flix complied readily.

"What say we put our heads together and see whether or not the two of us can't stop the Overlord's deadly game before it gets too far out of hand?"

"Agreed," Flix replied without hesitation.

"Not so fast," Nate cautioned cleverly, "I'm not done with you yet."

"I was afraid you might say that."

"When this nightmare is over, and when I begin impeachment hearings against Whetstone in the Senate, you must agree to testify against him even if it means going to jail for your part in the conspiracy."

"Agreed," Flix acquiesced, sighing deeply, "but can we go inside now? I'm freezing."

"Sure, *Gus*," Nate teased as they both got to their feet and went indoors. "By the way, did you make contact with Duncan?"

"Tried twice, but no luck. However, I did leave a message on his machine in your name. You asked him to meet you here as soon as practical."

No sooner had Nate nodded his approval and shut the front door behind them, than his comm began buzzing urgently. Exhausted by the day's events, he debated momentarily whether or not to even answer it, but the signal was insistent.

"Hello, this is Matthews," he barked brusquely into the comm. "Who is it? It's awfully late, you know, and I'm tired."

"Nate? This is Munson," the police chief reported in a somber tone. His voice had the quality of a man who had seen the light at the end of the tunnel and had found it to be that of an oncoming train.

"Yes, Chief, it's me. Frankie and I just got home. I hope you don't need him because he's already sacked out for the night," Nate grumped in an obviously irritated tone. "What's on your mind, Newt?"

"I may need your help after all," Munson confessed in a halting voice.

"Chief, as I told you before, I'd be happy to help. But didn't we agree this could wait 'til morning?" he persisted in an exasperated manner.

"No," the Chief declared firmly. "It cannot!"

Suddenly alert, Nate snorted, "Okay, I'm all ears." Even as he spoke, he flicked a switch on the side of the comm-unit to convert the instrument to speaker mode. Motioning to Flix with his free hand, Nate signaled for him to come listen in on their conversation.

"Remember those pictures?" Munson began timidly.

"How could I forget?" Nate snapped. "I told you they scared the bejesus out of me."

"After you left my office, I first had a bite to eat, then thinking about what you said, I began contacting the people in sequence, beginning with numbers 1 and 2. Given the late hour, I expected to call and find these people at home and in bed, but when their comm went unanswered, I sent a car around to check on them."

There was a long silence at the other end as the Chief stopped talking. All Nate and Flix could hear were the sounds of his labored breathing.

Impatient for an explanation, Nate exhorted, "What already? Damnit man, what happened?"

"They're both dead!" Munson abruptly blurted, his voice cracking as if he were going to burst into tears.

"Dead?" Nate exclaimed, stunned by the news. "My God!" he declared, looking hard at Flix for confirmation of his own worst fears. "How? How'd they die?"

"Dunno yet," Munson lamented. "Cursory examination reveals no obvious wounds, but forensics is not my specialty. On first glance, I'd have to say that both of them died from natural causes, only…"

"Only *what*?" Nate interrupted testily even as he paced anxiously about the floor.

"Two things," the Chief pointed out, regaining his composure. "First of all, the odds of two accidental deaths in one night are impossibly low. Vanishingly small, actually."

"And the second?"

"Each victim appeared to have been severely dehydrated. It was as if…"

"As if what?" Nate interrupted again, barely giving Newt a chance to talk.

"As if they had been left to bake in the hot desert sun," the Chief described, reminding Flix of the long, desperate march he and Tiger had taken across the Saudi desert a half century ago. "Their lips were dry and cracked as if they had run an awfully high fever, a fever which put them into the coma which eventually killed them."

"So, the package you received in the mail wasn't a practical joke *after* all," Nate commented absentmindedly as he thought of how Darna had looked when she died. "Cracked lips," he whispered to himself, thinking back.

"No gag, this," the Chief acknowledged, his migraine pounding. "This is serious stuff. Can I count on your help or not?"

Acting as if he didn't hear what Munson had said, Nate didn't answer.

"Senator? Can I count on your help or not?" the sheriff repeated nervously.

"You can count on us, Chief; we'll be at the station within the hour."

"Are you bringing your father along?" Munson quizzed, his attentive ears keying in on the plural in Nate's answer.

"No. Why do you ask?"

"You said 'we'—*we*'ll be at the station within the hour."

"That man I spoke to you about earlier—the intelligence officer—he has arrived. He's with me at this very moment. After I call my dad to have him come stay with Frankie tonight and after I swing by Musette's place to check on her, my friend and I will come to the station straightaway."

"All's quiet here, boss," Dirk reported from the alley a block away from the former Governor's wood frame home.

The security man was hunkered down in the front seat of his rental, speaking to the President on a mobile comm unit mounted against the car's dashboard.

"Maybe I misread Flix's intentions after all," Whetstone admitted to his flunky. "I would have wagered on his again seeking refuge with his old friend, Tiger Matthews. But perhaps there is another possibility. The tap you placed on Duncan's line yielded one very interesting call. According to the transcripts I was given, before leaving Washington yesterday, Senator Matthews left a message on Duncan's machine asking him to meet him at his house in Farmington. Maybe that's where Flix is going to show up as well. Why don't you switch your surveillance to the Senator's house instead."

"Whatever you say, boss," Dirk responded, delighted to have a change of scenery. "By the way," he continued in a worried voice, "while I've been sitting here with nothing else to do, I've had the radio on listening to the news. I'm confused by what I am hearing. Are there any new developments with regard to the situation in Hawaii?"

"The bloody Chinese fleet has taken up several stranglehold positions around the islands, and they have been turning back commercial flights. But as of yet, they haven't fired a single shot."

"What are they waiting for?" Dirk implored almost as if he couldn't wait for his country to be plunged into a full-scale war.

"I'm not exactly sure," the President admitted, "but even as we speak, I suspect the Chinese are testing my resolve with a demonstration of their strength."

30

REVELATIONS

By 8 a.m., the morning edition of the *Farmington Dispatch* was on the newsstands. It included a rather full account of the two deaths last evening—officially, they weren't being called murders yet—plus an interview with Chief Newton Munson wherein he disclosed the contents of the mysterious package he had received, and the existence of its intimidating message. The paper said nothing about the grasshopper.

But what the early edition did *not* include—what Munson himself had just learned—was the late-breaking news that there was in fact a *third* victim! Shirlee Winston, the spinster whose picture had a large number 3 emblazoned across her face in orange crayon, was found by a nosy neighbor after sunup this morning. Although apparently unmolested, Shirlee was discovered in her back yard, sprawled spread-eagle on her closely-manicured lawn, and naked as a jailbird. In death, she had the same bulging eyes and drawn, dehydrated face as the first two unfortunates. Neither her house nor her fenced-in yard showed any outward signs of unwanted trespass or of forced entry.

"Goddamnit the bastard moves fast!" Munson swore as Gustav Knapheide and Nate Matthews looked on after a short night's sleep in the station house. Sweat was pouring from the Chief's brow, and his shirt had two very large puddles where his armpits should have been.

"I feel so worthless," the former Boston cop lamented, hanging his head in shame. "I can't...I couldn't ...protect those people."

"Now, Chief," Nate interrupted unsuccessfully.

"Damnit, Nate, I *talked* to Shirlee last night. She was complaining of a cold, but otherwise, she was okay. I had Burt—he's one of my volunteers—drive past her house *twice* during the night. Everything was fine, and yet ...this morning she turns up dead!"

As if to punctuate his exclamation, an uncomfortable silence settled over the room as Nate and Gustav tried to figure out how to console him.

"Geez, Chief, it's all so very horrible," Nate sympathized, "but what else could you have done? Didn't you alert Shirlee to keep her doors and windows locked, and not to admit any strangers?"

Munson nodded, "I told everyone on the list the same thing."

"And now that the media knows," Gustav added soberly, "the entire community will be on guard. The townsfolk will contact you if they witness anything suspicious."

"Gentlemen, your kind words are comforting, but I feel as if I have failed this town! Goddamnit, Nate, I have three dead citizens on my hands! There is a serial killer roaming loose! Three corpses; no fingerprints; no murder weapon; no motive; not a clue!"

Squinting his eyes sharply in the Senator's direction, Munson charged onward like a bull, "Maybe it's about time you came clean with me Matthews."

"Whatever do you mean?" Nate countered in an innocent tone knowing full well what the Chief was alluding to.

"Yesterday you gave me some crap about Overlord Mao and some top secret run-in the two of you had; today, I have three dead bodies. I want to know what the hell is going on, and I want to know it now!" Munson boomed, slamming his fist against the top of his desk, upsetting his cup of java in the process.

Stealing a glance in Flix's direction, Nate struggled to

formulate an answer. "Well, Chief, boiled down to its essence, the story goes something like this: After Nolan's assassination, and after Whetstone refused to sign the Hawaii Treaty with China, Mao threatened to attack the United States with some newfangled virus they had developed if we didn't surrender the islands to them. Silas—I mean, the President—sent me to Beijing to tell the Overlord to fuck himself, a suggestion Mao apparently took a bit personally. He vowed that he would have his pound of flesh from me and that it would be a lesson I wouldn't soon forget…just like the letter says."

Even as Nate spoke, the Overlord's menacing words kept rolling through his head.

"And that's not the whole story, is it, Senator?" Newt taunted as he turned to look Gustav squarely in the face. "Have we ever met before?" the ever attentive Munson quizzed. "Because your face sure does look familiar to me."

"Never set eyes on you before today, Chief, of that I am sure," Gustav calmly replied, fearing his alias had been compromised somehow.

"That is undoubtedly true, Mr. Knapheide, only that's not your real name is it?" Newt challenged, ripping the wanted poster from the wall next to the door. True to his word, Whetstone had distributed Flix's picture to every precinct in the country. Shaking the poster furiously in one hand even as he drew his empty revolver and leveled it at Flix's gut with the other, Munson shouted, "With all due respect, General Wenger, give me one reason why I shouldn't lock you up right this instant!"

"Because we need his help," Nate intervened, trying to step between the two men.

"That's not good enough," Munson barked, easily shoving Nate aside.

"Because the man's wanted for a murder he didn't commit," Nate added, surprised by the Chief's strength.

"That's up to a jury to decide," Munson retorted, "not you!"

"Because Flix was with me when I went to China."

"Then *you're* as guilty as he is," the Chief reasoned, keeping his unloaded weapon trained on Flix's middle. It was a Smith & Wesson .357 Magnum, the standard gun of law enforcement officers.

"Because Silas hired some lowlife to kill his own wife, then had Flix framed for the murder."

"To what end?" Chief Munson cross-examined.

"To hide the fact that Whetstone himself was in on the plot to assassinate Nolan."

"My, my, what a yarn," Munson congratulated, waving Flix toward the cell occupied until yesterday by Nate's son.

"I know the gun's not loaded, Chief," Flix remarked, staring down the long, hollow barrel of the gleaming Smith & Wesson even as he raised his cane in self defense. "And I know you won't kill me, so let's just cut to the chase, shall we, and see whether we can't help each other out by solving both of our mysteries."

"What do you have in mind, General?" Munson interrogated, his tone becoming less belligerent.

"Even if the Overlord is behind these murders as Nate and I suspect, he's not the one doing the actual killing—some hired hand is. And the perp is not an ordinary Joe, of that I am sure. These are not simple deaths," Flix elaborated, "they are well-orchestrated homicides. And the murders smell of…well, I don't know…a forensics expert, perhaps."

"Chief, shouldn't we touch base with the state police or the FBI?" Nate butted in. "And shouldn't we place a bodyguard on…"

"Senator, just how stupid do you think I am?" Munson scolded, his headache burgeoning. "While you two were sacked out here on my couch last night, I called the Bureau's regional office, and I gave them a thorough report on what had happened up to that point. The liaison deputy promised me that a representative would meet us here at my office today at 10 a.m.," Munson summarized, glancing apprehensively at his wristwatch.

"And now," the Chief remarked sadly, a faraway look

misting his eyes as he sighed heavily. "And now I have to report Shirlee's murder to them as well."

"Begging your pardon," Nate interrupted hastily, "but I think we need…"

"Let me finish!" Newt shouted angrily at his friend, the tension in the room so thick you could have cut it with a knife. "Even before this fellow from the FBI arrives, we need to put bodyguards in place around the other seven targets. Which reminds me, you had better get a hold of Musette—she has called here four times since the *Dispatch* hit the mailboxes. She's frantic, and I told her you'd call as soon as you awoke."

"Quite right, I will," Nate agreed, "but if I may, I'd like to make a recommendation. If the killer is an expert in forensics like Flix says, I think we need a pathologist out here to help us. One of the perks my father enjoys as a former governor is the services of a top notch medical team out of St.Louis. They are on call twenty-four hours a day. One of their people could be here by airchop in less than an hour, and he might be able to help this FBI man pinpoint the cause of these deaths."

"Good idea; see to it," Munson ordered, gladdened by the suggestion. "And you," he observed, glaring sternly at Flix, "based on what I know of your reputation as a General and as the Chairman of the Joint Chiefs, for the time being anyway, you are worth more to me as a deputy guarding innocent citizens than as a burden of the state eating the taxpayers' food in my cell. But I promise you, after this nightmare is over, you and I will need to have another chat."

Nodding his head in understanding as Chief Munson crumbled the wanted poster into a ball and tossed it in the direction of the waste basket, Flix breathed a short-lived sigh of relief.

31

INVESTIGATION

Having just slipped his shield back into the breast pocket of his suit coat after showing it to Flix, the FBI agent sat fidgeting in Munson's straight-backed chair. From behind his horned-rim glasses the newcomer's dark eyes darted nervously from the Senator to the sheriff and back again. The man had intentionally avoided Flix's accusing stare from the beginning, figuring he wouldn't measure up in the old man's judgment.

"Yes, Chief Munson, I most certainly agree with your appraisal of the situation," the Federal officer confirmed, again shifting nervously in his seat as he squeaked out a smile. "You definitely do have a problem here in Farmington." The narrowness of his tie, the stiffness of his starched collar, and the freckles splashed across his thin face, suggested youth and inexperience.

"Well, what the hell are you and your FBI going to do about it?" Munson stormed, his bulk rolling as he gestured angrily across his desk.

"I suppose that we will launch a full-scale investigation into the circumstances surrounding these events, and…"

Now it was Flix's turn to blow his stack. He had been the one to demand the agent produce some sort of I.D.; he had been the one unwilling to believe the Bureau would send such a kid to handle an assignment of this magnitude. "We?" he challenged without introducing himself. "Tell me, young man, where is the 'we'? You have come alone, haven't you, Agent Fredericks?"

"Why, yes," the tenderfoot stammered."

Listening to Fredericks hem and haw, Flix wondered whether this might be the young man's very first field assignment. And the more he thought of it, the less he liked it, but given his own circumstances he reckoned there was precious little he could do to influence the Bureau's choice. After all, the FBI undoubtedly had more pressing cases on their docket than this one, and even if this *was* the hometown of a U.S. Senator and a former Governor, tiny little Farmington probably didn't command their best operative.

"Let me rephrase that," Fredericks continued. "*I* will launch a full-scale investigation into these mysterious killings, and I will report back to you in a few days' time with my suspicions," the agent offered even as a distinguished-looking man arrived at the door and waited patiently for his turn to speak. His overcoat was wet from the rain outside.

"A few days!" Munson exploded, displeased with the first man's timetable and completely ignoring the second man's attempt to squeeze in a word of introduction. "By then, half the *town* could be dead! Hell, they're ready to riot now. And why? Because the Freaking Bureau of Idiots sends me a damn youngster to do a man's job!" Munson was steaming.

Pausing long enough for the blood to return to his face, the Chief bludgeoned on, "Listen, Goldilocks, you go ahead and carry out your freaking official investigation, but make it snappy! I need some answers before anyone else dies...not after!"

Stomping from the conference room, his belly jiggling, Newt brushed past the newcomer standing at the doorway. From out in the hallway he yelled, "Three have died, Fredericks; if you don't get your ass in gear you may very well be number four!"

Even as Agent Fredericks sat on the couch stunned by the Chief's outburst, Nate contemplated whether or not there might be a way for him to wield his political influence in Washington to get a more qualified investigator on the job. With the FBI man staring blankly out into space and looking as if he might break into tears at any moment, the tall, good-looking stranger at the door cleared his throat to be heard.

"Have I come at a bad time?" the well-dressed gentleman questioned, edging his way into the room where Flix, Nate, and Agent Fredericks were still seated. The newcomer had the blond hair and the blue eyes of a SKANDIA.

"You must be Dr. Johannsen," Nate correctly guessed, recalling the description his dad had given him in their brief talk on the comm an hour ago. Dr. Johannsen was a renowned pathologist and a medical examiner of some acclaim. Nate hoped to convince him to perform the autopsies and run the necessary toxicology studies, but he had brought him here under false pretenses, telling him that Nathanial, Sr. was sick. "Thank you for coming on such short notice," the Senator continued, rising to offer the doctor his hand.

"Please. You may call me Wilhelm. I was surprised the taxi brought me to the police station. Is the Governor ill?" Johannsen probed, a worried look on his tanned face.

"Not exactly," Nate admitted, remembering the lie he had told Johannsen's secretary in order to get the doctor on an airchop out here. "His town is."

"I beg your pardon?" Wilhelm queried, putting his things on the empty chair next to Flix. "Perhaps you had better explain," he requested, stealing a glance at his expensive wristwatch. It was 10:30 a.m.

"Perhaps I'd better," Nate acknowledged.

And he did.

When Nate was through, Johannsen sat down heavily.

"Sorry for the subterfuge, Doc," Nate apologized sincerely, "but we needed the best man we could find, and you are he."

Swallowing a bashful smile, Dr. Wilhelm Johannsen glanced first over at Flix and then at the equally astonished Fredericks. "Well, kid," he declared, reaching for his coat as he rose to leave, "it looks as if we have got our work cut out for us this morning."

Responding as much to his own sense of duty as to the Chief's verbal thrashing, Fredericks nodded and followed the older man out the door. After getting directions from Munson, they went straightaway to the makeshift morgue set up at the funeral parlor to begin work on the case.

Although Johannsen was impressed by the extent of Fredericks' forensic skills, the doctor took sole charge of the bodies, while Fredericks tried to ascertain whether the victims were selected at random, or whether they were connected in any way. In an unsuccessful effort to unearth any common denominator in their backgrounds, the FBI man ran their names, their work and family history, their party affiliations, and a host of other essential variables through the databanks at the Bureau, at the IRS, and at the Census Service. When he was done, he hadn't learned anything they didn't already know. The only common factor linking these ten people together was that they all lived in Farmington, Missouri, the hometown of Senator Nate Matthews.

The good doctor's efforts met with equal success. Inasmuch as discovering the cause of death was of the highest order of importance, he was at once stymied by the utter lack of physical evidence. All the victims appeared to have met a nonviolent finish—there were no gunshot wounds for him to examine, no crushed craniums to study, no strangulation scars to scrutinize, nor any jagged knife lacerations to inspect. Nothing.

Undeterred, he went over the corpses with painstaking care, searching for fingerprints, or strands of hair, or specks of dirt—anything which might help him identify the perpetrator or the means of death—and still nothing!

By the time the five of them had regathered in the Chief's office early that afternoon, a crowd had collected outside the station house, and the town was in an uproar. With no progress to report in bringing the killer to justice, the normally complacent citizens of Farmington were edging toward hysteria and a sense of panic was beginning to grip the community; a lynch-mob mentality had begun to take hold.

"Ordinarily, the inhabitants of our fair town are not given to such outward displays of emotion," Nate observed after the Chief hung up with yet another angry constituent.

"Yes, I feel the tension myself," Munson admitted, confounded by the speed at which circumstances had unraveled the residents' self-control, "and I plan on taking several steps to calm the village's frayed nerves."

"Short of apprehending this fellow, what could you possibly do to control the situation?" Fredericks ridiculed in an uncharacteristically bold fashion. From the flushed look on his freckled face, he was obviously agitated by the mob outside and his own lack of success in finding a connection between the victims.

"Institute a curfew, for one," the sheriff quietly replied, unruffled by the younger man's haughty attitude.

"Newt, this is Farmington, not Boston," Nate argued strenuously. "Isn't that a bit extreme?"

"So long as I am in charge here, we will do things my way," the Chief emphasized as he ticked off on his fingers the measures he intended to put in place. "As I already said, beginning tonight, I am instituting an 8 p.m. curfew; secondly, I have set a round the clock surveillance on each of the seven remaining targets; third, I have deputized volunteers to patrol the streets until reinforcements from the state patrol arrive; and lastly, I have ordered a news blackout to prevent any copy-cat killings."

"Hah!" Fredericks taunted, throwing his arms up in the air with disgust. "What a cowboy you are! You propose to catch this guy with curfews and news blackouts?" Getting to his feet as if he were about to leave the room, he mocked, "I suppose, Marshall Dillon, you carefully instructed your watchdogs to make regular reports, and I suppose you armed these trigger-happy deputies as well."

Munson frowned. Despite his long-standing and well-known dislike for guns, he had intended to issue each guard—

Nate included—a long-barreled Winchester rifle or else a Remington 12-gauge shotgun from the department's cache of confiscated firearms. Now he wasn't so sure any more.

"Chief, the boy may have a point here," Flix interrupted as he watched Munson unlock the gun cabinet and place several shotguns on his desk.

"Nothing beats a 12-gauge shotgun loaded with OO buckshot," Munson objected. "At the range of a household gunfight, aim need only be approximate; you're going to *shred* the guy!"

"Hah!" Flix laughed. "There's one big problem with a shotgun, though."

"What's that?"

"You're going to catch hell from the victim's wife 'cause you're also gonna shred the lady's precious Chippendale sideboard…and the irreplaceable portrait of her mother."

Chuckling, Chief Munson turned to reply, but Fredericks spoke up first.

"Munson, why are you wasting our time with this crap? The doctor and I have work to do. Besides, this silly plan of yours will never stop him," the FBI man contended as he eased himself back out the door. "Deputized hicks with hunting rifles?" he chuckled lightly.

If Fredericks' words angered the Chief, he did not let it show when he spoke. "So what do you suggest?" he asked with rabbinical patience.

"Prayer," the agent advised as he and Dr. Johannsen left to go back over to the mortuary.

As the door swung shut behind them, the chief murmured, "I don't think I like that fellow too much."

"Indeed, there is something quite disagreeable about him," Flix concurred, a frown on his face. "And something decidedly suspicious as well."

"What's that, Gus?" Nate quizzed, gently poking his friend in the shoulder.

"If my picture was distributed to Munson here, and to every other law enforcement agency in the country, don't you think an eager new operative from the FBI would have seen it as well?"

"What of it?" Nate asked, not getting Flix's point.

"Well, if *Newt* recognized me so easily, why hasn't *Fredericks*?" Flix reasoned soberly.

"He's a scatter-brain," the Chief answered.

"Perhaps."

"What are you suggesting?" Matthews cross-examined.

"Perhaps he's not *with* the Bureau."

"Meaning what?"

"Meaning he bears keeping an eye on."

32

FEVERISH

Despite Chief Munson's determination in putting a halt to the carnage, the murderer seemed destined to complete his heinous dirty work. And despite Fredericks' advice as to the value of prayer, the reign of terror continued unabated even after their midday meeting broke up. No sooner had they gone their separate ways—with Nate leaving for Musette's place to watch over her, and Flix going to Nate's house to keep an eye on Frankie—than Munson was handed a news-bulletin. According to the dispatch, Phil Rugby, victim number four, had died in a fatal traffic accident on the outskirts of St. Louis.

After having dropped his mail off at the post box around lunchtime, Phil had come by police headquarters to talk over the progress of the investigation with Chief Munson. Inasmuch as he was next on the list after Shirlee, Phil had deservedly been in a panic. Thinking back upon it now, Munson remembered how flush the man's cheeks had been and how clammy his forehead had appeared. He looked as though he had been running a high fever. Though Newt had done his best to calm the frantic man down, there was nothing he could do or say to make Phil relax. And to make matters worse, when Munson had suggested he remain in protective custody at the station house, Phil had gone berserk and bolted, hoping to avoid his appointment with destiny by fleeing Farmington altogether.

Now, as Munson held the police dispatch in his trembling hand, he knew that Phil's bold dash to safety had ended in tragedy. According to the bulletin, eye-witnesses at the scene claimed that he had swerved into an oncoming gcar and lost control of his vehicle before plunging it into a bridge abutment. After the medics pried Phil's bloodied head from the windshield, and after a blood test proved that he was not intoxicated at the time of the crash, the local authorities traced him to Munson's jurisdiction on the basis of his license plates.

As Munson realized that he had yet another murder on his hands committed by a still unknown means, the furrowed lines etched in his forehead deepened even further. Lunging for the comm and encoding the number at the funeral parlor where Johannsen could be reached, Munson heard the scream of fire trucks wailing down the boulevard outside. Turning up the volume on the police-band radio with his free hand as he waited for the call to go through, he listened for the announcement of the street number the firefighters were racing to. Munson's heart sank when it came across the air. He didn't have to check the city directory to know who lived at 510 N. Spring—he had memorized the addresses of all ten of them— it was John Thompson, the man pictured on photograph number five!

Munson stood there as if in a trance. Why didn't it surprise him to learn that John Thompson's house had burned to the ground? Why wasn't he shocked to find out that the charred remains of Burt, his bodyguard, were discovered next to John's barbecued corpse in the burnt-out upstairs hall? Why wasn't he astonished when it was later disclosed that there was no indication whatsoever of arson? Had his many years of policing hardened him that much? Or was he just numb?

"Yes?" Wilhelm sighed as he answered the comm, breaking into the Chief's train of thought.

"Have you learned anything?" the sheriff implored hoarsely.

"Yes, I think so. How 'bout you?"

"Unfortunately I have," Newt admitted, struggling to

maintain his composure as the blare of fire engines receded into the distance. "There have been two more deaths."

"God no."

"After dinner tonight I want you to come up to the station and tell me what you have. If you talk to Fredericks, bring him along too."

"Until dinner then."

"On the surface, each killing has the appearance of being an accident," Chief Munson described, a look of frustration clouding his face. The embers had barely cooled at the Thompson place when he, Agent Fredericks, and Dr. Johannsen came together for this strategy session. Not wanting to leave Musette's side, Nate was listening in on an open comm line Newt had established for this purpose while Flix took a long overdue nap at Nate's house under Frankie's watchful eye.

"Granted, each death may have the *appearance* of an accident, yet each one was meticulously planned," Dr. Johannsen contradicted, his firm SKANDIAN build giving him an authoritative look. Although less than half a day had passed since the murders had first begun, the circles under his normally bright blue eyes suggested that the strain of the investigation was already taking its toll.

"What do you mean 'meticulously planned'?" Fredericks asked, surprised by the medical examiner's comments. The two men hadn't seen each other for hours and this was the first the FBI man had heard of Wilhelm's hypothesis.

"The autopsies I have performed so far show that in each instance the victim literally drowned to death in his own mucous."

"Yuk!" Nate blurted over the comm as Musette cringed in the background next to him.

"Not very pleasant to be sure," the doctor agreed, "but such asphyxiation is consistent with a debilitating case of untreated viral pneumonia. Only I have never seen anything like it in my life. The latency period for this virus is remarkably short, and the onset of pneumonia extremely rapid," Johannsen elaborated in a professorial tone.

"Though I have no proof of it yet," he continued as he paced anxiously back and forth across the floor of Newton's cramped vestibule, "I strongly suspect that both Phil Rugby's traffic accident and John Thompson's house blaze might well have been the chance byproducts of two delirious persons, each hopelessly confused by a torrid viral fever."

As Johannsen spoke, Fredericks shifted uneasily in his seat. He seemed to know more than he was telling.

"You mean like passing out in bed while smoking a cigarette, and setting yourself ablaze in the process?" Nate inquired over the speaker comm.

"Or falling asleep at the wheel while driving?" Munson chimed in.

"Precisely," Johannsen exclaimed, nodding energetically as if Nate could see him across the many blocks that separated them.

"And yet, the proximate cause of death was still this virus thing," the Chief summarized. "But where did the goddamned thing *come* from?" he asked perplexed.

"There are several possibilities," Johannsen pointed out. "The virus might have been delivered to the victims in something they ate; or they might have gotten it from something they drank; or it might have been transmitted to them through the air; or it might even have been *injected* into them."

"But I thought you said there were no marks on the bodies?" Nate questioned from the comfort of Musette's living room. She was sitting next to him with her arms folded neatly in her lap.

"True enough," Wilhelm conceded, "I found no puncture wounds whatsoever."

"Maybe the pinpricks were too small and we just overlooked them," Fredericks rejoined, thinking back to his own cursory examination of the corpses this morning.

"Perhaps," Johannsen nodded. "Nevertheless, I have eliminated injection as a possibility for an altogether different reason."

"Do come to the point," Fredericks demanded in an irritating manner.

"Shut up and let the man speak!" Munson bellowed at the frail FBI man before turning back to the medical examiner. "What reason, Doc? What?"

"So far as I could tell, there were no signs of a struggle at any of the crime sites. Not only that, there were no comms off the hook as there would have been if the victims had tried calling for help."

"Huh?" the Chief murmured. "You've lost me, Doc."

"Haven't you ever had a shot?" Johannsen quizzed, knowing full well that every adult had had his share of inoculations.

"Well, of course," he stammered.

"Did it hurt?"

"Yes, I see now what you mean," Newton admitted sheepishly, rubbing his shoulder as if he had just been given an immunization by needle.

"Well, I don't," Fredericks interjected angrily.

"It's just not that easy to shoot a hypo into someone's arm—or their butt, for that matter—without them feeling it. Believe me, I've tried. Even if they *had* been asleep at the time of the injection, the pain of the shot would have awakened them," Johannsen explained. "And no virus known to man works that fast—the prey would have had plenty of time to put up a struggle or else to call for help."

"Which leaves food or else airborne contaminants," Nate reasoned.

"Quite so," Johannsen agreed, "only I have decided to discard airborne sources from consideration as well."

"On what basis?" Fredericks probed, still red-faced from having just been told to shut up.

"Assume for a moment that our Mr. Thompson's watchguard died as the unintended victim of a negligent act committed by his delirious charge, and not as the result of being explicitly targeted by the killer."

"In English, Wilhelm. Please," Munson implored, his

head pounding again.

"I think what the good doctor is trying to say is that Burt perished in the chance fire which John caused when he fell asleep with a lit cigar in his mouth. Isn't that right?" Nate cross-checked, acting as if he were an interpreter.

"Quite so. I would submit that no airborne agent I know of can be delivered with such precision as to be considered effective against only one person at a time. These genetic nightmares are typically so lethal entire cities can be taken out with just one application," Johannsen declared in a clinical voice.

"So make your point already," Fredericks urged, a bead of sweat rolling off his forehead.

"My point is, this germ had to be imbedded in something these people consumed. I believe they *ingested* the virus which killed them," the medical examiner concluded earnestly.

"Intolerable!" Munson shouted, at his wits' end. "Impossible!"

"Why so?" Dr. Johannsen snapped back with a puzzled look on his face.

"Look, Doc," Munson argued, "these people were as different from each other as night and day! They lived lives as unlike one another as any you could possibly imagine. There's no way they could have all eaten the same food on the same day. Can't we just inoculate the remaining five against this goddamned virus and be done with it?"

"It may take a month or more just to isolate the strain," Johannsen correctly pointed out.

"We don't have that kind of time," Newt sighed.

"I know, Chief. I'm telling you—concentrate your manpower on finding out what Shirlee and Phil and the others ate or drank in the past several days, and I guarantee you will find your murder weapon. And—with a little bit of luck—you will find your murderer as well."

33

PRISONER

Keeping his eyes fixed on the rain-soaked street to see if he had been followed, Duncan bounded up the front porch steps of the modest house. The service attendant he had spoken to minutes earlier had said it belonged to his some-times adversary, Senator Nate Matthews. Like the rest of the nation, Duncan was oblivious to the siege that Farmington had come under in the past twenty-four hours. All that had con-cerned him in the last day and a half was getting out of Washington alive and responding to Nate's insistent sounding message on his machine. Even now, as he stood there under the protective canopy of the porch roof, it bothered him how little Nate had sounded like himself when he played back the recording.

Gently rapping on Nate's door as the sun settled slowly against the horizon, Duncan wondered whether this wouldn't be the perfect opportunity to try once again to enlist him as an ally in his effort to bring Silas down. Duncan was sure that with a little prodding, the recalcitrant Nate could be convinced to change his mind and join up with his cause.

Impatient to get inside where he couldn't be seen, Duncan raised his fist to pound a little harder on the door. But just as he was about to strike it with his knuckles, the door popped open and he was greeted by a pimpled adolescent.

"Is this the Matthews' residence?" he asked the youngster,

confident that the service station attendant had given him the correct address.

"Who are you?" Frankie challenged without introducing himself or acknowledging whose home it was. Gustav Knapheide, the old man lying inside on the couch, had insisted that while he took a nap, Frankie be extremely cautious about who he admitted to the house or who he spoke to on the comm.

"I'm a cohort of your dad's," Duncan explained. "That is, if you are Franklin Matthews and if this is Nate Matthews' house."

"Maybe it is, and then again, maybe it isn't," Frankie retorted haughtily, enjoying watching the older man squirm. "What do you want with my dad, baldy?"

"To speak with him if he's home," Duncan declared, absentmindedly touching the hairless crown of his head.

"Well, he's not!" Frankie roared, looking as if he were about to slam the door in the Senator's face.

By this time, Flix had been awakened by the commotion in the foyer. Recognizing Duncan's voice, he yelled from the other room, "It's okay, Frankie! Let the man in."

"Whatever you say, Gustav," Frankie shouted back. "Just trying to do my job like you said."

"Chrissake, Wenger!" Duncan exclaimed when he saw the General's face. "What are *you* doing here?"

"I thought my dad said your name was Gustav," Frankie objected suspiciously when the older man responded to the appellation 'Wenger'.

"It is, Frankie, it is," Flix assured the boy firmly, "but some of my fraternity buddies call me Wenger."

"This man's not old enough to have been in your fraternity," Frankie astutely pointed out, fancying himself as a junior detective.

"But his father was," Flix lied without hesitation. "He must have picked up my nickname listening to his father talk about me. Isn't that so, Senator?" Flix noted, urging Duncan to agree with his story.

Duncan nodded without comment.

Seemingly satisfied with Flix's explanation, Frankie drifted into the other room mumbling as he went. "Listen, Gustav, if it's all the same to you, Grandpa invited me to stay overnight with him at his place tonight. So if you and baldy here don't mind, I'll be shoving off now."

"I promised your father I wouldn't let you get into any trouble," Flix reminded the boy, "so don't let me down. And be sure to program your grandpa's number into the call forwarder in case Nate calls and I'm not in," he bellowed as Frankie went to the hall closet, knocking over an umbrella stand in the process. "Oh, and one more thing, don't forget about the 8 p.m. curfew Munson has ordered."

"You worry too much, old-timer," Frankie emphasized in a typical teenager's smart-alecky voice as he grabbed for his coat and hurried out the door.

"What's this all about, *Gustav*?" the Senator queried once Frankie was out of earshot.

"While I have been here in Farmington hiding out from the law, I have been using the name of one Gustav Knapheide, systems analyst for Computer Applications, Inc. out of Witchita, Kansas," Flix elaborated with a flare for the dramatic. "Duncan, if you must know, things have changed a great deal in the last couple of days." But before he could explain any further, there was a timid knock at the door.

"That must be Frankie," Flix pointed out, putting aside his usual safety precautions as he approached the front door. "You know how kids are—he probably forgot his favorite sweater or something."

Without taking the time to peer through the peephole in the door, Flix swung it open, only to regret his decision moments later. Staring him in the face was a mean looking, semi-automatic weapon. Standing behind it was a brawny man with bushy eyebrows.

"Step aside," the big man brusquely ordered, pushing his way into the foyer even as he shoved the door closed behind him. He held a Intratec DC-12 in his gloved hand. The black semi-automatic pistol had a 32-shot capacity and its stock glistened with a few drops of machine oil. Knowing how dangerous this pistol was at close range, Flix recoiled into the corner.

"Now that that damn kid's gone, I can finally take you in unobserved," Dirk anounced, his lips practically tasting the reward for his patience. "And, as luck would have it, our good friend Senator Duncan is here as well. How sweet!"

"You are a wanted man, General Wenger," Dirk clamored with obvious pleasure. "You are wanted for conspiracy in the assassination of President Nolan; you are wanted for the murder of Clara Whetstone; and now, you are wanted for the murder of Senator Duncan as well."

Without even flinching, the security man squeezed the trigger, allowing several rounds of ammunition to spit noiselessly from the gun. His face frozen in a look of horror, Duncan flew across the sitting room in a cavalcade of blood and torn flesh.

"You bastard!" Flix shouted, grabbing clumsily for the steaming barrel of the Intratec. It was hot with effort.

"Don't be a fool!" Dirk exhorted, deftly striking the former demolitions man in the kidney with a jab of his fist.

Collapsing painfully to the floor, Flix taunted defiantly, "Well, if you have come here to kill me, get to it you scumbag! I haven't got all day you know!" he murmured, gratified that when he arrived here last night he had had the foresight to hand over his book of codes and addresses to Nate.

"I'm not here to kill you, old man; I'm here to take you in. Whetstone wants you alive, but that doesn't mean I can't kick you around a bit first if you don't cooperate," Dirk underscored as he rammed his boot into Flix's side. "Do I make myself clear?"

"Perfectly," Flix croaked, gasping for air. "You're the asshole I saw in the stairwell at Bethesda, aren't you? You shot Clara, didn't you?"

"Indeed," the big man acknowledged, towering over Flix. "Now get to your feet, you fossil. I have a gcar waiting for us down the street."

"I can't get up without the help of my cane," Flix complained as convincingly as he could. "Hand it to me won't you?"

"Not so fast, Wenger. Silas has told me all about your nasty cane. If you wish, I'll stick it in the trunk for you so that you can have it later on, but for now, use this umbrella," he commanded, grabbing a long-handled bumbershoot from Nate's closet and sliding it across the floor in Flix's direction. "You and I have a long ride ahead of us so you had better not give me any more trouble," he barked, tossing Flix the gcar keys. "You'll drive. That way I can keep my eyes on you," he explained in a menacing tone as he waved Flix toward the door.

Taking one last look at Duncan's lifeless corpse, Flix nodded his assent as he followed Dirk's instructions with military precision.

"I'm telling you—concentrate your manpower on finding out what Shirlee and Phil and the others ate or drank in the past several days, and I guarantee you will find your murder weapon. And—with a little bit of luck—you will find your murderer as well."

As Nate hung up the comm after hearing Dr. Johannsen's analysis of how the killer had passed the virus to his victims, the walls of Musette's tidy bungalow began to close in on him. Ever since the sheriff's midday meeting had broken up and Munson had issued all the bodyguards a gun or a rifle from the station armory, Nate had been cloistered in Musette's house. As the afternoon had slipped by without any word of progress in identifying the culprit, a look of resignation had settled in on Nate's tired face. By the time of their just concluded dinner-hour meeting where Nate had attended by comm only, he couldn't escape the uncomfortable fact that his girlfriend was number eight on a short list where number five had alrcady mct a fiery demise.

Recognizing that in order to save her life, he might have

to face this murderous demon alone, Nate had done his best to steel himself for the unknown challenge which lay ahead of him. Unlike his friend Flix, however, he had not had any formal military training, and he wasn't sure if he was up to the job. His only preparation for such a siege was what Flix had taught him about self-defense and about the proper use of a gun. For the umpteenth time since lunch, he had glanced at the Winchester rifle lying poised on the mantelpiece and at the Luger waiting patiently for him on the front room table. Unfortunately, the two firearms had been cold comfort against the featureless killer still roaming the streets of Farmington unperturbed by the efforts being mounted to apprehend him.

Lost in uneasy thought, Nate had been startled by the sounds of heavy steps on Musette's front porch around 2 p.m. that afternoon. Alarmed by the clamor outside the door, he had jumped up and vaulted across the room to where the revolver was quartered. In his haste to grab for his gun, the address book Flix had given him fell from his pocket. Remembering the promises he and Flix had exchanged last night on the steps to his house, Nate had stooped to pick the secret folio up off the floor, even as he held his Luger at the ready. But Musette had waved him off.

"Forget that silly gun—it's just the mailman," she had announced calmly as he had surreptitiously slipped the enigmatic book under one of the seat cushions on her couch. "The letter-box is mounted on the wall next to the front door; that's why you hear him outside on the porch."

Thankful for the distraction, she had retrieved the envelopes and returned to the sitting room with an armful of letters and small parcels. But sensing her unease, Nate had made her put the pile of mail aside for the time being so that they could talk. And as a consequence, until they hung up with Johannsen a few minutes ago, the entire afternoon had been spent exchanging one light-hearted pleasantry after the next. After hearing his portrayal of how innocent people were drowning in their own mucous, however, their mood took an abrupt shift for the worse. Paralyzed by what he had told them, Musette and Nate just sat there, afraid that one or both of them had already been poisoned by the dinner they had just finished eating.

"Nate, I don't want to die," she exclaimed, her delicate brown eyes brimming with tears.

"You won't," he promised, though his heart was filled with doubt.

"Can't we just leave town?" she begged, her hand touching his. "Just run away?"

"Darling, you heard what happened to Phil. Don't you see? There's nowhere for us to hide. Out on the streets, we're easy targets, but here, at least we have the advantage of a familiar terrain plus we have the weapons to protect ourselves with."

Again his eyes darted to the opposite side of the room where the long-barreled rifle adorned the fireplace. It was a.44-calibre, magazine-style rifle with the stopping power of a small cannon. Gathering his resolve, he asserted, "We have to face up to this…and we must do it here!"

Putting one finger to his lips to shush Musette's blubbering, he suggested she attack the pile of mail still sitting unopened on the counter of the buffet. By this time, what little of the sun that could be seen between the rain clouds had drifted below the horizon.

"Boy, you must be popular," he commented as he brought her the huge stack of mail and she began rummaging through it.

"Looks like you are too," she retorted, handing him a piece with his name on it.

"That's curious," he commented. "Not that many people know that I'm here with you."

It was marked *Personal & Confidential for Senator Matthews Only*. Expecting that it was something of importance from his office in Washington, he eagerly tore open the pink envelope. But what was inside made his skin crawl.

The message was very ominous. And very personal. Musette trembled with fear as he read the typed poem aloud several times:

> So much to do,
> Dreams to pursue.
> If only you had the time,
> Killing Senators shouldn't be a crime.

Without a second's thought, Nate shot across the room and encoded the Chief's exchange on the comm. When at first a busy signal buzzed in his ear, he nervously rapped his fingers against the table even as he frantically depressed the resend key. Nearly in cardiac arrest by the time the call finally went through, Nate was practically incoherent as he struggled to inform the Chief of the threatening note. Once he was able to make Munson understand that the letter had sat there un-opened all day long and that time was now of the essence, the Chief sprang into action, promising Nate that he would be there within minutes along with a couple of officers from the newly-arrived state police.

Reassured by Chief Munson's pledge of reinforcements, Nate gave Musette a weak smile from across the parlor. But she turned away from him with a sour look on her face. By the time he had said good-bye to Munson and hung up the comm, she was doing her best to shut out the world and concentrate on the stack of mail he had set before her.

"Munson's bringing two men over here to stand watch outside the house," he pointed out earnestly.

"That's nice dear," she replied, feigning disinterest de-spite her obvious fear.

"What else would you have me do?" he retorted in a dispirited fashion, staring at the rhyme again in disbelief.

Avoiding his question, she asked, "Nate dear, why do you insist on sending out these stupid surveys to your constituents?"

In her hand she was holding a thick brown, official-looking envelope. Marked boldly across its face it read: Citizen Survey From Senator Nate Matthews, *Your* Voice in Washington.

Reading the typed poem to himself once more, Nate didn't pay close attention to what she was saying or to what she was holding in her lap.

"What, love?" he redirected absentmindedly. "What did you say?" he repeated, fidgeting in the uncomfortable chair.

"Why do you congressmen bombard us poor citizens with so much junk mail?" she cross-examined. "Questionnaires and such?" Holding the opened envelope up for him to see, she added, "Like this."

His eyes vacant, Nate stared at her from the other side of the room. Suddenly bursting from his chair, he screamed, "Stop! Put the goddamn thing down! Immediately!"

Terrified by his hysterical tone, she dropped the envelope to the floor, spilling its contents on the carpet at her feet.

"Nate, are you coming *unglued*?" she shrieked, shrinking into her seat.

"Yes, that's it!" he bellowed. "Don't you see?" he continued almost as if he were intoxicated. "It's the *glue*!"

34

SURVEY

Baffled by Nate's strenuous outburst, Musette intoned, "Whaaat?"

"From the start, I was convinced there had to be some way to piece this all together," Nate exclaimed excitedly, "and now I think I know how to do it!"

"Tell me," she demanded, staring at him with a look of shocked disbelief.

Energized by his insight, the Senator feverishly launched his explanation. "Johannsen told us that he suspected the murder weapon was a virus. He also said that if that were the case, it would have to have been transmitted to the victims via something they ate or else via something they drank. Keeping that possibility in mind, I asked myself what sort of food these people—and *only* these people—could have eaten. Answer? It couldn't have been store-bought food…"

"Why not?"

"Because there would have been no way for the killer to have controlled who bought what—or where they bought it. Therefore, it would have to have been order-out food."

"What do you mean?" she questioned, perplexed by his line of reasoning. "Like pizza?"

"Yes. But it could have been any number of things—pizza, poor boy sandwiches, Chinese."

"That's not very darn likely," she countered in her naive,

but direct manner. "I knew Shirlee quite well, and she was a stickler for detail. Everything she ate—and I mean everything—had to be prepared at home or else she wouldn't touch it."

"The same thing occurred to me, so I asked myself: What else—*besides* food—can typically be delivered to a person's home?"

"Perhaps drugs from the pharmacy," she volunteered, pacing back and forth across the room in front of the fireplace.

"Good thought," he complimented, following her graceful movements with his eyes. "I thought of that also. That is, until I remembered that Phil Rugby never *took* pills; he was deathly afraid of choking on one. And in thinking about it further, I figured there had to be *another* possibility. Perhaps it was something the victim didn't necessarily order, but would gladly accept from a delivery man anyway."

"Yes, I'm beginning to see your point," she smiled, for perhaps the first time that afternoon. "Well, how 'bout a bouquet of flowers from a florist then?"

"Forgive me, my sweet, but I thought of that one too. Even if that were true, let's face it, with flowers or something else along that line, we're back to an airborne agent which..."

"...which Johannsen ruled out as being unlikely," Musette interjected.

"Exactly. Plus, can you imagine a macho guy like John Thompson accepting an unsolicited delivery of flowers?" Nate probed as he chuckled lightly.

"What then?" she asked exasperated. "What would people willingly accept from a delivery man without questioning its arrival?"

"The mail," he answered matter-of-factly, glancing apprehensively at the voter survey still laying on the carpet.

"The mail?" Musette stammered, her voice a high-pitched squeak.

"Yes, it makes perfect sense, don't you see? The murderer *mailed* the virus to his victims!"

"What do you mean, he *mailed* it?" This time it was Chief

Munson speaking. He had just arrived at the front door of Musette's house with Agent Fredericks and two muscle-bound officers from the state patrol in tow.

"Chief, thank goodness you're here," Nate sighed in the middle of detailing his hypothesis. "As I was saying, maybe the offending germ is imbedded in the paper the survey was printed on; or maybe it has been stirred into the ink; or maybe…"

Walking over to where Musette had spilled the congressional survey out onto the floor, and being careful not to touch any of its potentially lethal pages, Nate studied the contents. His eye immediately caught on the brightly-colored postpaid return envelope, its pink hue identical to that of the alarming packet he had opened only minutes before.

Beginning again from where he had left off, Nate completed his unfinished sentence, "…or maybe it's in the adhesive. The glue you lick to seal the envelope shut!"

As Fredericks and Munson exchanged puzzled stares, Nate sang out excitedly, "Geez, fellows, that's *got* to be it! I'd wager my Senate seat that the gummed flap of this return envelope is *laced* with that God-awful virus. The enclosed questionnaire probably asks the recipient some penetrating questions, then begs the citizen to promptly render a reply along with a check no doubt—and when the unwitting, but conscientious, voter licks the envelope shut—bammo, he's infected!"

Animated by his tale, Musette and Fredericks both began talking at once.

"Since I touched the envelope, am I now infected?" she gasped nervously, running to the bathroom to wash her hands.

"Are you suggesting that someone on your Senatorial staff has been spiking your surveys with these damn germs?" Fredericks challenged anxiously, his eyes taking note of the rifle on the mantelpiece and the Luger on the coffee table in front of the couch.

"No, I'm not suggesting that at all," Nate retorted firmly even as he contemplated how Fredericks knew it was *his*

Senatorial survey they were discussing.

"What are you suggesting then?" Munson demanded, shushing everyone else in the room so he could hear.

"Senator Matthews didn't *send* out a survey to canvass his constituents," Nate asserted matter-of-factly. "And even if he *had*, he would never have authorized the use of bright pink envelopes."

"He didn't? I mean, you didn't?" Musette quizzed, her voice cracking as she returned to the living room, a towel still in her wet hands.

Even as Nate shook his head "no," they all gawked at the floor deliberating over what to do next.

After a long while, Fredericks finally broke the tomb-like stillness. "Chief, don't you think you should tell Nate about Charlie Jenkins?"

Snapped out of his zombie-like daze by the FBI man's comment, Munson declared, "Yes, yes, by all means. Nate," he said, turning to his friend, "while I was on the comm talking with you a few minutes ago, Fredericks here was on the other line taking a call from Doc Simpson. You might know him: he's the medic whose practice is over on Locust Street. It seems that Old Man Jenkins died in Simpson's office not an hour ago."

Nate was aghast. "Not another death?" he trembled.

"Jenkins had come in complaining that he was having some difficulty breathing. Doc Simpson told us that although Charlie was sweating profusely from an intense fever, he was nearly unable to examine the poor fellow because Jenkins was completely delirious. Apparently the man started ranting and raving, then with his arms flailing wildly about, he suddenly collapsed on the floor—dead. There was nothing Doc Simpson could do. He tried to resuscitate Jenkins but…"

Munson's voice trailed off into a whisper as bad memories of his days as a Boston cop came rocketing back to him. It was like a nightmare that just wouldn't end.

"Was it the virus?" Matthews asked glumly.

"Probably," he nodded. "I sent Johannsen over to Doc

Simpson's to check it out, but there's something else you should know," Munson added darkly.

"What's that?"

"Jenkins was number seven, not number six."

The confused look on Nate's face announced that he didn't digest the import of the Chief's comment.

"Don't you get it?" Munson clamored, the answer so blatantly obvious to him, he couldn't believe the Senator didn't see it too. "Jenkins...died...out...of...order," he intoned, enunciating each word slowly and deliberately.

When he was still greeted with a blank stare, Munson repeated himself, "He died out of order!"

Finally understanding the Chief's point, Nate exclaimed, "Geez, you mean Hans Toleffson is still alive?"

"Yes, goddamnit, that's what I have been trying to tell you!" Munson declared vehemently. "Your frantic call sounded so urgent, I rushed over here before I could raise Hans on the comm, but yes, as far as I know, he's still alive. And even if there *had* been trouble at his place, I'm sure I would have heard about it by now from one of my deputies. I have two men stationed on the street out in front of his house and they have a mobile comm in their gcar."

"Maybe you couldn't reach him because he tried to skip town like Phil Rugby did," Musette offered.

"We'll know soon enough," Chief Munson made clear, "because as soon as I'm done with you here, I am heading over to Hans' house."

"I'm going with you," Nate decided abruptly. "If Hans is still alive, I would hazard a guess that this bogus survey either hasn't reached him, or else it's sitting right there in his mailbox unopened. And I'll bet that if we have Johannsen run a toxicology on the survey—the paper, the ink, the glue, the whole shebang—he will find whatever poison or whatever virus all these people have been exposed to. Geez, but if this all hasn't become very personal!" Nate swore.

Seizing on that remark, Fredericks probed, "Senator, who do you think hates you enough to poison innocent people using a questionnaire supposedly distributed by your office in Washington?"

Nate's anger bristled at Agent Fredericks' unexpectedly mean question. As if he needed any more convincing, he suddenly decided that he too didn't like this obnoxious man from the FBI.

"Who, indeed?" Nate recited, his gray eyes narrowing and his keen mind racing. Up to this point, he had never revealed to Agent Fredericks the details surrounding his encounter with Overlord Mao Tsui, but there could no longer be any doubt as to who was behind these murders. With each passing hour of this nightmare, Nate had become more and more convinced that not only had Mao engineered this personal vendetta, the yellow-skinned bastard had also killed his wife, Darna. Maybe not intentionally, but he had killed her all the same. Somehow, somewhere, on that goodwill trip to China just before the election, she had visited a Chinese university or a research center or someplace where she had been exposed to the very same virus being deliberately unleashed here. Visions of their last moments together tormented him—her bulging eyes, her drawn and dehydrated face, the erratic, delirious movements, the fevered ranting.

Thoughts of revenge made their way clumsily to the surface, and Nate found the unforeseen emotion curiously fascinating. He had never thought of himself as capable of such hatred, such rage.

Directing his attention to Munson, he said, "Not that I don't trust the guards you have brought with you Chief, but I would feel a whole lot better if my friend Gustav and my son Franklin were to stay here with Musette while the three of us go to Toleffson's."

"You want *Frankie* to come over here?" the Chief asked surprised. But upon seeing Nate's determined face, he impatiently agreed, "Well, okay, but make it quick."

"Our house is just a couple of blocks over," Nate assured. "I'll call him straightaway."

"And while you do that, I'll radio Johannsen on the police-

band and ask him to join us there. Meanwhile," the Chief
continued with military efficiency, as he turned to address
Fredericks, "why don't you collect up Musette's survey?
There are evidence bags out in my squad gcar."

Within minutes Franklin and Nathanial, Sr. had arrived on
the scene, and after Frankie explained how he had been invited
to stay at his grandpa's house and how Gustav had instructed
him to switch the comm to call forwarding mode, Nate hastily
made a few introductions.

"Chief, you, of course, already know my son."

Nodding a perfunctory nod and shifting uneasily as Franklin
smiled politely back, Munson did little to hide his eagerness
to be on his way.

Turning to Fredericks, Nate elaborated, "My son Franklin
was the Chief's house guest for a spell, wasn't he Newt?"

The Chief grunted an unintelligible reply even as he edged
toward the door to leave.

"Agent Fredericks," Nate announced proudly, "let me
present you my son Franklin and my father Nathanial."

"Frankie, Dad, this is Agent Fredericks of the FBI, one of
the two investigators Chief Munson has brought in to help us
crack this case. Dad, you already know the other gentleman;
that would be Dr. Wilhelm Johannsen out of St. Louis."

The man and the boy shook hands. Studying the thin man's
freckled face and the dark eyes glaring at him from behind a
pair of horn-rimmed glasses, Frankie found Fredericks'
countenance strangely familiar. Still, there was something
distinctly out of place, something he couldn't quite put his
finger on just yet.

Scratching his head in confusion, Nate's son quizzed
Fredericks, "Have we met before?"

Almost too quickly, the FBI man replied, "Not that I can
recall. Perhaps my picture was in the *Dispatch*."

Sensing Munson's impatience to get to Hans Toleffson's
place as quickly as possible, Nate interrupted his boy's interrogation, "Son, I want you and grandpa to stay here with
Musette until I return. You can go back to his house after-

wards. I have a pretty good idea how these murders are being committed, and we are going there to check out my theory."

As the others stepped through the doorway and out of earshot, Nate whispered to Frankie, "Be nice—I like her!"

Smiling, Franklin nodded his approval.

"You don't actually know what this is all about, do you?" Flix probed as he plotted his escape. The two men were in Dirk's gcar about six miles from town, traveling eastbound on the main highway out of Farmington. Flix was at the wheel and his captor was sitting sideways on the front seat with his semi-automatic pistol leveled directly at Flix's middle. The magazine of the Intratec had a 32-shot capacity, a capacity reduced now by the two slugs imbedded in Senator Duncan's lifeless body.

Because it was impossible for Dirk to ride sidesaddle with both his lap belt and his shoulder harness firmly secured, the man's canvas safety belt hung limply on the seat next to him. Seeing it resting uselessly there, and relishing the comforting snugness of his own seat belt, the General had hatched a bold escape plan. If only he could get up the nerve, all he had to do was ram the passenger side of the gcar into the bridge abutment of one of the many overpasses along this stretch of road. Theoretically, without his seat restraint attached, Dirk would fly through the windshield while Flix would be spared a horrifying death. Theoretically.

And even if the airbag kept Dirk's head from punching a hole through the thick glass, the unexpected maneuver should come as enough of a shock to him that Dirk would either drop his piece or else take his eyes off his prisoner long enough for Flix to knock the weapon from his grip, thereby regaining control over the intolerable situation. Theoretically.

Flix imagined himself taking deliberate aim on the bridge support of the next overpass. He contemplated how it would feel to slam the accelerator to the floor; how Dirk's eyes would go wide with disbelief as it dawned on him what Flix was about to do; how his captor might scream out in anguish even before the collision took place; how the blood would spurt from his body once the evil act was done. It never occurred to him that he too might perish in the wreck.

"You don't actually know what this is all about, do you, Dirk?" Flix repeated as the highbeam of his gcar revealed yet another overpass not more than a mile away. Streaks of rain clouded the windshield.

"Wenger, you're really a piece of work, aren't you?" Dirk snapped haughtily, waving his fearsome-looking assault weapon back and forth as he spoke. "Everything's intrigue and deception to you isn't it, you old coot? Intrigue and deception. Tell me, you old fossil, haven't you figured it out yet?"

"What's that?" Flix inquired calmly, fixing his eyes on the steel and concrete structure three-quarters of a mile down the road.

"Whetstone will treat me like a *hero* for bringing you in. Don't you realize what's going to happen to you? The President means to hang you out to dry," Dirk explained matter-of-factly.

"Oh, does he now? I would have thought he'd have warned you about me. I'm sure he instructed you to take care that I didn't get hurt," Flix pointed out as he stole a glance at his dimwitted captor. The bridge was no more than 500 yards away now.

"He did; and I am."

"I have lived a long and fulfilling life," Flix sighed, girding his loins for the crash, "so if I were to die now, there would be no regrets. I only wish that I could say the same for you."

And with that, Flix jammed his foot onto the accelerator and aimed the right-hand side of the vehicle into the concrete upright of the bridge. The screech of metal against concrete was mind-numbing; the shrill outcry of his passenger, stomach-turning; but it was over in an instant. The last two sounds he heard before passing out were the swishing of his airbag as it filled with air and the squishing of Dirk's brain as his cranium crumbled under the force of the impact.

35

FISHING

Less than an hour later, the three men were back at Musette's house with good news to report. As luck would have it, Hans Toleffson had been on a tortan binge for days; he hadn't been sober enough to open his mail since before this whole affair began. In fact, the suspect envelope was still crammed in his mailbox between a pile of advertising circulars and a stack of overdue bills. Eager to get started with his work, Johannsen had taken it, along with Musette's survey, back to his make-shift lab at the morgue to begin testing them for a long list of possible toxins. Meanwhile, convinced that Nate was correct about the surveys being the source of the killer virus, Munson had dispatched an officer to each of the homes of the two remaining victims hoping to sequester their mail before the targets had a chance to act upon the lethal question-naires.

Sinking his bulk into an overstuffed chair in Musette's living room now that he had sent his officers on their way, and confident that his day-long migraine was about to come to an end, Chief Munson sighed, "Thank God, it's over."

"How can you possibly think this is over?" Nate gasped, dumbfounded by the Chief's remark. "Are you out of your mind?" he yelped incredulously, not believing his ears. "This isn't over, Newt, not by a long measure! We don't know the 'who' yet, and we just barely know the 'how'."

Even as Munson listened glumly to Nate's reasoning, Fredericks nodded his head in agreement.

"This is *personal*, damn it!" the Senator exclaimed passionately. "The son-of-a-bitch has been murdering people with envelopes brandishing *my* name! The killer has been striking at me! At my town; at my girl; at my friends! Mark my words, Chief; this is not over. Anyone nuts enough to have gone to all the trouble *this* fellow has gone to won't let it rest just because we have figured out how he has been doing it."

"Dad, what makes you so sure that this is personal?" Franklin chimed in, perplexed to learn that his father was the true target of this terror. "Who could possibly hate you enough to do this?"

"The Overlord, son," Nate answered coolly, stealing a glance in the direction of Agent Fredericks.

"The Overlord, as in that guy from China?" Franklin quizzed in disbelief. "Sure, Dad," he mocked, a note of skepticism in his voice. "Sure."

"I'm serious, Frankie, the Overlord, as in that guy from China."

"What did you do to *him*?" Franklin asked.

"Yea, son," Tiger echoed. "What the hell did ya do to 'im?"

"It's a long story folks, but in essence it boils down to this: though the public isn't aware of it, ever since President Nolan was killed, Overlord Mao has attempted to blackmail the U.S. with a germ warfare attack if we didn't agree to cede the Hawaiian islands to him. Being as how Whetstone had paved the way for me to become the Chairman of the Military Oversight Committee, I couldn't refuse him when he asked me to pay a visit to Beijing and call the megalomaniac's bluff. Mao took understandable offense at what I was ordered to tell him and he vowed revenge. In the beginning I hoped that it was just an idle threat; now I'm convinced this is part of his plan."

"*Part* of it?!" Frankie questioned, not realizing the full extent of what his father had to tell him. "You mean there's more?"

"Yes, much more," the Senator acknowledged, taking a deep breath before continuing. "I'm beginning to think that your mom…I mean…well, after her trip to the Orient, she died so suddenly…like…like, Shirlee Winston…or old man Jenkins."

In the tense silence which followed, Nate tried to reach out to his son, only the gap between them was far too wide. As if not talking about their grief would somehow lessen the pain, Franklin finally said, "Dad, would it be okay with you if I went back to grandpa's house now?"

Seeing his boy's dejected face even as he glanced in the direction of his own father, Nate replied, "Sure, Frankie. That might be a good idea. I'll call you and grandpa first thing in the morning."

Once Franklin and Tiger had said their good-byes and left, Nate picked up his explanation from where he had taken the detour. Addressing Chief Munson, he exclaimed, "Now do you understand why this is so personal? Mao won't break it off yet. I tell you—the game isn't over."

Remembering the cryptic message and the ten crudely numbered photographs which had arrived on his desk two days ago, Munson realized that the Senator was correct—the game really *wasn't* over. Recognizing that he couldn't abandon his friend with the culprit still at large, he declared, "Have no fear, Nate, together we will see this thing through until the end. I'll stay right here in the house with you and Musette, and if this bastard is still after you, mark my words, we'll catch the creep. As far as I'm concerned, the game ends right here!" the Chief boomed emphatically.

"Munson, don't get yourself so worked up over this," the FBI agent countered hastily. "Even if Matthews' theory on how these people became infected is right, and even if Overlord Mao *is* involved, Johannsen already told us it might take him months to identify the strain. In fact, he said we might *never* pinpoint the source. Without something tangible to link the virus to the killer, the murderer will escape scot-free."

"He's not going to get away," Nate retorted firmly. "This

villain wants to hurt me, and since he has failed thus far, he will
be back to try again."

"Don't you get it?" Fredericks argued strenuously. "It's
not important whether he gets you or not; he's making a
statement—a demonstration, actually—of the killing power
of his virus."

"You seem awfully certain of yourself," the Chief noted
suspiciously.

"We have to find a way to draw the culprit out into the
open," Fredericks claimed, ignoring Munson's insightful remark.

Senator Matthews stared hard at the thin FBI man. "You
want Musette to be a target don't you?" he probed with some
trepidation. "So you can trap this lunatic?"

Not wanting to hear the answer to that question, Musette
bolted abruptly from the room, a disgusted look splashed
across her otherwise pretty face.

Doing his best to soften the Senator's burgeoning anger,
Fredericks implored, "Please, Nate. Be reasonable. What are
we trying to accomplish here? Are we trying to neutralize the
'bug', or are we trying to neutralize the 'bug-man'?"

Nate was silent as he wrestled with his own worst fears. He
wished that Flix was at his side to help advise him on the right
thing to do. In fact, it was beginning to bother him that Flix
hadn't checked-in with him before now.

"I believe I'm beginning to see your point, Fredericks,"
Munson reluctantly agreed. "The scientists will have to be the
ones to eventually neutralize the bug, but we will have to be
the ones who apprehend the perp."

"Yes, yes, that's what I have been trying to say," Fredericks
interjected, a thin smile eclipsing his face as he saw that he was
about to get what he wanted. "We should worry more about
the man who is spreading the virus, than about the virus itself."

"Not so fast," the Chief interrupted, reversing his earlier
stance. "What if this virus—this bug, as you call it—is
contagious? Or worse?"

"What could be worse than it being contagious?" Fredericks

objected, his horned-rim glasses slipping down the slope of his nose.

"Like I told you before, the Overlord's bug was designed to be a weapon," Nate rejoined. "A genetic holocaust, actually."

"All the more reason why we must draw this scoundrel out in the open," Fredericks insisted, struggling to regain control of the conversation. "Countless lives may be at stake," the FBI agent emphasized.

"But only one of them is important to me, you bastard!" Nate swore, his arms outstretched as if he might assault the man.

Cringing at the outburst, Munson stepped back, wishing to avoid the inevitable confrontation.

"Be that as it may, there's no other way," Fredericks advised, pulling away from Matthews' iron grip. His words hung in the air like stale meat.

Scowling, Nate took a deep breath, then stomped into the next room where Musette sat quietly, her head in her hands. He looked at her, touched her hair, then spoke.

"Musette? Honey? Have you ever gone fishing before?" he inquired, doing his best to find a way to explain this to her without bringing on a rush of tears.

"Fishing? No, I never have," she answered dejectedly. "Are we leaving town after all? To go fishing?" she responded, suddenly turning hopeful. "I can be packed in fifteen minutes," she bubbled excitedly, rising from her chair, ready to go.

"Well, no, not exactly," Nate sputtered hesitantly, unsure how to explain their intentions. "Agent Fredericks wants us to go fishing right here," he detailed as he completed the analogy. "And he wants you to be the bait."

"Bait?" Her innocent eyes blinked, revealing her fear. "Isn't there any other way?" she pleaded, the tears streaming down her cheek.

"Fredericks says we need to draw the butcher out into the open. Fredericks says we need to capture him alive, if at all possible."

"Which means what?" she cross-examined, preparing herself for the answer.

"Which means that Munson will dismiss the guards posted outside, and we will sit and wait."

"Wait?" she blubbered. "Wait for what? Wait until the house is broken into? Wait until we are *murdered*?"

"Perhaps," he replied unsympathetically.

"Are you crazy?" she screamed incoherently.

"Vengeance always embraces a certain degree of insanity," he answered without elaboration.

Knocked out cold by the impact of the crash—his face and hands caked with the blood of his former captor—Flix lay there stunned on the seat for a long time. The inflated airbag had kept the car's steering column from piercing his chest, and the safety harness had kept his head from punching through the windshield; nevertheless, in keeping with a trauma-avoidance scheme Mother Nature had spent a million years perfecting, Flix had passed out. By automatically shutting down all but the most essential internal functions until such time as the danger had passed, his body had succumbed to evolution's programmed response during times of crisis. It was a condition know to medics as shock. And, as any Boy Scout manual would correctly point out, the standard first aid treatment for shock would be to "lower the head and raise the tail," a procedure intended to assure that an adequate supply of blood was kept flowing to the brain. Unfortunately, strapped upright in the seat as he was, and pinned behind the cushiony expanse of the airbag, the recommended head-down positioning was just not to be had. As a consequence, consciousness returned slowly, and it took former pyrotech specialist, General "Flix" Wenger a long while to clear his mind.

Confused by the white pillow obstructing his field of vision, he thought for a moment that he had died and gone to heaven. In his heart, though, he knew that given all the bad things he had done in his life, heaven wasn't in the cards for him. Not until the pain of his throbbing head made itself known did he fully recognize where he actually was.

Unclasping the safety belt from around his body, Flix fell from the gcar and onto the damp ground. Shocked back to reality by the smell of petrol and the high beam of an oncoming vehicle, he began to reconstruct exactly what he had done. Staggering to the rear of the gcar, he pried open the crumbled trunk and recovered his cane from the luggage bin. Though he couldn't be sure just how far it was back to Farmington, he knew that he had no choice but to return there as swiftly as possible. Confident that with as much hiking as he had done over the years, his old legs were still in good enough shape to make the trek, Flix set off in the dark, every joint in his ancient body wracked with pain. In some ways, it was not unlike the desperate journey he had made across the desert so many years ago as a young man. Only now the stakes were much, much higher.

36

PASSION

"Goodness gracious!" Musette exclaimed. "What in the world does *that* mean?" she demanded, making reference to his remark embracing vengeance and insanity. Even in her anger, she could see the pain in his eyes.

"I guess all I'm trying to say is this: for Mao, the game isn't over yet," Nate murmured as he tensely fingered the Luger which Flix had entrusted to him before this bad dream first began.

"We're next," Nate asserted matter-of-factly as he nervously popped the magazine in and out of the Luger's stock under the disapproving eye of Chief Munson. "And there isn't a damn thing I can do to change that."

Stung by his callousness, Musette slapped him hard across the face, then turned and ran upstairs. Feeling completely alone in the world, she flung herself on her bed and began crying her eyes out.

"Go to her," the Chief advised, having quietly witnessed the exchange.

Reluctantly acknowledging Munson's directive with a nod, Nate deposited the Luger on the end table next to Musette's long sofa and timidly followed the sounds of her sobbing up to the next floor. As he climbed the stairs to her bedroom wearing his heart on his sleeve, Nate heard Agent Fredericks excuse himself for the night and leave the house by way of the front door. Moments later, as the dejected Senator stood in the hallway outside her room, a clock somewhere on the lower level chimed 8 p.m.

Confronted at her doorway by a new explosion of tears, Nate struggled to find a way to take back his thoughtless words, but before he could even utter a sound, she started in on him.

"Do you have to be so God-awful blunt when you speak about death?" she blubbered from her bed. "This isn't a game to me; this is my life we're talking about. You sound as if you could care less whether I live or whether I die!" she yelled, what little makeup she wore streaming down her cheeks.

"That's just not true," he objected strenuously, feeling wretched inside. It had not been his intention to be mean or insensitive to her; it had just come out that way. Musette was the best thing to happen to him since Darna had died, and he wasn't about to lose her on account of his own bullheaded stupidity.

Crossing the threshold into her room, Nate apologized, "I am truly sorry, Musette. You know perfectly well that I cannot possibly live without you. I need you, and when this is over, I want you to consider being mine on a permanent basis."

"Permanently?" she warbled, taken aback by his suggestion. "Is this a proposal of marriage? Is that what you are trying to say?"

"Yes, I guess that's what I'm trying to say," he admitted, pinching himself to be sure he was awake before sitting down on the bed next to her. Pressing her hand against his as he dried her tears with his sleeve, her dark hair splashed against his arm.

"Oh, Nate, you are the most wonderful man I have ever met," she bubbled excitedly. "Nothing I can think of would make me happier," she confessed passionately, "but have you considered Frankie's feelings in all this?"

"Geez, Musette, what in the world does Franklin have to do with it?" he cross-examined, unsure what to make of her.

"How can I possibly be the boy's mother if he doesn't like

me?" she lamented.

"What makes you think he doesn't like you? Did he say something nasty while I was gone?" Nate challenged, ready to scold his boy for being a smart-aleck again.

"I can see it in his eyes," Musette pointed out dolefully.

"Oh, don't be silly! Frankie likes you well enough, only he hasn't gotten over the loss of his own mother yet. Heck, it's only been a couple of months," he explained. "I promise you, in time, we'll work it out."

"And how about you?" Musette probed. "Have *you* gotten over Darna's death? As you said, it's only been a couple of months."

"No, I haven't gotten completely over her yet," he reluctantly admitted, "but I'm doing my best. None of which means I'm not serious about wanting you."

Reflecting fondly on the first time the two of them had been together, Nate leaned over and kissed her wet and willing lips. Trying to be a gentleman on that occasion he had held back, but considering what had happened to them since, and what might happen to them yet, it seemed as if those had been two other people, two other souls. Though he couldn't deny wanting to be intimate with her now, he dismissed the rush of lustful thoughts as being out of place. Unfortunately, his libido got the best of him, and as he sat there contemplating the firmness of her bed, his eyes fell upon the fullness of her breasts. Fantasizing that she was but a willing nymph put on this earth solely for his pleasure, he slowly undressed her in his mind even as he cupped her magnificent breasts in his athletic hands. In his imagination, he sighed how wonderful she looked naked and how delicious she smelled. But upon hearing the footfalls of Chief Munson pacing back and forth on the floor beneath them, Nate was snapped rudely out of his steamy daydream.

"It seems warm in here," he murmured, shifting his gaze toward the window and away from her.

But reading Nate's thoughts, she leered naughtily at him from across the bed. "Ignore him," she suggested in obvious reference to their chaperone downstairs.

Even as she spoke, she slowly unbuttoned the top clasp of her delicate chemise exposing the creamy white skin of her neck. When she reached out and touched his thigh provocatively, he gave a start, trembling uncontrollably as an overwrought teenager might.

Caressing her face with both his hands, he found her quivering cheeks to be hot with passion. Grabbing her firmly by the shoulders, he kissed her as if he would never have the opportunity to do so again. She responded by pulling him on top of her as they both sank onto the mattress.

Sucking playfully on his ear even as she disengaged herself from his arms, she rose to close her bedroom door. Flipping on the radio to cover the sounds of their lovemaking, she returned to his side, her body scented with the aroma of a woman in heat. Egging him on, she said, "Take me now, and for many years to come." Unable to resist her lustful advances any longer, he put up no further resistance.

Downstairs, Munson heard the click of the door as it swung shut. Smiling to himself, he reclined on the long sofa to begin a well-deserved and overdue nap.

The first mile of his journey back into town was probably the toughest. His legs hurt, his back was sore, his head was throbbing, even his insides were in pain. Flix was wet and he was cold, and to add insult to injury, every now and again a passing gcar would splash muddy rainwater up on him from one of the puddles leftover from yesterday's storm.

As he lumbered along the highway, leaning heavily on his cane, Flix reckoned that whoever was behind the killings in Farmington was not about to break it off until they had finished their grisly business. Figuring that Overlord Mao was out to ruin Nate for his role in supporting Whetstone's policies, Flix wondered what the impact on Nate would be if his girlfriend were now harmed so closely on the heels of his wife's death. He also questioned whether the humiliation and the embarrassment of the Senator's association with a wanted felon like himself might not be enough to force an ignoble end to Nate's political career. Without ever meaning to, Flix had compounded Nate's difficulties immeasurably, and between the strain of the two events, Matthews might find it easier to resign his Senate seat than face the challenge of explaining his actions to a disbelieving public. Such a resignation would almost certainly even the score for Mao, and considering what had gone down between him and Silas, it might satisfy Whetstone's corrupt objectives as well. Clenching his fist in determination, Flix decided that no matter what it cost him personally, he had to prevent this from happening. For an instant, he even debated whether the two men—Mao and Silas—might not be working together somehow to discredit both him and Nate. Was there perhaps some sort of double cover up, or was Flix still in shock from the accident and just imagining the whole thing?

As he trundled along the side of the road under the watchful eye of the moon, Flix's worried mind was shrouded in doubt. He wondered whether Nate had paid any attention at all to the lessons he had tried so very hard to teach him, lessons in self-defense and lessons in common sense. Fearing for the safety of his protégé, Flix replayed the events of the last few months over and over again in his mind.

"I need you," the newly-elected Senator had exclaimed. "I am in desperate need of a seasoned adviser."

"I guess all I *really* want to know," the Vice President had insisted, "is can he be trusted?"

"To achieve the desired effect, it must be a public assassination—a very public assassination," Flix had spelled out for Whetstone in their meeting.

"Why would a luscious young thing like yourself be interested in an old duffer like me?" he had asked the blond bombshell, too naive to recognize that he was being had.

"Let me ask you something, young Matthews," the retired General had challenged. "Do you know what America is actually all about?"

"And is the Congressman expecting you?" the uniformed

man at the gate to the medical center had asked.

"Sooner or later they'll come looking for me," he had explained to the Senator, "and when they do, the only thing which will keep me among the living is that book. Hide the damn thing somewhere, and don't tell me—or anyone else—where you've hidden it."

"On one condition," Nate had bargained.

"Name it," Flix had answered without faltering.

"You must agree to testify against him even if it means going to jail."

"On one condition," Flix repeated, the words echoing deep within his brain.

"You must agree to testify against him."

As yet another gcar drenched him with a splash of cold, dirty water, Flix picked up his pace, his objective clearer than ever before.

37

WORDS

Evening became night, and the moon shone through the bedroom window casting a ribbon of light across the pair of motionless forms nestled closely together beneath the sheets. Their hurried bout of passion having quickly run its heated course, the two animated lovers had collapsed into an exhausted sleep unaware of the tragedy being played out one floor below them. After a time, one of the figures stirred, opened his eyes, and sighed contentedly, his moonlit body throwing an eerie shadow against the wall behind him. Studying the contours of his companion's tranquil form by the light of the moon, he silently climbed from the bed, showered, and dressed.

When he arrived at the head of the stairs, the house lights were extinguished and the place was inexplicably quiet. Though he wasn't frightened by the darkness, the absence of any sounds was alarming. Even the roll of the Chief's snoring would have been reassuring. Instead, his heart sank as he recognized that the drama was about to resume. When an involuntary chill ran down the length of his spine, Nate trembled at the thought of what might have happened while he had been upstairs in bed with Musette.

Not knowing where the wall switch was, and not wanting to wake the Chief from his slumber, Matthews guided himself hesitantly down the darkened flight of stairs. As he reached the bottom rung of the staircase, he made every effort to visualize where he had left his two weapons earlier in the day. Thinking back, he remembered placing the rifle on the mantelpiece where it would be easily accessible, but, for the moment, he couldn't reconstruct where he had stashed the Luger.

Realizing that he was an inviting target standing there out in the open, he racked his brains to recall the precautions Flix had taught him in their evening sessions last winter, precautions he should observe if he was ever threatened by an intruder.

"Get down!" Flix's words shouted back at him from the darkness.

Hugging the wall as he had been taught, Nate crouched low against the floor.

"Survey the situation!" Flix ordered from across the miles, his military training revealing itself.

With his heart pumping like mad deep within his chest, Nate studied the front room. Though it wasn't completely pitch-black, the irregular shadows played terrible tricks on his inexperienced eyes.

"Get a weapon! Protect yourself!" Flix urged as if he were standing right there next to him guiding his every move.

Searching the darkness for a familiar landmark, Nate wondered whether he could make it to the fireplace to grab hold of the long-barreled rifle he had left sitting there.

The room's stillness was disturbed only by the muffled sound of his own shallow breathing. Rising cautiously to his feet, Nate warily crossed the floor to the center of the room, then edged swiftly along the back side of the long couch. It was situated to the left of, and perpendicular to, the fireplace.

"If you must move, move quickly," Flix instructed him.

Certain that no furniture lay between the far end of the sofa and the nearest corner of the hearth, Nate eschewed all caution and strode purposefully toward the mantle. In his haste, he was caught off-balance when his foot unexpectedly struck a large, unseen object laid out upon the floor. Stumbling over it, he slammed his head brutally against the rough, brick facade of the fireplace. Blood oozed from the nasty gash.

Afraid he would pass out from the stabbing pain, Nate fought bravely to remain alert. In spite of being dazed and bloodied by the fall, and in spite of being unable to see the corpse's features, he was certain that he had tripped over the Chief's body. The realization made him hot with anger, and he didn't need Flix's prodding to remind him that there wasn't any time to shed the tear he felt for his good friend; that now every second might count. Operating suddenly on pure animal instinct, Nate bolted upright and grabbed for the Winchester rifle.

But it wasn't there!

In a frenzied panic he searched the mantelpiece, knocking over one of Musette's favorite porcelain dishes in the process. "Damn!" he swore out loud upon hearing it crash against the hardwood floor and shatter into a hundred pieces.

Realizing that his weapon had been intentionally moved, fear gripped at his bowels. But just as he was about to make a wild, desperate dash back up the stairs to where Musette lay sleeping, Nate sensed another presence in the sitting-room with him. He was no longer alone!

A distressingly familiar voice hissed out of the night at him. "Who is there?" it asked, though it already knew the answer.

His mind swirling, Nate refused to reply.

"Is that you, Matthews?" Fredericks probed from somewhere on the other side of the darkened room.

Doing his best to eliminate the dread from his voice before answering, Nate replied, "Yes, Fredericks, it's me. Why are all the house lights out? Why are you sitting here in the dark?"

"It's nighttime," the FBI man declared menacingly. "What are *you* doing down here? And what, may I ask, are you doing over there by the fireplace?" Chuckling lightly in that arrogant tone of his, he added, "Looking for something?"

Ignoring the obvious taunt, Nate redirected, "How long have you been down here?"

"Actually, I never left," Fredericks droned cockily. "I just waited outside on the veranda until things quieted down in here, then I took him."

At least twenty feet separated the two men, yet Nate could feel the footfalls as Agent Fredericks edged furtively closer.

"What time is it now?" Nate inquired of the figure somewhere in the darkness in front of him.

"Around 10 p.m., I believe, but I wouldn't let that worry you too much—as far as you are concerned, it's time to die."

Despite his throbbing head wound, Matthews strained to concentrate. Hoping to sidetrack his opponent, he questioned, "Is there a light switch on the wall there behind you?"

"Farmington has ten streets, you know," Fredericks rejoined ominously, leaving the lights extinguished.

"What did you do to the Chief?" Nate queried, although he had already guessed the sad truth.

"It was my fondest hope to murder one person for each street," Fredericks replied insanely, "but you messed that up for me."

"Where's my rifle?" Nate quizzed, but he didn't wait for the madman's answer. Flinging himself over Munson's motionless form, he landed unceremoniously on the hardwood floor behind the oversized couch. Jarred noticeably by the impact, his jagged gash opened further, sending a confused fog rolling through his battered head.

Shaking off the haze, Matthews began frantically frisking Munson's inert body for the unloaded police revolver the law enforcement officer always carried. Even as Nate struggled to roll the heavy man over, he tore at the dead man's clothing, praying that the Chief still toted a box of shells in his button-down pocket.

Fredericks' steps drew nearer.

In his haste, Nate ripped the buttons from Munson's shirt; they splattered noisily against the floor. He heard Fredericks scramble for position along the opposite wall. Propelled by fear, a megadose of adrenaline rocketed through Nate's system, triggering his "fight or flight" reflex.

Desperate now, he jammed a round into the Chief's Smith

& Wesson; then another; and then another. Clicking the chamber shut, Nate held his breath, waiting for his adversary's next move.

The wait was short-lived. Within moments, Fredericks discharged his gun in Nate's direction. But handicapped by a darkness of his own making, the Federal agent missed his target, the bullet from his FBI revolver slamming harmlessly into the arm of Musette's couch.

Between the glint of the revolver's steel barrel and the report of its silencer-muffled blast, Nate was given the opportunity he needed to hone in on his opponent's position. Focusing his attention on that exact spot, he pulled the trigger of the Chief's .357 Magnum twice in rapid succession. The recoil of the powerful piece threw him stumbling backwards half a step.

Then, as Fredericks returned his volley from across the dimly-lit room, there was an explosion of sound and a flash of light.

Catching a glimpse of the man's spectacles, Nate fired again. Only this time, he must have struck home. Holding his breath so as not to give away his position, Nate heard a pair of dull thuds as Agent Fredericks staggered back, first against the wall, and then against the floor.

"Got you, you bastard," Nate swore triumphantly as he scrambled to his feet.

38

CONFUSION

By this time, the roar of the gunshots on the lower level had awakened Musette from an otherwise peaceful post-coital nap. Blissfully unaware of the circumstances which awaited her in the front room, she was still scantily dressed and half asleep when she reached the top of the stairs. Groggily flipping on the downstairs light, she was greeted by an appalling, gut-wrenching scene.

Directly in front of her at the bottom of the stairs lay Fredericks, his blood splattered across her beautiful hardwood floor and onto the wall behind him; cradled in his stilled right hand, its silencer still smoking, was his automatic; next to him lay Nate's Winchester. Laying behind the couch in a dark pool of crimson, his shirt torn asunder, and his leg folded up beneath him in a queer, unnatural fashion, was Chief Munson. And hovering over the Chief, his busy hands fumbling to reload his weapon, stood Nate. But not until she heard him groan and saw him lean heavily against the sofa, did she realize that he too had been shot!

Frozen in place by the horrible truth, she wanted to scream, but no sounds emanated from her constricted throat. The smell of death which adorned her front room was so fresh, it was incomprehensible. Staring blankly at the blood dripping from Nate's gouged forehead and at the widening rose-colored stain on his white shirt, she clasped her hand over her open mouth confused as to what she should do next. With no inkling that Agent Fredericks was the one responsible for unleashing this bloody nightmare in her house, she logically reasoned that the actual perpetrator was still lurking nearby, ready to pounce on her and on Nate at any moment. Torn between rushing to Nate's side or retreating to the safety of her room upstairs, she debated who she could call for help. With the Chief already dead, and the FBI man seemingly so, she decided that Nate was her only hope against the unseen assailant, and that darkness was their only ally.

Taking a quick mental picture of the location of Fredericks' body at the foot of the steps and of Nate's crouched figure by the fireplace, Musette flipped the house lights off once more, then darted swiftly down the flight of stairs. In an instant, she was at her lover's side.

"It's...all...over," he mumbled deliriously, his speech slurred by the shock of the bullet wound. "Fredericks is dead."

"Are you nuts?" she whispered angrily, trying to shush him. "The killer is still loose somewhere in the house."

When he started to object, she instructed, "Get down, Nate, and for God's-sakes, be quiet. By the way," she whispered urgently, "have you reloaded your gun yet?"

Even as he resisted her attempts to wrestle him to the floor, he grunted a weak, "Yes."

"Damnit woman," he declared with all his strength. "Let go of me! It is over! Fredericks was the murderer, but I killed him first," he grimaced as he clenched his battered shoulder with his free hand. "Only now I need a medic. Be a dear, won't you, and call Doc Simpson for me?"

As his meaning sunk into her bewildered head, Musette sprang into action, dashing first for the light switch, and then for the comm.

Even as she encoded the three digit emergency number for the hospital, a voice behind her boomed, "Put it down!"

Thinking that Nate was out of his head as a result of his gunshot injury, she didn't turn around to argue with him; she concentrated instead on putting the call through to the medics as quickly as possible. While it occurred to her that his intonation had sounded strange, with her back to the room, she didn't give it a second thought.

"Put it *down*!" the man ordered again, more fiercely than before.

On hearing the voice for a second time, she realized that the person shouting at her wasn't Nate after all. A shiver ran down her spine as she slowly turned to face the stranger, the comm still in her hand. As she stopped short, her naked body barely concealed beneath the cover of her flimsy underthings, she couldn't believe her eyes— Fredericks was standing over them snickering! Although he had been bloodied by one of Nate's bullets, evidently the wound hadn't been lethal. Clutched in his arm was the rifle he had snatched from the mantelpiece earlier, the same one she had seen laying next to him when she stood at the top of the staircase minutes ago. In his hand was Flix's Luger, its cold, dark metal suddenly looking very ominous.

Stunned by this awesome turn of events, Nate's mind raced as he silently debated how to regain the advantage. Considering that his blood-covered right hand clenched his bullet-mangled left shoulder, even as his pain-numbed left hand hung uselessly at his side, the odds for success appeared long. Nevertheless, there was one possibility. In that clammy, almost lame left hand—a hand hidden from sight by the fabric-covered arm of the sofa—he felt the pleasantly cold steel of Munson's revolver. Nate had had just enough time to reload it before the bogus FBI man had come to.

Confident that Fredericks could not see the Smith & Wesson from where he stood, Nate took a deep breath. Searching his inner self for the reserve of strength he needed to see this thing through to the end, he gritted his teeth. Even though the gash on his forehead smarted, he did his best to mount a feeble grin as he spoke.

"I take it you're not with the FBI," Nate began, bargaining for time.

"No, no, I'm afraid that you are wrong," the thin man

responded mischievously. "I *am* with the Bureau. How do you think I got this swell bullet-proof vest?"

Tearing open his shirt for both Musette and Nate to see, Fredericks revealed a dull-colored Stromberg vest. It was top of the line and had two good-sized dents in the kevlar where Nate had shot him. Seeing the indentations, the Senator flashed a weak smile—he knew that even in the dark there had been no way he had missed hitting the FBI agent. Considering the stopping power of Munson's revolver, and considering the narrowness of the range between the two men, the impact of the shells against the impervious vest had apparently rendered Fredericks temporarily unconscious. Regrettably, the two pointblank impacts hadn't done any permanent damage. Nate's final shot, however—the one which accounted for all the blood spewed around the room—had struck him below the lip of the protective vest in the meaty portion of the thigh.

"But being in the FBI is just a cover for something much more sinister, isn't it?" Nate cross-examined, still pressing for time. While he spoke, the Senator shifted his enfeebled left hand just enough to twist the orientation of the heavy gun he was gripping. "Do you work for a mob boss?" Nate probed, hoping to keep the man talking a while longer.

"No, wrong again," Fredericks scoffed. "I'm a military scientist by trade. A mercenary. I design nasty little viruses and dandy biowarfare weapons for a living."

"But why develop such beasts?" Nate interrogated, needing to stall for just a bit more time. "What good can it possibly serve?"

"*Good?*" he spat contemptuously. "Microbes are weapons, my dimwitted friend, weapons. An efficient means for killing a great many people cheaply and without great risk to one's own armies. I once thought as you do; I too once worked for Uncle Sam at the Fort Detrick arsenal; now I freelance. These bugs, as you called them, were originally intended to be used in times of war by the United States against her enemies, only…"

"But what do *you* want with these nefarious germs?" Nate

questioned as he lifted his right hand off of his blood-caked left shoulder. Even as he did so, he stole a sideways glance at Musette. She remained frozen in her corner of the room looking pathetically vulnerable.

"You're not real bright, are you Senator?" ridiculed Fredericks indignantly.

"I guess not," Nate reluctantly agreed, wishing Flix was here to help him out of this mess.

"The government I represent now is blackmailing your pitiful United States of America with these little microbes I've perfected. If my bosses don't have what they want by the end of the week, we will unleash a plague of biblical proportions upon your fair land."

"A plague?" Musette cried out, not seeing Nate's right hand move ever so slightly.

"Not a plague actually; more like an epidemic," Fredericks detailed, seeming awfully proud of himself. "At this very moment and in this very town, my bio-team is incubating billions upon billions of these viruses in thousands of specially treated petri dishes. When I give the word, they will be distributed to hundreds of pre-selected locations all across the country. After being in place for thirty-six hours, the viruses will become active and then the Overlord will have his vengeance upon you," Fredericks elaborated, smiling narrowly. "Indeed, I am told he intends to be here personally for the final act."

"I smelled his foul hand in this from the start," Nate admitted, "but why the melodrama with the package to Munson and the photographs and the tainted surveys and all that? In what possible way could killing these ten people advance Mao's blackmailing scheme?" Nate asked angrily, his blood boiling with rage. "These murders serve no purpose, damnit!"

"Au contraire, mon ami, they serve a very important purpose: Mao wants to embarrass and discredit you. He wants you, your friends, your town, and your reputation to suffer. As for how I chose the ten victims, I can assure you that, except for *your* little tart here," he mocked, pointing in Musette's direction, "all the choices were entirely random; as I said before, one faceless stranger per street. All we're after are the islands of Hawaii."

"You're insane," Nate muttered under his breath.

"Hang up the comm, dearie," Fredericks ordered, leveling Flix's Luger at Musette even as he holstered his own piece. "It's time for you to die, sweetheart; my viral monsters impatiently await my return."

"You bastard!" Nate spat. "Leave her out of this."

"Oh no, I'm not a bad fellow at all," Fredericks smirked. "Didn't I allow you sufficient time to finish screwing her while I politely sat down here and waited? I didn't want her to die unfulfilled, you know."

Dropping the comm noisily to the floor, Musette began sobbing uncontrollably. The sound of her moans catapulted Nate into action.

Ignoring the intense pain radiating from his shoulder, Nate swiftly passed the loaded gun from his impotent left hand to his lethal right one. Mindful of Fredericks' unstoppable Stromberg vest, he took deliberate aim at the man's beady little head and calmly squeezed off a single round just like Flix had taught him at the shooting range.

Although only an instant elapsed before Nate's bullet punched a nasty looking hole in the thin man's cranium, he was too slow by a factor of ten. There was nothing Nate could do to prevent the tragedy from happening. By the time the Senator had taken the FBI man out, Musette had already crumbled to the floor in a ragged heap of nightie and blood. Shattering Nate's dreams for the future, the echo of Agent Fredericks' shot reverberated throughout the house. He dashed to her side without delay; however, she seemed all but gone already.

"Stop him, my love," she pleaded haltingly. "Stop him ..."

For an exhausted man who was soaked to the skin, the lights of the town seemed reassuring and close at hand. Flix had been making steady progress for nearly three hours now and aside from being hungry and looking like hell, he was none the worse for the wear. Knowing that Whetstone had to be stopped and knowing that only *his* testimony could accomplish that, Flix had pushed on through the night despite formidable odds. Twice he had even turned down offers of a ride so he wouldn't have to answer nosy questions as to why an old man in his condition happened to be walking alongside the road at this hour.

Though Flix could not possibly have had any idea what Nate was up against at this very moment, he did know that Overlord Mao was behind the whole murderous scheme. And even if Mao and Whetstone weren't in cahoots as he had earlier suspected, they were each dangerous parasites gnawing at the fabric of humanity. Like common roaches they deserved to be stomped out, and only he could manage their extermination.

As Flix reached the outskirts of Farmington, grateful for having survived the ordeal, he heard the wail of an emergency vehicle racing across town. A sixth sense told him that there was trouble afoot and that he had better find out from Chief Munson what was going on. Heading for the nearest public comm, Flix tried to call the Chief at the station, but there was no answer. Figuring it was too late for anyone to be still manning the comms, he next tried to reach Nate at Musettes's house. All he got was a busy signal. Frustrated at finding the comm off the hook, he decided to ring up his old friend, Tiger Matthews. Considering the dead body stretched out in Nate's foyer, Flix didn't want Frankie returning home from his grandfather's place in the morning and discovering Duncan's body lying there in a hardened pool of blood. Curiously, there wasn't any answer there either.

39

LOCUST

By the time the haggard-looking Senator had reached the ambulance company on the comm, Musette's face was white and her body had gone limp in his arms. Though Nate was admittedly no medic, he had learned enough first aid in his life to take someone's pulse and to wrap a nasty cut, and he promptly put both those skills to work. Pressing his first two fingers against her wrist, he made the horrible discovery that her pulse was too weak for him to feel. Even so, not wanting to give up hope completely, he began applying direct pressure to the wound, hoping to staunch the flow of blood with his palm. Fearing the emergency vehicle would not get there in time, his eyes filled with tears, and for a very few long seconds, he knelt there beside her, his body shaking with rage.

Within moments, though, the wail of the approaching siren snapped him out of his trance. Although he was heartened by the sound of the oncoming rescue team, it occurred to him that he could not remain there in the house waiting until the emergency vehicle arrived at her doorstep. For starters, the medics would undoubtedly take one look at the him, and once they saw the seriousness of his wounds, demand that he be admitted to the hospital for treatment. And that would probably just be the beginning of his troubles! Inasmuch as he was bound to be considered the prime suspect in no less than two unexplained murders, once the doctors released him, the police would more than likely hold him over without bond until they could sort things out. Either way—if he got detained in the hospital or if he got detained in jail—the results would be the same, which is to say, disastrous! If he didn't get straight to work ferreting out the location of Fredericks' secret laboratory, it would mean that the Overlord's biological blackmail of America could continue unchallenged. *That* musn't be allowed to happen!

All of this and more roared through Nate's head in the disheveled moments after he first heard the sounds of the approaching medic-van. Deciding that the worrisome petri dishes had to be found and destroyed, and that he had to be the one to do it before they could be set out to infect the population, Nate tightened Musette's makeshift bandage in place, kissed her clammy cheek good-bye, and staggered weakly outside into the shadows by way of the back door. The moon was high in the sky, its brightness cheering the cursed night.

Gazing up at the heavens, he stared glumly at the stars. Believing Musette was all but lost, grief scrambled his brains, preventing him from thinking in an orderly fashion. Wondering what kind of God could take, first his wife from him, then his lover, he shook his fist angrily at the moon. "What do you *want* from me?" he screamed at the edge of hysteria. "How much pain must one man be expected to stand? Is there to be no justice?" he demanded, wandering aimlessly out of Musette's back yard even as he strained to recollect bits and pieces of his discussion with the assassin.

"How had Fredericks put it?" he mumbled to himself out loud. "'My viral monsters impatiently await my return' ... Geez, what does that mean?" he petitioned the omniscient sky.

Crossing the street at the next corner, Nate answered his own question. "That must mean they are close by," he decided as he replayed more and more of their final conversation through his blurred mind. "'At this very moment and in this very town...'"

"...in this very town..."

Even as the ominous words lingered on the edge of Nate's

tongue, the logical, right-half of his brain began running the names of Farmington's ten streets through the fogged-over left-half.

The right-half started down the list. "Pine, Oak, Elm, Locust, Maple, Main, Birch…"

"No! Back up," the left side interrupted abruptly. "What was that last one?"

"Birch," the logical side replied.

"No, you idiot, *before* that," the impetuous half chided.

"Maple? Main?"

"Before that."

"Locust?"

"Yes, Locust."

"As in a *plague* of locusts?" the sensible half reasoned, remembering how Fredericks had used precisely that word.

"Naw, you jerk, that's too simple. It can't be."

A moment later he had changed his mind. "It *has* to be!" the right-half exclaimed.

"But there are *dozens* of homes along Locust," the left side bellyached. "It could be any *one* of them. Couldn't we just sit down and rest for a while?" it sniveled pathetically. "I'm getting kinda tired."

"No!" the voice of authority boomed. "We have to figure this out! We have to figure out which home it is."

Before long Nate found himself stumbling along the sidewalk on the north side of Locust Street. He had no idea what it was he was looking for. A clue, perhaps. A suspicious-looking truck, maybe. Something. Anything.

It was very late, his shoulder was throbbing, he had lost a lot of blood, and his mind was numb with grief. He had heard the scream of the siren as the ambulance had run up Main Street from the medical center and toward Musette's house two blocks over. The shrill whine had triggered an unwanted flood of tangled images. Time and time again, her ashen face glared up at him, blaming him, hating him. Finally, exhausted by the labor, he sat down on the curb, shut his eyes to blot out the pain, and was instantly asleep.

But the torment didn't stop with the closing of his eyes. Over and over again in his dreams he revisited the anguished scene in her front room, torturing himself each time over the outcome.

"You were too slow," the left side snarled in an accusatory fashion. "Too goddamned slow!"

"The Chief was already dead," the logical half retorted, trying to defend himself against the allegation. "What could I do?"

"Musette is dead, you dolt!"

"Granted, but so is Fredericks."

Then other images started crowding in on their exchange: Franklin has been arrested. Each victim literally drowned to death in his own mucous. You think the Overlord is *bluffing*? If you don't offer him an honorable way to back down, Mao is liable to take his anger out on me personally. Musette, oh sweet Musette. Ten photographs. Petri dishes. You broke into the *Sanders*' place? She hasn't a pulse. Lab coats. Munson keeps bullets in his pocket. Horn-rimmed glasses. Test tubes.

Shivering, Nate jerked suddenly awake. Though he hadn't been out long—the bright moon was still overhead—it had been just long enough for him to become drenched in a disquieting bath of sweat and nighttime dew. More importantly, it had been long enough for his subconscious to ferret out the solution to his problem.

In his disheveled nightmare, Nate had remembered the men in the lab coats, the men his son Franklin had told him about. Last Friday, on the way home from school, Frankie had literally run into a man wearing a white laboratory coat, a man lugging a heavy box of test tubes in his arms. At the time, Franklin had decided that the authoritative looking fellow was a part of the EPA's water-survey team, but now Nate knew better. His son had run into *Fredericks* that day! Only a scientist could properly ready the germ cultures for distribution, nurturing the lethal viruses to maturity, and only a scientist would have the audacity to think of using such a plague as a weapon. Fredericks was that scientist!

With a sudden burst of newfound energy, Nate jumped to his feet. Now he knew *precisely* which residence he was searching for—the house next to the one his son had broken into! It was one of those gothic, rural-style homes with a porch out in front like his own, plus several ground-level windows servicing the basement. His objective clearly in mind, Nate started moving in that direction as quickly as his unsteady legs would carry him.

40

POWER

As he surreptitiously approached the wood-frame, farm-style house, Nate could see that the basement lights were aglow as if someone were hard at work downstairs. Considering what time it was, he found it curious that anyone should be up and about so late at night. But remembering what Frankie had told him about the evening he broke into the Sanders' place next door, Nate decided to investigate. Edging his pain-wracked body along the bushes lining the foundation, Nate flattened himself against the wet ground and peered into the cellar through one of the undersized casement windows.

Although he couldn't observe the entire room from where he was crouched, the far wall was stacked from floor to ceiling with what appeared to be dozens upon dozens of tiny microwave-ovens. On first blush this discovery made absolutely no sense to him, until he recognized that the box-like appliances weren't microwave-ovens at all, but rather the incubators Fredericks had spoken so fondly of. Figuring that these incubators were programmed to maintain the dormant viruses at just the right temperature until it was time to unleash their horror upon an unsuspecting populace, a plan began to take shape in the Senator's mind. Although he didn't know a great deal about biology or about genetics, common sense dictated that if he could alter the temperature settings on the brooding ovens, he could either freeze the cultures—or fry them. The only problem was: How to reach the knobs?

Not only were the basement windows far too narrow for a man of his size to easily pass through, upon silently testing the front and back doors to the house, he found them bolted shut. Worse yet, even an amateur could tell that both the doors and the windows had been alarmed, and in his agitated state he imagined that a contingent of unseen guards lurked inside, waiting to pounce on him if he entered the premises. Stymied as to how to proceed, Nate didn't know what to do until it occurred to him that he didn't have to actually break *into* the house to lower the temperature settings on the incubators. All he had to do was *shut off the power*!

Plotting out a strategy in his head, his eyes traced the route of the power line from the utility pole at the corner of the lot, across the moonlit backyard to the far wall of the house, and then down along the wall where it fed into a circuit-breaker box hanging about five feet above the ground. Although he had never considered himself much of a handyman, his dad had taught him enough about home repair for him to know that for each electrical circuit inside an older home like this, there was a disk-shaped fuse lodged in the junction box hanging on the outside wall. All he had to do was select the right one and unscrew it.

Visualizing the solution to his problem as he strode across the lawn in the direction of the circuit-breaker, Nate quietly reasoned, "No fuse, no power...no power, no incubators...no incubators, no viruses!"

Throwing just enough light over his shoulder for him to work, the moon watched as he quickly defused the box. Deciding to leave nothing to chance, once Nate had pulled all the fuses, he smashed them with a rock one by one. Then, retreating to the safety of the bushes, he waited in trepidation for a siren or an alarm to announce the interruption of power.

As he sat there shivering in the damp night air, expecting a guard to come charging from the house at any minute, his guns blazing, Nate contemplated how he would defend himself without a weapon. But when nothing happened, he assumed that the terrible ordeal was over, and that he had won.

After a few more moments of reflection, however, the painful truth reasserted itself—not only had he *not* won, he still had a score to settle with Overlord Mao. Indeed, it wasn't long before a fit of rage had taken possession of both sides of his brain.

"Who is going to pay for all the senseless killings?" he bayed at the moon like an animal. "First my wife, then my friend Munson, now my woman—the murdering bastard must be forced to square accounts with *me*!" he howled, his voice cracking. "Fredericks was just a hired hand; it's Overlord Mao that I want. How can I prove that the son-of-a-bitch is responsible for all of this? He—and he alone—must pay!!"

Putting aside the torment of the festering bullet wound which had torn his left shoulder apart, and ignoring the ugly gash engraved upon his forehead, Nate summoned an unfamiliar reserve of animal hostility. Marching resolutely toward the front of the house, his angry eyes shone red.

Even as he pounded up the sidewalk intent on breaking into the house and finding the necessary evidence to tie Overlord Mao and Agent Fredericks to each other and to the killings, a figure inside the house was racing up the stairs from the cellar, determined to learn why the lights in his basement laboratory had been extinguished. The two ballistic missiles collided on the front porch.

Though the newcomer was temporarily caught off-guard by Nate's unexpected appearance, the wiry Oriental was the first to recover. "Ah, we meet again," Mao remarked, his flowing mustache twitching suspiciously. Then suddenly more sure of himself, he mocked, "Do my eyes deceive me, or are you the silly man who seeks neither power nor money?"

"Yeah, that's me, you bloodsucker, and I am going to enjoy this," Nate promised, cocking his fist. There was such a fire in his eyes, even his son wouldn't have recognized him.

"Am I to fear for my life from a man who seeks the truth before all else?" the Overlord ridiculed in his scratchy voice, his scrawny hands carving out karate moves in the night air.

"You haven't the stomach," he taunted.

"Is that so?" Nate replied, remembering his words to Musette. "Vengeance always embraces a certain degree of insanity."

"What does *that* mean, you pathetic little man?" Mao taunted again, aching for a fight. He had come all this way for satisfaction, and now he was about to have it.

"No truth is more genuine than revenge," Nate spat back as he uncoiled his fury and began beating the thin man mercilessly. It wasn't even a contest.

Although the Overlord fought back at the start, the Senator was far too strong—and far too unhinged. In fact, the truth be known, Nate was completely out of control and the Chinaman quickly abandoned any hope of overpowering his assailant. Resigning himself instead to shielding his vital organs from the inhuman onslaught, the Overlord tucked his head into the fold of his crossed arms. But even that tactic was hopeless, and before long, Mao collapsed under the brunt of Nate's relentless pummeling.

His fists numb and covered with blood, Matthews had beaten the Overlord to within inches of his life when two someones grabbed him roughly from behind.

"Dad," the first voice exhorted firmly. "Stop it! You're killing him!"

Acting as if he hadn't heard his son's instructions, Nate punched the despot yet another time.

"Damnit, Dad, stop hitting this guy," Frankie pleaded, tightening the grip on his father's arm.

Nate's eyes were blank, devoid of emotion. Not even Frankie's hand on his badly mangled shoulder made him wince. All he could do was glare at the whimpering figure curled up beneath him in the fetal position.

"For God's-sakes, Nate, you have won," a new voice explained. "You don't need to *assassinate* this piece of slime."

At long last the words of his son and of his adviser began to make contact with Nate's consciousness and he quit kicking at the slant-eyed man. Moving away from the inert body, Nate covered his swollen eyes with his bruised hands; the cathartic tears came easily.

"She may live," Frankie urgently pointed out even as Flix added, "It's too early to tell."

Either Nate didn't comprehend what his son was saying, or else he wasn't paying attention, because he just sat there like granite, his eyes a blur.

Undeterred by his father's muted response, Franklin struggled to make him understand. "The FBI man you introduced me to at Musette's house seemed strangely familiar somehow, but it didn't come to me until after I had fallen asleep at grandpa's. When the shock of recognition finally hit me, I tried to call and warn you, but her line was busy. After I woke up grandpa, we got dressed and hurried over there together. When we arrived on her front lawn, we heard what sounded to me like gunshots. It made us plenty scared so we waited outside until things quieted down, but by then your buddy Gustav showed up and we all dashed inside to see what we could do. When Gustav saw what had happened to her, he started giving her CPR. Luckily, someone must have called for a medic because an ambulance arrived on the scene within minutes. Once they took over, Gustav and I hightailed it out of there, while grandpa stayed behind with the medics to see if he could be of some help. I knew you'd come here since this is where I first ran into that fellow from the EPA or the FBI or wherever he was from. Anyhow, if your friend Gustav hadn't shown up when he did, she would have been a goner for sure. As it is, *he* looks like hell."

"Gustav?" the Senator inquired in a bewildered tone, still in a daze from his harrowing experience. "Gustav who?"

"Your friend from D.C.—Gustav Knapheide. Don't you remember? He was the guy sitting on our porch last..."

"Oh, you mean *Flix*," Nate exclaimed as he turned to face the older man, a look of recognition dawning in his eyes.

"That's not what the other guy called him," Frankie countered in a combative voice.

"What other guy?" Nate asked, beginning to pay more attention to the goings on.

"The guy that came over just before I left the house for grandpa's," Frankie explained without elaboration.

"Senator Duncan," Flix interjected. "He came to Farmington like we asked him to, but your man Dirk shot poor Duncan right before my very eyes."

"Dirk killed Duncan?!" Nate exploded, quaking with fury. "How can that be?"

"Hell, Dad, there are dead bodies all over town," Frankie yelped, almost as if he were getting a kick out of the whole thing.

"Jesus God," Nate cursed as the tears started to roll down his cheek. "What have I done?"

"Don't cry, Dad, it's over now," Frankie consoled, grasping his father's hand firmly. "Besides, they said she might live."

"What?" Nate interrupted, a breath of energy surging through him. "What did you say?"

"The boy said Musette might make it," Flix repeated, "but it doesn't seem as if *you* will. Are you okay?" he asked, studying his protégé in the moonlight. "That arm of yours doesn't look so hot."

"I guess Fredericks must have winged me, but I'm sure Doc Simpson can patch me up. How about you? As Frankie so aptly put it before, you look like hell."

"It's a long story, Nate, but I too shall make it," Flix replied confidently.

"You sure went berserk on this fellow," Franklin observed proudly as he stooped over Mao's crumbled frame. "Who is he anyway?"

"Overlord Mao Tsui," Nate and Flix asserted in unison.

"Give me a break—*the* Overlord Mao Tsui?" Frankie cross-examined. "As in from China? Is this the guy you were telling me about? What are you going to do with this slime-ball?"

"This bastard not only tried to have *me* killed, he did kill

Munson…and your mom. I was well on my way to evening the score when the two of you showed up."

"This is the guy who killed my mom?" Frankie lamented anxiously, his voice becoming melancholy.

"His viruses did," Nate declared. "I'm not a hundred percent certain, but it may have been an accident."

"I don't care," Frankie clamored. "Let's finish him," the boy urged, raising his boot to stomp on the helpless despot's head.

"I have a better idea," Nate submitted, glancing toward the house. "There are some tiny little friends of his in the basement to whom he should be warmly introduced."

Grinning from ear to ear, Flix set down his cane and helped Frankie hoist the Chinaman onto Nate's good shoulder. As the three men entered the house, they agreed that no truth was more genuine than revenge.

41

THE BRAZEN RULE

"Flix, I'm ashamed of what I did to Overlord Mao the other night. What a terrible way for someone to die."

"Ashamed?" the General exploded furiously. "He deserved it! You shouldn't be ashamed, you should be proud. It took guts to do what you did."

"My father always taught me to live by the Golden Rule," Senator Matthews explained as the suborb descended through the clouds into National Airport after the short hop from Lambert Field.

"Oh you mean that rubbish from the Gospel of St. Matthews?" Flix questioned, a mischievous look plastered across his face. "No pun intended, of course."

When Nate didn't react, he added, "The one about doing unto others as you would have them do unto you?"

"Yes, that's the one," Nate recited as he shifted uneasily in his seat. Though the bullet hole in his shoulder had been plugged and sutured firmly shut by Doc Simpson, and his left arm was now immobilized in a sturdy sling, he was still plagued by a dull ache where he had been shot. So far, the speed-healing drug had done nothing to lessen his pain, but thanks to the Acceleron tablets the doctor had prescribed, it would only be a matter of days before the stitches could be removed. With a little luck, by then he and Flix would have this nasty business concluded, and Nate could return home for

Frankie and Musette. Due to the seriousness of her wound, it would be some time before she would be allowed to travel.

Picking up from where he had left off, the Senator quipped, "I take it you're not a big fan of the Golden Rule?"

"Let's just say it makes for a rather humbling existence," Flix reported pensively. "There are other philosophies, other schools of thought, every bit as workable and every bit as admirable as the Christian, but there are none quite so narrow-minded."

"Do tell," Nate clamored as the suborb came to a rest outside the terminal. It was a sunny day, and from low-Earth orbit Washington had appeared clean and hospitable in a way it never could from close up.

"When asked his opinion of repaying *evil* with kindness, the Chinese philosopher and teacher Confucius, replied, 'Then with what will you repay kindness?' He believed—as I do—in something called the Brazen Rule."

"I've never heard of that," Nate admitted bashfully as he unbuckled his safety harness and gathered his things. "What in the world do you mean by the 'Brazen Rule'?"

"Repay kindness with kindness, but evil with justice," Flix clarified in his eminently sensible tone. "That is, do unto others as they have done unto you. Reward others with tenderness when they are nice to you; punish them with brutality when they are not."

"That doesn't sound like a very forgiving philosophy," Nate criticized, still struggling with his guilt over Mao's death.

"It is the most human of all canons, my friend. Tit-for-tat, and nothing more. Unlike the moral code of a tyrant, *my* golden rule allows for compassion."

"Tyrants have rules?" Matthews asked as the cabin was depressurized and the air-lock unhinged. They had a long day ahead of them, and he was grateful for the conversation.

"Yes, and I should know, because I have faced a great many tyrants in my life. The code of men like Ali Salaam Rontana or Adolf Hitler or Silas Whetstone is the Iron Rule.

It is the unspoken precept of the powerful. Do unto others as
you please, so long as you do it unto them before they have a
chance to do it unto you."

"That is cold," Nate asserted, shivering involuntarily, "ice
cold."

"Indeed. It is cold and it is calculating and it is brutal, but
it is the law of the jungle and the motto of the bully. Suck up
to those above you, and intimidate those below you."

"Which gets us where?"

"Which gets us in front of the Senate's Select Committee
on Assassinations this afternoon at 2 p.m. We have a story to
tell and it's about time for it to be told."

"Geez, Flix, aren't you scared?" Nate asked.

"Of testifying? No, not really. It's my duty. Besides, I owe
it to you."

"Do you think they'll believe us?" the Senator quizzed as
the two men limped their way from the suborb and climbed up
the ramp into the terminal. Between the sling on Nate's arm
and the bandage on the General's bum leg, the two of them
looked as if they had been in a war. They were quite the sight
as they worked themselves through the airport. Already a pack
of reporters were trailing behind them.

"For God's-sakes, Nate, don't be silly!" Flix scolded,
resting on his cane. "After Wilhelm's interview with the *St.
Louis Herald* hit the teevee news last night, you became a
celebrity, an instant national hero. The entire *country* is
waiting to hear your story. Thanks to your bravery, we are no
longer on the brink of war with China. With Mao out of the
picture, a struggle to control his vast empire has pitted the
brothers Ling and Chang against a dozen other contenders. To
protect the Chinese mainland from invasion, the fleet which
had been holding Hawaii in a stranglehold has been recalled
and—for the moment anyway—the blockade of the islands
has ended. Not only that, the local insurgents' dream of a
Hawaii Free State have been temporarily thwarted as well."

"Still, once the genie has been let out of the bottle, so to
speak, it will be darn hard to put it back in," Nate countered

somberly. "Sooner or later the Hawaiians will want to secede from the Union."

"That's tomorrow's problem, Senator," Flix stated as they rode the escalator down to the lobby level. "Today, the Presidency is yours for the asking."

"I don't want it," Nate asserted defiantly.

"I don't blame you," Flix acknowledged dismally. "In its present weakened condition, the Presidency is a no-win job."

"Which reminds me," Nate interjected, "where was Johannsen off to in such a rush after the interview?"

Patting the pocket of his uniform which again held the enigmatic black book he had recovered from beneath the cushion of Musette's couch, Flix declared, "On my direction, Wilhelm took the tainted surveys to one of the research labs I had listed here in my folio of off-budget operations. You told me that Fredericks had once worked for us at the Fort Detrick biowarfare lab, so I figured that if an antidote existed for whatever germ Mao and him had conjured up, Johannsen would find it there. I gave him high enough security clearance plus all the key codes he could possibly need to access the data-files of every biowarfare laboratory in the country."

"And you?" Nate cross-examined. "Where are you going when this is over?"

"Back to Maine where I belong. You don't need me around to help you anymore, and with my testimony against Whetstone being given in exchange for immunity from prosecution, I've decided to retire permanently from public life. Besides, I haven't been to a lobster bake in years."

"But there's so much that still needs to be done," Nate pleaded as they made their way through the busy airport and out onto the street. "I can't do it all without you."

"Oh, yes you can," Flix retorted as they boarded the waiting limousine one step ahead of the reporters. "I've done my job. Don't you see? It all makes perfect sense to me now: I had to save your father that day in the desert so that you could be here to save America today," Flix justified emphatically. "And that's just what you are about to do; by sinking Silas, you will be saving all of us—including me."

Nate smiled a narrow smile and nodded his head. "So, Flix, what are you going to tell the committee to do about Whetstone?"

"I'm going to tell them that he is guilty of high treason against the good people of the United States of America, and that he should be arrested and put in jail. I am going to tell them that if we don't start facing up to our responsibilities, America will balkanize herself like every great empire before her. I am going to tell them that unless we stop feeding our people bread and circuses, we will spend ourselves into bankruptcy. I am going to tell them that unless America begins to apply the Brazen Rule in our dealings with other nations, the Iron Rule will be applied against us with much harshness. Capisce?"

Nodding his head as they drove away from the curb, Nate thought of what Flix had told him earlier. "It is the most human of all canons," he had said. "Reward others with tenderness when they are nice to you, but punish them with brutality when they are not." How true.